ALL HE WANTS FOR CHRISTMAS...

Gift-Wrapped

GOVERNESSES

Three magical dreams come true from favourite
authors Sophia James, Annie Burrows
and Marguerite Kaye!

GOVERNESSES

Sophia James

Annie Burrows

Marguerite Kaye

First published in Great Britain 2012
Mills & Boon, an imprint of Harlequin (UK) Limited,
Eton House, 18-24 Paradise Road, Richmond, Surrey TW9 1SR

GIFT-WRAPPED GOVERNESSES
© Harlequin Enterprises II B.V./S.à.r.l. 2012

The publisher acknowledges the copyright holders of the individual works as follows:

Christmas at Blackhaven Castle © Sophia James 2011
Governess to Christmas Bride © Annie Burrows 2011
Duchess by Christmas © Marguerite Kaye 2011

ISBN: 978 0 263 90231 0

25-1012

Harlequin (UK) policy is to use papers that are natural, renewable and recyclable products and made from wood grown in sustainable forests. The logging and manufacturing processes conform to the legal environmental regulations of the country of origin.

Printed and bound
by CPI Group (UK) Ltd, Croydon, CR0 4YY

Christmas at Blackhaven Castle

Sophia James

Sophia James lives in Chelsea Bay on Auckland, New Zealand's North Shore with her husband, who is an artist, and three children. She spends her mornings teaching adults English at the local migrant school and writes in the afternoons. Sophia has a degree in English and history from Auckland University and believes her love of writing was formed reading Georgette Heyer with her twin sister at her grandmother's house.

Chapter One

*'Everywhere and at all times, Christmas has been
the season of miracle and surprises...'*

*Blackhaven Castle, Essex, England
19 December, 1812*

Lady Seraphina Moreton came to Blackhaven Castle on
the edge of the worst storm to hit Essex in living memory.
Hailstones as large as golf balls had pelted the carriage
roof and the snow at each side of the winding country
lane was deep.

'Not an omen, not an omen,' she whispered to herself,
repeating it over and over again as the coach jolted violently and stopped. Before her the castle loomed, walls tall
and dark. A single light was held by a figure standing on
the large front portico.

Blackhaven. It suited its name, forbidding and isolated.

Seraphina drew in breath. She must not be seen to be criticising. She must place a smile on her face and be unremittingly merry. Was that not what Mrs Jennings at the agency had impressed upon her? 'No sour faces in this profession, miss. The client is always right and beggars cannot be choosers.'

Beggars like her! The panic that lay beneath her careful veneer was only just buried. She wanted to run from this place across the frigid ground and away from a world that was increasingly indecipherable to her.

Instead, she waited until the door was opened, lifted the hem of her velvet cloak and stepped out into the night, the servant with the lamp indicating the care needed on a patch of frozen ice as she followed him into the house.

Trey Linton Stanford, the sixth Duke of Blackhaven, stood against the windows in his library, turning as the woman entered, accompanied by his man Elliot. He had seen her alight from the coach, her hair the colour of the burnished angel wings that graced the stained-glass panels in the family chapel and bright in the falling dusk. He hoped like hell that she was not beautiful, was not young and was not one of those governesses who placed a false smile upon their lips and never let go of it.

When she came closer, however, and pale blue eyes met his own, he knew himself to be sorely disappointed on all three accounts. He swore soundly beneath his breath.

'Welcome to Essex.' He could hear the lack of charity

in his words, but did nothing to alter the tone. Six governesses in three years and this one looked to be the most fainthearted of the lot. His sons would eat her up in a day. 'I am Blackhaven.'

'I thank you for the kindness of the offer of a position here, my lord. My name is Miss Sarah Moorland, and I hail from London.' She curtsied with grace, her voice holding the cadence of a genteel upbringing as she went on. 'I shall, of course, do my very upmost to be the sort of teacher you desire for your children, sir, as this post has arrived at a most opportune time for me.'

Trey almost smiled at that. Almost. He could see desperation in her eyes. 'You have experience, then, in the role of a governess?'

The flush in her cheeks told him she had not, though to give her her due she did try to dredge up something. 'I have often minded the children of friends, my lord, and found the experience most rewarding.'

'Indeed.'

Silence followed the word, though a frown deepened on the delicate lines of her forehead as he came into the circle of bright light thrown from the lamp on his desk. Damn, he kept forgetting about his appearance in the company of strangers until he saw the reaction on their faces.

'I was hurt in Corunna under Moore, and I apologise for any fear such a visage might engender.' The explanation was the one he gave to all who looked at him in the way she did, word for word rolling off his tongue like a remembered poem.

'Oh, it is not your countenance I frown over, my lord. My brother was killed in Rueda in the same campaign you mention and such an injury reminded me of him. You were lucky to at least be able to come home.'

A surprise. He seldom enjoyed them any more. To be called *lucky* was a new experience, too. For the first time in a long while he laughed. The sound was rusty and broken.

'You say this post arrived at an opportune time. Why?'

'My father has recently passed away and my only remaining brother found he had not the space to house me.'

'Marriage was not an option, then?'

Her face reddened from top to bottom, fear in the quiet blueness of her eyes. Deciding now was not the time to pursue such a topic, Trey switched subjects altogether.

'My boys are nine, seven and five. They need tight control and good discipline. They wake at six and go to bed at eight. If you can teach them something of literature, mathematics and science, I should be well satisfied.'

The uncertain nod of her head told him such subjects were probably as much a mystery to her as they were to his sons, though under the circumstances he could ill afford to be strident. Someone to watch over chaos was the most he could ask for. Eton should see to the rest. 'Your room will be on the same floor as the children's though a night nurse is employed. Breakfast will be served in the downstairs salon at seven and the hours of schooling are between nine and six. Weekends, apart from Saturday morning, shall be your own; if you wish a ride to the nearest village you only need ask. Are there any questions?'

He watched while Miss Moorland mulled the rules around in her head and was surprised when she nodded. None of the other governesses interviewed had ever asked anything more of him.

'Do you travel back to London much, sir?'

'Never.'

Waiting for chagrin, he got relief instead and as she pulled at the front of the cloak he noticed that her fingernails were short.

His leg ached from standing and he longed to sit, the cold gnawing into his bones as pain. All he wanted was some solitude and a stiff brandy, but she did not look as though she were finished.

'I would also like to ask if you would allow me to bring a small dog into your house, my lord? She has nowhere else to go, you see, and…'

'How small?'

The cloak fell back and the russet head of a mongrel came out from between balding velvet.

'It seems one is already in my house, Miss Moorland.'

'I know and I am terribly sorry, sir.' Her cheekbones were hollowed in anxiety, eyes beacons of absolute entreaty as she stared at him. 'But I promise she is the quietest dog in the whole world and she loves children.'

'A paragon, then.' The disordered world of his house

was becoming even more disorderly. Miss Moorland's bare hands were white knuckled and shaking, but short of throwing the small animal out into the cold there was very little else that he could do. God, the dog looked as frightened as its mistress with its timid stare and down-turned mouth. The only hound he had ever owned was his father's cast-off mastiff and that canine had been both surly and dangerous.

He did not like dogs. He did not like surprises. He did not like forced joviality or the further promise of future chaos.

However, the newcomer was not quite finished. 'Would there be any chance, sir, of a tit-bit from the kitchen for Melusine? I know it is late, but she is hungry and it has been a very long journey.'

Two things hit Trey simultaneously at her request and both interested him. She was as hungry as her dog but had not asked for her own succour, and she knew the obscure legends from the house of de Lusignan.

Melusine. The dragon princess. A beautiful woman by daylight and a serpent by night. Beautiful and secretive. The same might be said of Miss Sarah Moorland.

'You will both be fed in a few moments and your duties tomorrow shall only be light ones whilst you recover from the trip.'

Lord, what had made him say that—the tip-tilted nose or the dimples deepening in her cheeks every time he did her a small kindness? Her hair in the light of his lamp was shining spun gold, a few of the pins loosened and allowing strands to fall unbound to her waist. He wondered what his wife might have made of her and then dismissed the thought completely. Catherine Stanford had been a woman who seldom thought of anyone else, her death mirroring her selfishness in life.

She had caught pneumonia in a gown that would have been better suited to a London whorehouse. She had gone to a party, riding home on horseback afterwards through the darkness with a neighbouring lord. Trey had arrived at Blackhaven three days later, war-shocked and sickened from the storms the British sea transports had endured across the Bay of Biscay, his left cheek red, raw and infected.

He might have taken her to task for such inappropriate actions had she lived beyond the following week. But she had not and the rumours of her faithlessness had swirled about the chapel even as he had buried her, the neighbouring earl inconsolable in the front pew.

On the day before the coming of the Twelfth Night, no less. He had always hated the Christmas season since.

Seraphina turned away from him, trying to regroup. *Do not cry*, she told herself firmly. *All men hate tears and this one will be no exception*. But she was tired and hungry and scared and the bravado she had worn like a shield all the way from London was beginning to crumble at an alarming rate. Melusine's warm body next to her own was shaking, a result, she suspected, of too little food and too much travelling. If her dog should be sick on the expensive Aubusson rug beneath her feet, they would both be tossed out. The thought made her swallow as the duke watched her intently.

He was beautiful, though the scar across his cheek gave the comeliness an edge of menace and threat. No small wound that, no easy recuperation either. His wife had died three years before at Christmas, the woman at the agency had impressed upon her, so this time of year would hold hard memories.

Yet he had not bade her gone, even with her dog, and had also promised them both some supper. She swallowed again and felt some small hope return. He did not travel to London at all, and this place was as isolated as they came. Perhaps she would be safe for a little while until she could devise a better plan and escape England altogether.

No. She could think of none of it until she ate something for the dizziness was back, whirling around her head in a cloud.

The door had opened, too, three small children peering through behind it, their eyes as dark as their father's.

Reaching for the back of the sofa to steady herself, Seraphina's fingers felt too strange to grip and then she was falling down and down and down, the room spinning as she went.

Trey caught her, scowling at the knowledge that she was hardly even the weight of his oldest son. The threadbare velvet in her cloak enveloped him and her animal had made a last-moment leap for safety and sat panting in one corner of the library, the whites in her eyes brushed with fear. Her tail had a strange bend to it.

'A dog?' Gareth, his youngest son, rushed over to sit before it, his hand reaching out with care whilst his brother David tossed a variety of cushions from the old sofa, leaving a bed on which to place this unexpected visitor. Terence, his middle child, did nothing but stand and stare and Trey's heart tumbled in recognition of the familiar lack of response.

Already Miss Moorland was coming around, the colour in her cheeks pale. A thin beading of sweat covered the skin above her top lip and plastered her fringe to her forehead. She looked younger and more vulnerable than she had done awake, the darkness of her lashes a contrast to her hair. When Trey untied the fastening on her cloak to try to give her more air, he saw that the white dress she wore was at least two sizes too big. The pieces of the puzzle of Miss Moorland were not adding up somehow, for the leather in her boots was fine and skilfully fashioned—as fine as her voice and the one pearl she had on a silver chain hanging around her neck.

'I fainted?' Her query was laced with horror as she tried to sit up.

'I would stay lying down for a moment if I was you.'

She ignored him. 'Melusine?'

'Is in the corner looking about as alarmed as you are. My son is tending to her.'

'Thank you.' The pulse at her wrist raced and Trey thought she might very well faint again. Placing her hand down, he stood.

'Gareth, bring the hound to Miss Moorland, please. Pick her up. I am assured by this lady that she is the kindest of dogs.'

His youngest son pulled the small animal towards him by the collar, making his best attempt at lifting it, but just as he was about to secure it in his arms, the thing bounded straight out of them and on to the circular table next to the sofa, tipping both it and the ancient urn of Great-Uncle Tobias, with the ornate porcelain-twisted handles and painted woodland scenes, and sending them headlong to the floor.

A thousand pieces shattered around the room in a single loud explosion, causing the hound to simply draw into itself and urinate all over the rug, her whines of apprehension becoming more insistent as a hush fell in the library.

Then Terence began to laugh, a sound Trey had not heard him make in three long years and so foreign that he could not believe he was hearing it. The dog, understanding that one member of the human population in the room was not about to kill it, sidled immediately up to his middle son and waited patiently to be lifted into a careful embrace.

A miracle.

A wonder.

The answer to his prayers.

Though Miss Sarah Moorland, newly arrived from London and now sitting open mouthed on his burgundy-velour *chaise-longue*, looked very much as if she was going to be violently sick.

Chapter Two

'Is she a Christmas fairy, Papa? Is that how she mended Terry's voice?'

The smallest boy stood in front of her, dark eyes watching warily. The oldest child joined him.

'Did she bring us the dog as a present?' His voice was imbued with the hope that only children knew how to engender. Even the one who held Melusine looked interested in her answer, though the spell was broken as the Duke of Blackhaven shepherded them away to a further distance.

'This is your new governess, Miss Moorland, and her dog, Melusine.'

'How old is she?' The finger pointed at her puppy looked decidedly grubby, a large and untended cut across the skin above the thumb and Seraphina sat forwards, her mind clearer and the dizziness in her head lessened now, though nausea still roiled in her stomach.

'A year old. She was born in late November and I found her on my bed on Christmas Day.'

'Who put her there?'

She had never quite understood how Melusine had come to be asleep in her chamber with a spotted ribbon tied beneath her chin as the sun had come up. Certainly it would not have been her father's or her brother's doing and her mama had been a long time dead.

'Someone who knew I needed her, I think,' she replied, and left it at that. She suspected it to be the cook at Moreton Manor, for the woman had always been a faithful servant.

Blackhaven was watching her carefully, measuring her person, weighing her up. After such a start, Seraphina was afraid that she would be thrown out on her head before the night fell properly, the darkened freezing landscape of Essex completely foreign. If this was to be the case, then it had all been for nothing, this flight, this subterfuge, this foolish dash into the countryside with terror on her heels and freedom on the horizon. The wet patch on the rug seemed to be growing before her eyes.

She had failed. Miserably.

'Did you come down the chimney, then?' The oldest child observed her person as though she might disappear, and looking at her smudged white gown Seraphina could see how such a thought could occur. The part of her personality that found a story in everything resurfaced, surprising her, for it had been a long while since the joy of fantasy had taken her in its grip, and she could not understand how, in the middle of one of her darkest hours, such a trait might flourish.

'No, for I would have been much dirtier if I had, of course. Real fairies would make themselves so tiny so that not a single spot of grime might spoil their dresses because everyone knows that fairy wings are very accurate in the art of flying.' Trey Stanford looked away, though not before she saw the waning hopes of her teaching the exact sciences to his sons written on his face in a heavy frown. But she could not care. Imagination had a place, too, in the minds of small boys such as these ones.

'Miss Moorland will be here until you go up to Eton after the Yuletide season and I expect the best of manners from each of you.'

Lord Stanford sounded as if he had had enough of conjecture, a man who dealt only in facts and reason, and when an old woman came to the door he instructed her to take his children along to their room despite all amount of protest. As the portal shut the silence lengthened.

Melusine had gone with them, trailing behind the boys with a decided interest. Seraphina hoped her dog would be safe, but under the circumstances thought it unwise to voice her worries. Finally, the duke spoke.

'My son Terence has been mute since his mother died. A laugh was a good start, I think.'

Seraphina was left speechless at the enormity of this confession.

'I had not thought of a pet, you see, but your dog seems

to have broken through his reserve. My children have had
a great loss and their reactions to it have all been different.'

Given the tone of his voice, she thought that the loss had
been his as well, a man left now struggling with the remains of life. Lord, and how well she understood that difficulty, the tattered remnants of her own torn into shreds.

Trey Stanford was tall, much taller than she had first
thought him to be; as the light scent of spice filled the air
between them she breathed in, a feeling of safety gar-
nered in the action. His library was filled to brimming
with books and a piano stood to one end of the room,
ivory keys well used and worn—a home that was not just a
showpiece. Did he play? He did not give the impression of
a man who spent a lot of time indoors, his body hewn into
the hardness of much exercise. She looked away quickly
as she noticed he watched her.

Shards of porcelain beneath her boot brought her back
to reality. Would wages be docked for the breakage of such
an expensive treasure and should she as 'help' be offering
to clear away this mess?

The rules had changed around her as well and she chas-
tised herself for not taking more notice of the hierarchy
of service in her father's house. The place of a governess was undoubtedly strictly observed in a ducal mansion
such as this one. Another problem to overcome. She had
not foreseen the enormity or the complexity of her change
in station when she had decided upon it. Sitting here, she

wondered if she should have run for the port of London instead and jumped on the first ship on an outgoing tide.

A trolley heavily laden with food arrived, the aroma of chicken and coffee and newly baked bread making her mouth water.

'I can take it from here, Mrs Thomas.'

The servant's eyes flicked across to her own, curiosity and regard written within them, the ghost of a smile on her lips before she bobbed and turned towards the door. Another younger maid came to quickly tidy the broken urn and mop up the unfortunate puddle, finishing the task in less than a moment and following the older woman out.

Lord Blackhaven indicated the fare on the table. 'After you help yourself we will talk, Miss Moorland. Your dog shall be fed in the kitchen.'

Relieved that Melusine was to be given a meal, Seraphina piled her plate with food as high as she deemed polite and sat down.

'What was your brother's name?' His lack of small talk made caution surface, his presence filling the room to bursting.

'Andrew.'

'Andrew Moorland? Which regiment did he serve with?'

'The 18th Light Dragoons, sir.' Lord, pray that the duke was not a soldier within those ranks as well or her ruse would be up.

When he shrugged his shoulders and leant back against the chair, she relaxed. In another life she might have asked what regiment he marched with and what the conditions had been like on the Peninsula at that particular time, just to give herself a better idea of the place where her beloved brother had fallen. But that life was long lost to her and a servant who had come to care for children would have no place in the asking of it. So instead she stayed silent. She was aware that he was observing her most closely.

'Have we met before? You look…somewhat familiar.'

She reddened again, the curse of her fair skin and blonde hair. She remembered him, of course, for she had seen him once a good seven years ago, before he was injured and when his wife Catherine had conquered the *ton* with her beauty. Seraphina had been thirteen and gauche when he had stopped her wayward mount from bolting across a newly laid garden off the Row in Hyde Park. She had thought then that he was like the princes in her storybooks, handsome, kind, brave and wonderful.

He would not remember. It was her mother he would have some recall of. Elizabeth Moreton. A rival of his wife. An Original. Every man who had ever laid his eyes upon her was entranced by her beauty and kindness, except for her husband, Seth Moreton.

But she wouldn't think of this now, here in a room full of books and music and the smell of spice, here in a castle far from London and the dangerous jealousies of men. Swallowing, she took a drink of lemonade.

'There are probably many others who look like me, sir.'

She had the feeling he wanted to say something else,

but did not. The clock at one end of the room ticked loudly into the silence and farther away in the house there was the sound of a crying child. She saw how he tilted his head to listen until the noise stopped.

A watchful father. In this light the scar on his cheek was wide and reddened—the mark of fire, perhaps, or a wound that had festered and been left untended. She did not dare to ask him of it.

'Did the agency tell you that you are number six in a long line of governesses?'

'They did, sir.'

'And did they tell you of the reason many left without notice?'

'No.' Seraphina shook her head. The woman at the agency had cited unresolved differences when she had asked and made it clear that she would divulge nothing further.

'The Castle is haunted, it seems. The science of such a possibility belies any rational thought, but belief is injudicious and once an idea is seeded…' She saw resignation on his face, a man who spoke of the supernatural with no true belief in any of it, but she could not leave it just at that.

'I have always been interested in the metaphysical, my lord, and there is much in life that cannot be simply explained away.'

'Such as?'

'Six governesses, perhaps?'

His brows rose alarmingly and she fancied the dent of

a dimple in his chin. 'Your dog, of course, is named after the Phantom Lady of the de Lusignan family.'

'I am surprised you should know of this, sir, without having the need to revert to a book. Usually I have to explain the connection.'

'Melusine, one of three sisters cursed with an undisclosed flaw.' He shifted on the seat and looked directly at her. 'I think I comprehend the secret nature of your dog already, Miss Moorland.'

'And what is that, my lord?'

His answer was quick and firm. 'Chaos.'

Her laughter was like music, soft and real, as joy lit her face. Where had he seen her? How had he known her? Trey's mind sifted back through the years, but he could make no placement whatsoever. Moorland? The name was without memory. He would ask around, of course, though he had no wish to return to the crush of the city.

Catherine had dragged him down to London a number of times and it had always been the same. She had loved it and he had loathed it. He wondered how he had ever been foolish enough to ask such a woman to be his wife. Granted, she had given him heirs to inherit the Blackhaven fortune and titles, but little else in joy or comfort—a woman whose looks belied a nature that was selfish and cold.

He had vowed to stay well away from beautiful women ever since and yet here was one now laughing in his library, her dirtied white gown many sizes too big and an honest, self-confessed belief in the truth of ghosts.

Sarah Moorland had worn rings on her fingers until quite recently, the sun-touched skin on the first joints of her third and little digits showing white. Both hands now pulled at the fabric in her skirt. Nerves, he supposed. Every fingernail was bitten to the quick.

It was the small details that gave a person away, he ruminated, the experience he had gained during his time with Wellesley as an intelligence officer brought into play. Sometimes he wished it was not there, this innate distrust of human nature that kept him isolated from the sort of discourse that others favoured.

'You seem well schooled in the classics, Miss Moorland. What brought you into the profession of governess?'

'Necessity, sir.' The truth of such an answer was written all over her face.

'Where was it your brother lived?'

There was a slight hesitation before she offered up the name of Oxford.

'My sister is from those parts. Once I knew the area well.'

Worry filled blue eyes and the same wash of redness that he had come to expect when she gave him any personal information whatsoever made her face flame.

Another thought chased the first one as memory clicked into recognition: Lady Elizabeth Moreton!

That was the woman she reminded him of; her colour

of hair and eyes were exactly the same. But it was more in the way she looked at him, chin tilted upwards with regard. Almost regal.

Sarah Moorland's mother? Moreton and Moorland. Anderley Moreton, a young man shot through the head under the push forwards by General Stewart at Rueda, when the 18th Light Dragoons had surrounded the village after dark. Her brother? Andrew? Lord, it all fitted save for one thing.

Why was this Moreton daughter here posing as a governess of no means and little substance when clearly she was a lady of the very first water?

Necessity, she had said and looked as if she meant it. Tipping up his glass, he swallowed the remains of his fine brandy as his housekeeper came into the room and announced that the new governess's sleeping quarters were ready and that she was there to show the way.

The chamber Seraphina was led into was beautiful, large and airy with tall windows looking out onto the hills, the view reminding her a little of Moreton Manor, the Moreton country seat.

The housekeeper continued to fuss about, plumping cushions and picking up non-existent lint from the scrupulously clean waxed floorboards. When the woman turned towards her there was curiosity in her dark brown eyes.

'If there is anything else you might wish for, you just need ask, Miss Moorland.'

'Thank you, Mrs Thomas, I shall.' This seemed to calm the servant, though as she gained the door she stopped, a look of resolution on her face.

'The boys have imaginations, miss, vibrant imaginations that set all the other governesses to odds with them because they could not understand enchantment. But I'd be thinking you can see things bright in the air around you that others tend to miss. At least I hope you do.'

With that she disappeared and Seraphina stared after her. The whole day had been awash with emotion and this small part of it was as confusing as the rest.

She had slept in the corner of a building on her last night in London, tucked under the overhang of an eave and frightened out of her wits in case anyone should find her there; now she was here in a room that was more than adequate with a servant confiding much about the nature of her charges.

Sitting on the bed, she felt a cloud of comfort envelop her, the icy rain beating against the windows as though it might never cease. Everything here was a warm reminder of how her life had been once before...

No!

The only way she had survived the past weeks had been to not think. She shook her head, but with this small quiet amidst the larger chaos her mind returned again to the horror of her last days in London.

Lord Ralph Bonnington, the Earl of Cresswell. Even the name scared her. Her father had made certain that they were left alone in the front room of the London town house, no care given for her safety; the large florid-faced man with the balding pate and beady eyes telling her exactly what he wanted out of this unexpected opportunity. She had bitten his lip when he had pressed in unbidden, demanding much more than she was willing to give, his hands ripping the bodice of her best gown in a rough attempt to sample that offered by her father in an agreement to save Moreton Manor. The sight of her skin had sent the earl into frenzy and he had forced her to the couch and laid himself on top of her, his hand across her mouth to stifle noise.

The heavy metal ewer had come into her grip as she struggled against him and she had used it to good effect on the shiny top of his head. It had been easy then to simply open the window and escape.

Her father, Seth Moreton, the Earl of Banbury, had shot himself the next evening; she had seen it in the papers as she roamed the back streets of London, trying to decide what to do. Mrs Whittle's Agency for Prospective Governesses had solved the problem.

Lying back, Seraphina felt hot tears scald down the side of her eyes and disappear into her hair at the temple. 'Mama,' she whispered softly, 'Mama, I need you.'

Trey sat in his library, listening to the rhythms of his house: the creak against timber from the elm-tree branch too low on the eaves; the hiss of a spark in the grate where a final ember flared. Heavy rain slanted in from the west, widening the Crouch River, he supposed, as it made its way to the sea.

The natural progressions of nature on land held in the Stanford family name for centuries, and his sanctuary.

In the hallway outside the library a servant hummed a carol softly. Crossing to the piano, Trey laid his hands down on the ivory keys, letting them sink into other music to block out the Yuletide notes.

Once he had loved Christmas. The thought surprised him, but Catherine had found the season a burden with all the effort required and so it had been largely forgotten about altogether. He was certain that Lady Moreton would be the sort of woman who might attack the idea with vigour: the Christmas pudding, the decorations, the charity visits and the long table full of food and family.

Standing, he walked to the window, looking at the snow deep around the house, bands of rain slanting against the light from his library. Terence had made the jump from the land of the still and the silent and his governess had undone years of aristocratic manoeuvring by mysteriously leaping backwards into an unexpected servitude. Uncertainly, he lifted his finger to the shadow of himself in the glass. He should send her back to London on the morrow, the trail of intrigue woven about her wearisome and unwanted, but there was something that stopped him.

She was Elizabeth Moreton's daughter and her ghost would not allow him to simply turf her out into the winter cold. Besides, there was something about his new governess that was beguiling. Swearing under his breath, he turned to find his best bottle of brandy.

Chapter Three

20 December

The maid brought her down to the dining room in the morning and Seraphina saw that the duke sat there already, a plate of breakfast before him and no one else at the table.

Surely as a governess he did not wish for her to be joining him for the first meal of every day? She remained still as she gained the room, uncertain as to what was expected.

'Please have a seat, Miss Moorland, for I would like to talk to you,' he said as he folded away the paper he had been reading. When she hesitated, he looked around. 'I take it your dog has been whisked off by the boys. A jaunt through the park should do Melusine no harm and a full breakfast may do you some good.'

The servant held out her chair and Lord Blackhaven waited as she sat, his calm menace more easily seen in the new light of day. The scar across his eye was reddened, the angled planes of his cheek moving under a pull of muscle and there was a tick visible around the damage. As if by magic the two footmen who stood at attention to each side of the hearth disappeared, though she had seen no sign from him to make this happen. Outside through the tall windows the day looked much brighter than it had yesterday.

'Your references are more than salutary, Miss Moorland, though were I to guess their origin I would say that they all came from the same hand.'

The drink Seraphina had taken a sip of was swallowed with a gulp at his words, shock leaping where caution had lingered. 'I do not know what you mean, sir.'

His dark-velvet eyes caught her own. 'The hand of a woman who, by her own admitted necessity, took this position of governess and far from London?'

When she did not speak he went on regardless. 'I worked in intelligence and part of my mission in Europe was deducing which written orders were fakes and which ones were original. The job requires a special attention to the sweep of letters, you understand, and the repeat of line. Put succinctly, I do know a forgery when I encounter one.'

'I see.' Her heart was thumping wildly. 'Under the circumstances, would you like me to leave then, my lord?'

He smiled. 'And have Terence revert again into silence when your dog disappears with you? Oh, I think not... Lady Sarah?'

She stood at that, barely able to breathe. He knew her name and station as well? He knew exactly who she was? Would he turn her in as an impostor and send her back? Would he summon the law and have them deal with something he would have no mind for? A hundred questions surfaced and she wanted to run, but her feet seemed carved of wood. The reputation she had in London was hardly salubrious.

'You could flee from this room and this house as certainly as you fled from London, my lady, or you could sit down and listen to what I have to say to you. Which is it to be?'

Seraphina sat, the sweat between her breasts building in fear.

'Good, I had rather hoped that you might do that. We both have our secrets, I would guess—undisclosed mysteries that tie us to a particular path or a preferred option. You need employment and I need a governess, for the probability of finding another with your long list of accomplishments would be slim until well after the Epiphany. So I propose a truce. You stay and tutor my boys until the end of January, after which I shall see to it that you are transported to the place you next wish to travel to and nothing more said of any of it. A month. Lodging. Food. A wage and no questions?'

She could only nod, for his terms were more than generous.

'Is Sarah your first name or is that a lie, too?'

'Seraphina. It can be shortened to Sera, though the spelling is different.'

'Then can you promise me that the law shall not arrive on my doorstep any time soon demanding recompense for some ill doing on your behalf?'

Horror threaded her words. 'If wrongdoing was committed, it was not my own, my lord.'

'Your father's, then. Seth Moreton, the Earl of Banbury. I had heard that he was having money problems before he...died.'

He was kind in the description of death, she thought. 'Lengthy card games tend to encourage bankruptcy, just as brandy addles the brain. He had a hankering for both.'

'Such excesses had come to my attention.' His anger was evident. 'My sister will arrive in three days' time, for as the daughter of an earl I should not wish your reputation to be ruined by the lack of a chaperone, even given your reduced circumstances. A letter has left this morning asking for her presence here.'

Ruined? Sera looked up. There were some things the powerful Lord of Blackhaven had no notion of, after all.

'Margaret is a stalwart for the correct and the acceptable. With her residence in the house your name shall stay safe.'

Safe? As in the same argument of shutting the gate after a rampaging stallion? At this moment all she wanted was to be in her sitting room at Moreton Manor, next to her beautiful mother, embroidery in hand. The way it used to be before everything changed. Instead, she was in the home of a duke who was as clever as he was dangerous, hiding from a miscreant who in all probability was even now prowling the streets trying to find her.

Time.

She was running out of it as fast as the Duke of Blackhaven was guessing every sordid detail. She couldn't breathe with the worry of it all, the woman she had been once replaced by a stranger she barely recognised.

To her alarm tears welled in her eyes, pooling and rolling down her cheeks to fall upon the soiled bodice of her much-too-big gown, and she could not stop them as all the horror of the past few weeks came crashing in upon her. Here, she was safe for one whole long month, no questions asked and board and wages given.

It was a miracle.

'Essex is a long way from London, Lady Seraphina, and the heavy snows of winter are making themselves felt. If it is security you are worrying about…?'

She shook her head as he went to stand by the window, the furthest point in the room from her. He was embarrassed by such a show of emotion, probably. He wanted a competent governess for his boys; instead he had got a watering pot of a woman who was not only a bland copy of her beautiful mother, but a pauper to boot.

She must not forget her station again, so she was careful in her reply as she gathered her lost composure. 'I should wish for anonymity here if this is at all possible, my lord?'

'You prefer to stay as Miss Moorland, then?'

'I do, sir.'

'Sense tells me that there must be a further reason for your flight?'

The clock on the mantel ticked loudly as he waited, the caution in his eyes illuminated by the windows. Because he did not press her as he was justly entitled to, she found some of the truth to give him. 'Moreton Manor, the Banbury country seat, was lost by my father on a single game of cards, so he tried to retrieve it by offering another inducement to the man with the winning hand.'

She saw the exact moment he worked it out.

'You.'

When she nodded he swore.

'Lord Ralph Bonnington was not one with any sense or honour, you understand.'

'Did he hurt you?'

'I left before he could.'

'So you would hide for the rest of your life because of the poor judgement of your parent and the disgraceful behaviour of a card sharp?'

Some plane of guilt shifted inside Seraphina at his interpretation of the whole conundrum. She was penniless and homeless, but her father's demise had been of his own making and not of hers. Still, there were parts of her explanation that were missing and she had hit Bonnington hard.

'No, my lord, but I would like a job that allowed me the time to consider my options.' She felt stronger already, more in charge, her more-familiar hopefulness reasserting itself at his calm and measured sense.

When he smiled she felt her cheeks flush. Even with his ruined cheek he was easily the most beautiful man she had ever seen, the lines in his face angled to perfection. Thankfully, though, a movement outside the window caught her attention. Melusine approached the house along the drive, two pink ribbons tied to her tail and three small boys jostling behind her. As she came closer Seraphina saw she carried a bird in her mouth.

Every motherly instinct surfaced and she was out of the room and away, hurrying to save the tiny prisoner before Melusine tired of it.

Trey watched her, running again and almost tripping on the hem of a gown that looked as though it had been made for a woman a good six inches taller than she was and at least two stone heavier.

She was so damned alone, save for the mongrel dog with the crooked tail. That was it. And now it looked as though she was after another soul to rescue. Lord, there would be a whole menagerie of creatures at Blackhaven for Christmas, he thought, like some emptying of the Holy Ark at the very end of a bleak and frozen world. Despite meaning not to, he called to his man to bring a blanket and followed.

The shoes she wore allowed her little traction on the ice though she regained her balance as she almost lost it and pressed forwards, shouting instructions to the dog who seemed to have no mind to obey.

She shouldn't have come outside in these satin slippers Seraphina thought, as she met the noisy incoming group, because already her feet were freezing and she was sliding on the ice.

'Drop it,' she said, her voice as gruff as she could make it, though her hound seemed to have no intention of obeying her. 'Drop it,' she said again, but Melusine simply ran the other way, the hysterical squawks of the bird egging the dog on. The boys tried to catch her, but missed as a flurry of snow from a nearby tree whitened the scene.

'Stop.' Blackhaven's order.

For the first time ever the dog obeyed a command, sidling over to the voice of authority and laying the wet bird carefully at his feet.

'Good dog.' The duke's hand came down to pat Melusine's ears before he lifted the now-silent bird into his palm, his sons picking themselves up and gathering around him to look.

'Melusine jumped into the pond, Papa. I think she was saving the bird because it was caught in the middle of the ice.'

'There were no others there, either.' The youngest child joined in David's story. 'And it was shivering and cold, like it is now.'

'It…is…scared—' Terence had his own interpretation of events '—because its mother…is dead.'

Like his own, Seraphina thought, and saw the duke reach out to bring his second son closer, his hand curling around thin shoulders.

'We shall make certain then that she is fed when we are back inside,' she said, 'for all birds love mash, fruit and vegetables finely sliced. It is a known fact.'

Four sets of identical eyes fastened on to her own at this imparted knowledge.

'Is she another girl, then?' Gareth asked the question.

'I am not exactly certain.'

The small bird struggled suddenly, then stood and spread its wings before flying up into the air and away. Heartfelt laughter rang around the bowers of pines and bare oak branches as they watched its flight, ungainly at first, but growing in competence with practice. Such mirth echoed the spirit of the season, amusement softened by the deep snow of December.

Like a real family, happy at Christmas. Oh, how Seraphina wished it could have been true!

Her feet came from beneath her as she took a step to watch the trajectory of flight; finding a hidden ditch, she fell into a soft snow drift. When the duke turned and smiled she rolled a ball of the whiteness before she could stop herself and sent it straight at him. The missile exploded against his legs and he stooped to make his own projectile. The boys followed. She was outnumbered and outclassed, but, as the sister of two older brothers who had perfected the art of martial attack, she was more than able to defend herself.

'Do you surrender?' she shouted as one of her snowballs hit Gareth in the chest.

'No,' he yelled back and came closer, rolling one huge missile. Both other boys followed suit, though she had Trey Stanford in her camp now, before her, sheltering her, the flurry of his shots matching his sons.

She could hardly speak for laughing, the barks of Melusine adding to the noise, and behind on the top step of the porch she noticed a row of servants observing the chaos.

Life.

This was how it should be.

Not hiding out for fear of what others might say about the loss of Moreton Manor and the death of her father, but living it regardless with laughter and energy and four days left until Christmas.

She would never forget this moment, she thought to herself: the joy of it and the fun, though drips of freezing ice down her back made her gasp.

'That's enough, now.' The boys obeyed their father as surely as Melusine had and when he bent to help her up his hand was as cold as her own.

'Do you surrender?' The same words she had used before, but said differently, and her heart beat in her throat as a sharp ache of want pierced her body, for him, for Trey Stanford and his steady, honest goodness and his offer of safety for a month. She could barely breathe with the promise of it and her grip tightened.

The moment was lost, however, as Terence moved forwards to give his help.

'Thank you, kind sirs,' she said, threading her arms through each of theirs and, with Melusine and the other two children running in front, they repaired to the portico where Mrs Thomas, the housekeeper, called out the enticing promise of hot chocolate and sugar-covered currant buns in the blue salon with a roaring fire.

Much later Trey lay down upon his bed fully clothed and booted, his valet dismissed for the evening whilst he mulled over the extraordinary day. His childhood had been dour and strict and he had let his own children go wild after their mother had died because of it. All advice had railed at him to send them up to school, but he had not wanted to let go of them.

He had revelled in seeing them as he had today in the snow, joyous, happy and carefree, the small dog yapping her head off and Seraphina Moreton aiming her snowballs like a professional.

He found it difficult to understand how she had managed to stand upright for so long in those ridiculous smooth slippers of hers, for even in boots with a thick and furrowed sole he had had trouble with the balance.

Wiping his hand across his face, he frowned. Lord, if Terence had not appeared when he did he might have picked Lady Seraphina up, daring the world to hurt her again or make her sad.

Leaving the thought there, he rose, gazing at the lights in the opposite wing of the castle. She would be in the room now, overlooking the valley. He wondered if she looked across the rolling hills to the ocean and its islands close in beside the promontory of rocks.

Blackhaven was his land and his home. Catherine had always hated the isolation. He could not have imagined her running out to save a wounded bird or throwing a snowball and laughing when the ice crept in down her back. The artifice of court seemed muted in the only daughter of an earl renowned for his pretensions and his imprudent ways.

Aye, Lady Seraphina Moreton was a puzzle.

Over hot chocolate she had told the boys that they could help her find holly tomorrow, pine boughs and mistletoe to decorate the castle's hearth for Christmas. His sons had looked at him, expecting a refusal, but the bright anticipation in his new governess's face was hard to deny.

The quiet sound of music came from beneath him, the servants in the kitchens, he supposed, singing of Christmas hope and glory, the stars above and the Stanford property spreading out below as far as the eye could see.

Star of wonder, star of night,
Star with royal beauty bright
Westward leading still proceeding
Guide us to thy Perfect Light.
Exactly here!

What did Lady Seraphina sleep in? he wondered, for the bag she carried when she arrived had been small. Did she take her slumber in nothing at all?

God, the woman was making him into a man he did not recognise. She had come as his governess, a position she had gone to great lengths to reassure him she wanted, and as the lord of the house he had a duty to allow her safety at Blackhaven.

He was a gentleman who understood the responsibility of honour and power. She was here for the while it might take to send her onwards and he only wished that the swelling region around his groin might recognise the fact.

Chapter Four

21 December

Seraphina opened her bag and brought out the only other dress she owned. The white gown was beyond repair and she doubted that even Mrs Thomas with her varied skills could rectify it.

Her sister-in-law, Joan, had given it to her as she had explained the difficulty in housing even one more family member. Seth Moreton's gambling had taken a toll on everyone, she had lectured, when she had extracted the yellowing garment from the back of her wardrobe and handed it to Seraphina—a replacement for the one Bonnington had ruined.

'The man should be shot, of course. He should be hanged, drawn and quartered for his ill use of you, but who are we now to demand it? It is finished, Seraphina.

Your brother is washing his hands of everything that was his birthright and you would be more than wise to do the same.'

Bernard had not appeared, but Seraphina had seen her eldest brother's shadow beneath the door in the hallway outside and she had known that he was hiding. Confrontation disturbed him, but the thought of a penniless dependent probably worried him more.

The Moretons had neither money nor land left and a city that prided itself in both would not receive them well. Joan had even refused the use of a carriage to take her back into London, reasoning that every pound was to now be counted if they were to survive the penury that would surely follow. Seraphina had left the house and walked the mile into town, her hat pulled full down across her face so as to avoid any notice.

There had been marriage proposals, of course. Her first Season had been awash with offers, but her father had demanded she wait for the one that could not be refused and when his own foolishness had tarnished their name, all promises had been quickly withdrawn.

Even before Bonnington she had been an outcast, she realised, the few dresses that her father had allowed her to procure constantly changed by her own hand to make them appear different.

The dark-blue gown she took out now was one of those dresses, three years old but well cut and made of worsted velvet, which she had to admit was in places thinning badly. The cook had smuggled it out with Melusine when she had chanced one final call at the Moreton town house before leaving London.

At least she would not trip over the hem, she thought, combing her hair and winding it into a long plait tied with a bright red ribbon. But she must be very careful with the condition of the dress; after this, there was nothing else left.

The duke was waiting downstairs, but this morning he looked ill at ease, a man caught by company he did not desire. When she smiled at him his frown deepened.

'Good morning, my lord.'

'Miss Moorland.'

As he remained silent she filled in the awkward space between them with chatter.

'Today with the children I shall begin on a lesson of botany. The plants that signify Christmas all have their own tales attached and the boys should enjoy the stories as we gather them.' She added a 'sir' when he still declined to answer, for the *détente* that had been so apparent yesterday had disappeared overnight.

'Then I hope you have a fruitful day.'

'You will not accompany us?'

He shook his head and stepped back. 'Don't go down by the pond the children spoke of yesterday. The ice is thin and my men cannot begin the job of placing up a barrier until the morrow.'

'Of course, my lord.'

'The hills to the back of the castle can also be cold and

windy. Do you have a thicker cloak than the one you arrived in, Miss Moorland?'

'I do not, sir.'

'Then ask the housekeeper to make one of my late wife's available to you. She had quite an assortment from memory.'

'Oh, it would hardly be—'

He cut her off. 'My marriage was not a love match, Miss Moorland. I would divest myself of all Lady Blackhaven's clothes if I could do so easily, but Mrs Thomas insists they have hardly been worn and that it should be a great travesty. You would be doing me a favour by taking at least one garment off my hands.'

Some of his words held an accent of Europe, Seraphina thought when he spoke, and she wondered just how long he had been stationed there. His hair was wet this morning, pulled back into a tight queue, a style far from fashionable. It suited him entirely.

He looked like a man too big for the room, though there was a grace about him that was also apparent. She imagined him on the battlefields, sword drawn and at the ready. He had been decorated for bravery on the Heights of Penasquedo in the final fiasco before the British retreat at Corunna. Perhaps it was there his cheek had been injured.

Not a love match! There had been rumours of the lack of emotion between the Lord and Lady of Blackhaven, but Catherine Stanford had played the part of duchess with aplomb, her clothes always of the latest vogue and her face unmatchable. Every man had adored her. Even her mother had been outshone by the beauty of the woman.

'David informs me that you wish to decorate the castle hearth with bounty from the forest. I will assign a man to help you with the cutting and another to drag back what is found.' His eyes were caught by a movement as Melusine slunk in behind her and sat at his feet.

'It seems your hound has finally been tamed, Miss Moorland.'

'I promised her a bone if she was obedient.'

When he laughed their eyes met. In London she had been plagued by dandies, their only thoughts those of the elegance of their clothes and the pleasure of the moment— minions who followed the Regent into hedonistic pursuits of little importance: *Eat, drink and be merry for tomorrow we may die.*

Trey Stanford was different. Even as a thirteen-year-old she had been able to recognise the fact. Had her mother, as well?

Lord, were Elizabeth and he once lovers? Is that why he had helped her mother so substantially when nobody else would? The thought was horrifying. Was this also the reason he was pulling back this morning, an edge of wariness on his face and in his words? Like mother, like daughter, though Elizabeth's vivacity and *joie de vivre* had always eclipsed her own.

The bright and joyous world she had built up in her mind overnight came crashing down upon her. Lord Blackhaven would not join them in their search for Christmas greenery and he was very obviously readying himself for a coach ride away from the castle.

Another thought chased in upon that one. Would there be news of Ralph Bonnington, the Earl of Cresswell, at the destination he was bound for? Please God, let the man not have died from the blow to his head! No, the impact of the ewer had been substantial, but the bone of his scalp had held and there had been many a time with her brothers as a youngster when she had clouted them as hard. Worry swamped reason and of a sudden she wanted Trey Stanford to stay close, away from the gossip and a world that was not kind.

As a governess, however, she had no mandate to question his movements or ask for his presence here. She was a nobody now, a pauper mired in debt and scandal.

'I shall be back before the evening sets properly. Is there anything you might wish for in Maldon?'

She shook her head and then stopped, her mind running on to the pursuits of the day. 'Ribbon, my lord, and sweets. I have promised the boys a tree, you see, like the one King George allowed Charlotte. My mother used to speak of it—a giant yew erected inside the Queen's Lodge at Windsor with its sweets and nuts and candles.'

'I am astonished such a tree did not burn down the palace.'

When she smiled the air between them lightened. 'Ours

shall be an evergreen fir bough, my lord, and the candles can stay on the mantel.'

'And where shall this tribute to the oncoming Yule be placed?' The tone in his voice suggested resignation.

'Mrs Thomas proposed the room downstairs to the left of the front portico.'

'My father's favourite haunt. I imagine him turning in his grave at the thought of the Christmas spirit displayed in the very spot where his ancestors railed against anything festive.'

'It could, of course, be changed, my lord?'

'No, leave it, for there is a certain retribution at the thought.'

'You did not like your father?' The new habits of servitude were not ingrained yet and there was a sadness about him that was beguiling.

'I impose few rules on my sons because as a child I had to obey so many. He was a good man underneath, though, a moral man.'

'Then you were fortunate that he cared enough to worry. My own papa barely knew my name.' *Until he signed it away on a piece of paper, promising her into unholy matrimony. Like horseflesh at Newmarket, no emotion save greed in any of it.*

'That I find hard to believe,' Trey Stanford said obliquely, knocking his hat against his thigh. 'But for now I bid you farewell, my lady.' The lines around his eyes creased at her title as though he found irony in her situation; indeed, in a gown that had been remade and remodelled so many times the stitching lines were beginning to fray, Seraphina felt perhaps there was.

'Thank you.'

He turned at her words. 'For what?'

'For allowing me to keep at least a measure of pride here.'

'One cannot take away that which was never lost in the first place, my lady.'

'I will bear that in mind when I wrap myself in the borrowed cloak then, my lord.'

'Aye,' he said, 'you do just that.'

This time he did not tarry as his man came forth and they both disappeared through the portal that led to the front steps.

She never said or did what he expected her to, Trey thought as he walked through the snow to the carriage. He wondered if it was deliberate, this knack of hers to throw him out just when he was beginning to understand her, her pale blue eyes laced at times with the fear of saying the wrong thing or inciting anger.

Hell, he would like to have laid his hands around the neck of her father and brother and squeezed hard, so little care they had taken with her. The dress she wore today was, if possible, even worse than the one she had on yesterday, the seams on the side of the bodice showing through to her white chemise. A ruffled velvet over-layer hid some of the damage, but the overall effect was unlike anything he had ever seen a lady wear before.

Catherine had been a woman whose wardrobe was full to bursting and one who was never happier than when taking a new shipment of ornate and expensive clothing. He grimaced. Would Lady Seraphina be slighted if he asked Mrs Thomas to select a few of the winter gowns his wife had never worn and take them to her room for appraisal?

Pulling his hand across his eyes as he felt the movement of the coach, he breathed in. He wanted Seraphina Moreton happy. He liked her smile and the deep dimples in each cheek, apprehension and alarm making way for the sort of joy he had long since forgotten. Part of him wanted to bang on the roof of the carriage and order it back so that he might go and find the Christmas greenery that she had spoken of, and the laughter. But he had promised her ribbon and candles and sweets and the look in her eyes when he had done so made the mission as important as any he had ever undertaken.

She seemed to be pulling them together, all of them, the boys, the dog, the servants and...him. Even the castle was to get a Christmas face of festive greenery and colour. He should say stop, of course, should halt such a transformation before the shape of their lives changed in such a way that they would be for ever stranded when she left them.

Which she would!

This isolated backwater of Essex would cease to be a haven for her before too many weeks had passed and the city and all its pleasures and amusement would call again. Was that not the way of beautiful young ladies, even one who was temporarily down on her luck?

The sun on the snow was harsh and the eye above his damaged cheek watered as it often did against such brightness. The gunpowder had burnt into his skin in Corunna, the sea voyage on the retreat through the storms of the Bay of Biscay stinging the weeping open wound with salt. He had arrived back in Essex just on the end of the Epiphany to find his wife had cuckolded him before dying, his sons left alone for months whilst their mother had sashayed her charms in London with numerous and adoring swains.

A hopeless wife and mother. Sometimes he wandered down to Catherine's marking stone in the small graveyard just to make sure that she was actually gone. Such a sorry thought made him sit forwards and he was glad that his man rode on the box seat outside.

Loss. Love. Beauty. Betrayal. Death. And now nearly Christmas.

The thought had him turning to look at the fir trees lining the driveway of Blackhaven, his practised gaze picking out one that might be the perfect specimen for candles, nuts and sweets.

Chapter Five

The evening drew on and still Trey had not come back to Blackhaven Castle; the children were tucked into their beds and the light had faded long past into darkness. Seraphina had made some ground with the boys today, yet they remained distant and suspicious of her, despite all that she had done to try to win them over. Terence had been a little more forthcoming but the others had made it plain that they should like her gone. Still, she was not a person to give up easily and tomorrow when they decorated the front parlour she would make certain to tell them all the stories she had read of Christmas cheer.

She had thought of the duke many times through the day, expecting to see him in the mid-afternoon. But he hadn't arrived even as the clock ticked on into midnight. Was he safe? Had the coach overturned? Did he freeze in the snow, waiting for aid that would not come? Cursing her vivid imagination, she shook away such doom-say and stood at her window, searching for a light. 'Lord, let him be safe,' she prayed over and over again, the flames in the hearth burning down to embers before she saw movement.

A moment later there was a flurry of action beneath her window as people ran out, the horses lifting their heads and prancing to try to keep the cold at bay. Packages were transferred into waiting hands and then Trey alighted, his cloak billowing as he mouthed instructions she could not hear.

When she changed her position to see him better he looked up and Seraphina knew that he saw her, but was unable to move. The force of his glance had left her shaking.

Why had she not met him three years ago on her first Season out when he might have seen her as she wanted him to, her father still solvent and a hundred suitors at her feet? Now, life bent her into a different woman, worry written in her eyes every time she looked in the mirror.

It was so ironic. When all seemed lost and hopeless she had arrived at the house of an honourable man who would help her as her own family had not, who would shelter her without question until the end of January. The truth of it made her frown.

'Please God, do not let him have been my mother's lover.' The words tumbled into the dark, standing on the edge of it like arrows piercing a growing want that blossomed inside her. For him. For Trey Stanford, the sixth Duke of Blackhaven. Seraphina had known her mother had a suitor because Elizabeth had told her so, once late at night when she had come to her mama's room and found her crying. The ring on her finger had not been her father's, and her anguish was such that no amount of help could assuage it.

The following week they had buried her and her father had taken to the bottle in earnest.

Her parents, lost to death and to scandal. Biting at the nail on her thumb, she sat down again on her bed and listened as the noises below faded into silence.

Trey had seen her face at the window looking down, caught into stillness, her hair like a halo around her head, gold and wheat and pale pure flaxen. He would have liked to mount the stairs and knock on her door to see her blue eyes widen as she heard the reason as to why he had returned so late.

Ralph Bonnington, the Earl of Cresswell, was telling the world that Lady Seraphina Moreton had attacked him, unprovoked and unexpected, her anger at the loss of Moreton Manor so acute she could not countenance his windfall. He had been found by two of his friends, almost unconscious, according to the paper, and now demanded she be brought to trial.

Running his hands across his face, Trey strode into his library, helping himself to a liberal brandy to chase away the cold. For now, the winter protected Seraphina, kept her safe away from others and all the gossip that had ensued. Each paragraph on the first two pages of *The Times* had speculated as to where Lady Seraphina had gone. Beneath the banter was another more dangerous thread. Trey imagined Cruikshank's caricatures in 'The Scourge' depicting the fallen daughter of a bankrupt family engulfed in ignominy, ruined and exposed to the delight of those who exchanged tittle-tattle on the dance floor. A young woman's reputation would not recover from such a public drubbing and Seraphina Moreton looked too fragile to weather any of it.

Refilling his glass, he sat before the fire, thinking.

Margaret and her husband were due to arrive in two days' time and his sister was no fool. She would recognise Lady Seraphina and when she did…?

Small footsteps behind had him turning. Gareth stood in his nightwear, his hair tousled and his eyes sleepy.

'I noticed your light from my window when I woke up, Papa, and I needed to ask you something.'

Trey already knew what was to come next. It was always the same question, every single time.

'Mama loved us a hundred thousand times over, didn't she?'

Settling his smallest son on his lap, he brought a blanket from the chair beside him to wrap away the cold.

'A millions times over,' he replied in the same vein, the truth of Catherine in London caring not a jot for her three small boys nowhere near his words.

'Terry thinks Miss Moorland likes us, too?'

Now this was new. He nodded and waited.

'He thinks we should, maybe, keep her?'

God, sometimes his children almost broke his heart with their want for a mother, though the small pitter-patter of paws saved him an answer as Melusine's head poked around the corner.

'Her dog wishes that you were in bed with him, Gareth,' he replied as he stood to carry his son back to the nursery.

22 December

The Duke of Blackhaven looked different this morning as Seraphina came to the breakfast table, for his hair was loose around his face, giving the impression of a pirate from the dangerous South Sea Islands. However, his jacket was double breasted and the beige superfine in his trousers well ironed.

Her own attire was unforgivably dowdy, the rips on her skirt repaired badly and her only pair of boots still damp from the deep snow.

'Mrs Thomas says that you declined the use of the gowns she laid out on your bed?'

'I did, sir, for the ones I own shall suffice.'

'If it is because you do not wish to wear my wife's clothes, my housekeeper assures me she could fashion something from the many bolts of fabric that are stored in the attic. She is an expert seamstress by all accounts.'

Seraphina felt herself hesitate. A new gown that was

neither too big nor badly torn for Christmas was tempting and she was so very tired of wearing what she had.

'I could take the cost of the fabric from your wages.'

His suggestion made her blush because she knew that such a thing would be far and above any money she was earning as a governess.

Yet temptation lingered. Reaching for her grandmother's single pearl on the chain around her neck, she slipped it off so that it lay in the palm of her hand. She had always worn this piece since Elizabeth had died and it was undeniably precious. Yet reality beckoned, too, in the shabby dress she had on, the seams beneath her left arm so frayed she could no longer repair them.

'If I put this down as a surety for the sum of the fabric, I could accept your offer.'

He shook his head. 'I have no need for it.'

Her gaze met his, amber-gold in the daylight, drawing her in. She felt her body respond to his glance, a throb of want dancing like flame warmth across her skin. When he stepped back the disappointment stung.

'You look like your mother. Did you know that?'

Her heart thumped at the question, coming as if on the surge of desire. 'Were you her lover, then?'

Discomfort shadowed his face. 'How much did you comprehend about Elizabeth's life?' His voice was wary.

'Enough to realise she was unhappy with my father. Enough to see her spend hours getting ready at night and not return until the morning.' She had never told anyone that before, but it did not feel disloyal here to speak of such things. The duke had known Mama, after all, and he had helped her when others had turned away. Besides, it might have been he who kept her occupied nightly.

'People deal with an unhappy relationship in different ways and for Elizabeth it was through enjoying the company of my cousin before he died. Terence. His name was Terence.'

Relief allowed the breath she hadn't realised she was holding to escape. 'The same as your son?'

'Aye, he was named after him. We were brought up together like brothers and the last thing he said to me was "look after Lizzy".'

'So you gave her money when Papa would not?'

'The bills were piling up and your father had refused to pay them, but in the end it was not such largesse she needed at all...'

Seraphina understood what he was saying. Her mother had gone to Moreton and raced her horse fast across the track above the cliffs. Fast enough for it to lose its footing and for Elizabeth to be transported to the place her lover had already been taken to? Other things became explained as well: her father's lack of grief, an escalating gambling habit and his anger.

'Thank you for telling me the truth.'

He smiled and held her gaze, just the two of them here in the breakfast room, the day drawing into coldness and the new snow falling outside. Buffered by nature and locked

in by the forces of winter as it laid its arms about the countryside in a white blanket of cold, Seraphina felt…altered.

Life at Moreton had been fraught and uncertain, the arguments and anger constant. She had always been frightened. She knew this absolutely because here, at the castle,
she wasn't, the disquietude of her home life replaced by
hopes and promises drawing her in as she anticipated what
was to come.

But there was something today in his gaze that was hidden, and when he began to speak she knew that the details
of the past few weeks had caught up with her.

'Yesterday in Maldon I saw a copy of *The Times*. The
man you mentioned, Ralph Bonnington, is telling the world
that you struck him when he offered you all the assistance
and support that your father had not.'

'Assistance? My God.' She stood as she said it, a sick
feeling of horror slicing into disbelief. 'He said that?'
Anger darkened her vision. 'I hit him on the head with a silver ewer because he was trying to…' She could not go on.

Trey came closer and reached out, putting her hand into
his, the gentleness felt in the action making her heart ache.
'The man is a charlatan and a cheat—as no one knows
where you are yet it seems you are safe.'

Relief flooded through her and her fingers clutched his.
She wished he might bring her closer and kiss her hard
on the lips, like the men in the romances she sometimes
read at night, no choice in it but need and want and taking.

But his fingers stayed still, a light pressure denoting

only comfort and consolation. She wanted to push up against him and demand so much more, a breathless hunger nearly undoing her. Instead, she moved back, smoothing out her rumpled skirt for something to do before she had to look at him.

'He is a large man with a lot of money. If he comes here to make trouble…?'

'He won't.'

The certainty in Trey's voice was so comforting. There were, after all, many other things he could have said and to have someone watching out for her was a new experience. A wonderful one! When her glance finally met his she reddened and looked away, his integrity and decency stealing into her bones as delight. She wanted to thank him for such belief, wanted to bring him into the joy of the Christmas preparation that she had spent much time in planning.

'We are dressing the tree this afternoon, my lord. The children would be happy if you might come and help us.'

'And you, Miss Moorland. Would you be happy, too?'

Confusion made her stammer. 'Your h-h-height would be a great aid in placing the angel on the very top of the tree.'

When he smiled she felt her world turn and hated all the hopes that rose unbidden.

Her reputation was lost and she was without a dowry. Her wealth consisted of what she wore, which was far less than satisfactory, a single pearl that did have some worth and a dog who was only now learning to sit still. A hundred pounds, she reasoned, the few notes she owned tucked into her pocket after pawning all her rings and a bracelet—the sum total that stood between her and ruin.

Resolution swept through her. Trey Stanford, the Duke of Blackhaven, could not possibly be interested in her and she could not jeopardise this posting by imagining that he might be. Regaining her lost composure, she smiled at him in the way of an employee who was both professional and distant and excused herself from his company.

Three hours later the smell of pine filled the room as Mrs Thomas brought in a plate of Christmas pies.

'Baked in the dozens to strengthen their charm,' she said, 'and good luck for the twelve months of the New Year, sir.'

Surrounded by red-and-green ribbon, a pile of gold-and-silver paper and balls made from the dry branches of last year's climbing wisteria, Trey was knee-deep in spangle as he looked at the tree.

Ginger-and-butter shortbread had been strung with twine, the delicacies embellishing an already over-embellished greenery.

Seraphina Moreton had no pattern of demanding the fir dressed in a particular way as Catherine had been wont to on the few times she had bothered. Everything went, according to the governess's philosophy, so that even the broken offerings the boys had put their hearts into creating took their place alongside the expensive and irreplaceable heirlooms collected by the Blackhaven ancestors for generations.

There was hardly a pine needle still on show and the angel on the top that he had had the task of securing looked down on a hotchpotch of colour.

His children loved it.

'Have you ever seen such a tree, Papa?' David asked him and his father shook his head in honesty.

'Never.'

Seraphina Moreton laughed as he looked over to find her watching him, Melusine jumping at the foil on a lower branch, then nestling in a pile of paper.

'I like the red apples best.' Terry pointed out his efforts, three matching misshapen balls with sprigs of gold drunkenly hanging from the top.

As leaves, he supposed. He made much of nodding.

'The stars are mine, Papa.' Gareth brought a folded silver shape away from the riot of others behind it. 'Miss Moorland helped me draw them. I could make some for your library tomorrow.'

'Indeed.'

'We have mistletoe as well.' David took a sprig from a box at his feet and placed it carefully on his hand. 'Where should we hang it?'

'Above Miss Moorland,' Gareth screeched. 'Then we can all give her a kiss.'

'Above Papa,' Terence amended. 'Then she could give

him one.' His oldest son was already counting as he walked over with the mistletoe.

'Twelve berries. Twelve kisses. You can have the first one, Papa.'

A vibrant red blush crept up Lady Seraphina's cheeks, but with three boys baying for a kiss Trey felt it easier to do so. He had meant to place a light peck on her cheek, just a small token to fulfil an expected duty, but he found the soft fullness of her mouth instead and his world exploded.

She felt his finger against her cheek, light as air, question in the last second before his lips slanted against hers, the full force of an unexpected magic making her press in. Trey Stanford was hers for this moment under a tree laden with Christmas and in a world of colour, the taste of him strong and real, his fingers at her nape, the shape of his body full down the front of hers, as a deep pain of need entwined itself into all the corners of her heart. He was neither careful nor gentle nor calm. He was masculine fervour tempered with steel, a man who knew his way around a woman and taking the chance of appetite even with his three children watching on.

Seraphina was breathless when he broke away. Kissing was nothing like she had heard it to be: tepid, shallow and lukewarm. It was hot and ardent and fierce, the meeting of souls through a joining of spirit, a giving and a taking. As amazement bloomed she heard the shouts of the boys and David plucked one berry and threw it in the fire. It sizzled against the embers, a slight puff of smoke and then gone.

When she chanced a quick look at the duke, he seemed unaffected by all that had just happened as he took the mistletoe and placed it above the door-well a good few feet away. He did not look in her direction once.

'Aunt Margaret and Uncle Gordon should arrive tomorrow. We will surprise them beneath it.' His voice was even and mellow.

Gareth screwed up his face. 'No, they are too old to kiss, Papa.'

'No one is ever too old, my lad. You'll find that out one day.'

All the boys laughed as Melusine barked, chasing her damaged tail around and around until she caught it, teeth clamped in dark red hair. She had been a quiet dog until she had come to Blackhaven, slinking around beneath the anger of Seth Moreton and the distant haughtiness of the Moreton servants. Here she hardly ever stopped, following the boys from room to room.

The kinder face of chaos, she thought, remembering Trey Stanford's words about her dog. The Christmas pies Mrs Thomas had made were still warm and the smell of spiced ale drifted in from the kitchen.

Last year she had been alone all of the day, her father asleep with a headache that he had acquired through a late night of gambling and the only food that was special a cake procured a good month before the season began. She had stood at the window of the Moreton town house overlooking the park and thought that she had never been as lonely.

This year the joy of the season shone on the boys' faces,

the decorations they had spent all morning fashioning bright and festive.

And she had been kissed. Her first ever. The throb of it still covered her lips, though she did not dare lift her fingers to touch them in case the duke noticed.

Her glance went to the mistletoe surreptitiously. Eleven berries left! Eleven kisses left! The thought made her blood rush fast.

Trey saddled his horse and rode across the frozen afternoon whiteness towards the river, the same place he often went when he needed to think, the gnarled avenue of bare brown oaks both peaceful and ancient.

He should not have kissed Lady Seraphina, should not have allowed such a thing to happen because now it was all that he could think of, her softness and her warmth and the startling force of energy that had passed between them unbidden.

'God help me!' His words to the grey and leaden sky as the consequences of such action unfolded in his head. He wanted to feel again what he just had, the ache of something other than the indifference and inertia that had hounded him for so long in his marriage to Catherine. He had never loved nor even liked his wife. A marriage arranged by his parents and hers to amalgamate the lands around Blackhaven into one solid and powerful block. When he looked to the horizon in every direction the soil was his—paid for in deceit and sham and loneliness.

Catherine had been unfaithful from the first month of their marriage and he should have left then, but David was already on the way and there was some honour in him that he could not just sever.

He had gone to Europe the following year and stayed there until the night Terence was conceived. Gareth was the child of one of her many other lovers when all relations between them had broken down, but he had never told anyone this and raised the boy as his own.

Secrets. How they destroyed one with the bile of anger and disappointment.

And now more secrets, dangerous ones with the weight of the law behind them and a man who was after his own scrambled retribution. Seraphina Moreton would need to be protected and she would require help to win against such a one as the Earl of Cresswell. Her fragility required armour and someone fighting in her corner who did not obey the rules.

Like him.

But how? The kiss under the mistletoe was a start because she must have felt exactly as he did. She had not met his eyes after it and he had not wished to find hers. Some things were better left for the quiet chance of talking later, so that she was not frightened again as she had been in the lurid attempts on her person by Ralph Bonnington.

Promise beat under his musings. He wanted her beneath him, knowing the curves of her body and the scent of her womanhood.

There had been other women since Catherine, he could not deny it. The sweet opiate of forgetfulness was easily procured, even with a ruined face.

But not for a while. It had been months since he had left the county of Essex and he had never liked to bed the local women. Too close to home. Too complicated.

Until now. Until a woman installed in the very centre of his world had whet with a single kiss an appetite long dulled under a sprig of mistletoe and the watchful eyes of his sons.

God in heaven. He swore again, but this time he laughed too. He felt alive again, interested, the ennui that had plagued him for so many years lifted.

'Seraphina.' He shouted her name and heard his voice echoed back to him through the barren outcrop of rock and muffled in the deep and thick December snow. It had the ring of salvation.

Mrs Thomas knocked on her door in the afternoon and she held a candle encased in glass because the skies had darkened and rain was threatening.

'The master asked me to show you the bolts of fabric in the attic, Miss Moorland. He said you might choose some material for a Christmas gown and if we are to have any hope of finishing it we would be best to get on to it as soon as we can.'

The thought crossed Seraphina's mind that Lord Blackhaven might be regretting his earlier kiss and allowing her some recompense in return for it. She swallowed down such a conclusion and tried to take stock of her situation.

'I haven't the means to pay you for the work, Mrs Thomas, and I am not certain yet of the amount of my wages.'

'Oh, never mind that,' the housekeeper returned softly. 'The boys are happier than I have seen them in a long while and that is the best payment I could ever receive. Now, come along and we will see what we can find.'

Ten minutes later Seraphina felt as though she were in some Aladdin's cave, myriad rolls of fabric leaning against the walls, some still bound in tissue paper but many partly unravelled as if the person who owned them had just been there deciding on her choice of colour.

'Lady Stanford was a woman who liked a great deal of selection. She was always buying from the travelling salesmen or the gypsies, as well as getting fabric sent up from London. Velvet, as you can see, was a special favourite of hers, and lace. The Brussels lace here cost a right fortune, I can tell you.'

'Then perhaps I should look at something less costly?'

'And have the moths burrow their way through this? Nay, the hue will show up the depth in the gold velvet of the gown and would suit the shade of your hair. If we do not cut into it now, it could stay unused for another decade and by that time there would be nothing of it left at all. Save dust. Such a waste.'

Unravelling the bolt, Seraphina felt her breath hitch. Catherine Blackhaven's taste in fabric was unparalleled and she had rarely seen lace so fine. Still, tempting as the gift was, she wondered at her own ability to pay back the cost of it.

'The duke said you could have your choice, Miss Moorland. Were it to be mine, I should most certainly select these ones.' The Brussels lace was in her left hand and the golden velvet in the right.

Without waiting for a reply, she bound the length around Seraphina's waist. 'If the skirt was full and the bodice tighter, you could use the lace here and here. Lady Catherine always favoured a scandalously low décolletage, but on you we could fashion a gown in a manner that was more classical.'

Mrs Thomas's words gave her an opening. 'The duke's late wife was a beautiful woman. I saw her in London a few times with my mother.'

'And the beauty went to her head until it was all that she could think of. It was why the master was in Europe for so long, with a bride who cared for nothing save herself.'

'But the children?'

As if catching sense, Mrs Thomas shook her head. 'I am the housekeeper, Miss Moorland, and I should remember my place.' Winding back the gold so that even more of the colour was on show, she nodded sagely. 'Blackhaven

Castle needs laughter and joy again and if the cost of that is a few yards of fabric, then it comes cheap.'

When Mrs Thomas undid the handles on a sewing bag she had placed on the floor, Seraphina saw scissors, pins and thread, and the promise of a gown that was neither too big nor too tight overcame reticence. With real anticipation she slipped off her old dress and stood in her many-times-patched chemise and petticoats as the measuring and fitting began in earnest.

The wind had died down and the rain had held off, though the clouds were thick and dark above as Seraphina sat on a wooden bench in the ornate inner gardens of Blackhaven as the evening was about to fall.

Reaching out to the bare wood of a bush beside her, she smiled as she touched the vibrant orange of a rosehip, the only colour besides green and black and grey in the snow-tossed square. It was good to be outside at the end of a long and noisy day, the silence of the place welcomed as she tucked her chin into the worsted wool of her borrowed cape.

The kiss from the morning turned in her mind, again and again, compelling and intense. She had kissed Trey Stanford back, too, pressing herself against his body like a wanton woman. The thought had her eyes opening and she stared into the amber glance of the very man she dreamt of.

'I saw you come out here through the window of my library,' the duke explained, gesturing to a room behind a row of barren espaliered fruit trees, light showing through diamond-panelled windows.

His hair this evening was tucked carelessly into the generous collar of a military coat: a soldier, a hero, a man whose very accent summoned the amount of years that he had served in Europe for England. She imagined just what he must have experienced.

'It was quiet out here, my lord, and a sheltered place to rest.' She wondered if she should invite him to sit, but he seemed restless, his fingers playing against intricate gold buttons in a line down his front, the same fingers that had caressed her neck and threaded through her hair as he had kissed her.

No. She must not think of this now, for she sensed a barely held anger broiling beneath the careful surface.

'My sons like you, Lady Seraphina. Gareth informed me last night that he wished we might keep you.'

Astonishment leapt quick, though he was not finished.

'I have no wish for them to be disappointed again, for they would not weather it. The boys' mother was...' He hesitated. 'She was not the sort of woman who held the maternal instincts in high regard, you understand, and they have suffered. Therefore, if you feel in the light of what happened today that you no longer wish to remain at Blackhaven Castle until the end of January, I would provide you with transport back to London and a generous stipend for the trouble taken for coming here in the first place.'

For the only time since she had met him he looked

slightly abashed, a peer of the land who was also a father and a man.

'I should also like to say that I have come into the gardens to find you in order to personally apologise for my lack of regard.'

'You speak of our kiss?' Anticipation sizzled amidst an unsettled anger. If he should say their kiss was a mistake or an error or a lapse in judgement, she would scream because to her it was none of those things. To her the very soft rightness of it still made the blood race in her veins, and the hope of more was in her answer. 'I could have refused your advances, Lord Stanford, easily, but I found myself not wishing to.'

At the words Seraphina stood, the evening wrapping around them both and her breath white in the half-light when she spoke. 'I do not consign what happened under the mistletoe as an error, but see it as a gift that was precious to me beyond words.' The vulnerability creasing his face made her reach up to his cheek and place her finger across the hard angles.

He felt warm even despite the chill, a twelve-hour stubble roughening his skin: a man who was solid and reliable and honourable. 'If, indeed, there is anything I might say, it would be to ask you to kiss me again,' she simply stated, standing on her tiptoes so that he might have better access to all that she offered him. She could no longer be careful or circumspect or judicious. She wanted him, his taste, his feel and his warmth. She wanted to know again that which she had in the room full of Christmas, the ache of delight filling every part of her body with heat.

The shards in his eyes lightened from brown to gold, melting into response, and his lips came down to hers, the slam of need attesting to a control he had suddenly lost hold of.

His tongue met her own, duelling against entry as he deepened the kiss, changing that which she offered into something else. Wonderment and lust. She felt his hips move even through the thick layers of wool between them, asking for what men and women through all the centuries had sought to understand in an elemental promise. When she answered back, his voice broke hoarse into the silence, her name whispered fiercely before his lips returned to take—only them in the world, only this feeling of an utter and precise truth, far away from the specifics of any dividing fact or faith. Together, and for this moment, everything was perfect.

A wintry blast of wind brought her back though, the facade of Blackhaven looming above, darkened in the dusk and watching. The bricks of the newer annexe addition glowed almost black and she fancied the shadows of those at work in the castle flickering across some of the small light in its windows.

Understanding her reticence, he let her go.

'You are right, for this is neither the place nor the time.' She thought he might stop there and walk away. She could see he meant to from the gleam of distance in his eyes, but he did not go. Rather, he began to speak again and in a tone she had never heard him use before. 'I am only a man, Lady Seraphina, and every time I look at you I am reminded of the fact, but know that if you wish me to stop any of what has begun between us…I will.'

The memory of Ralph Bonnington, she supposed. It was Trey Stanford's way of telling her that he was nothing at all like him. She was speechless as he bowed his head and left because his troth was exactly that which she wanted, and because the compliments he had given her were so unexpected.

He liked her and so did his sons! Even a new blast of snow did nothing to diminish her happiness as she turned the strange conversation over and over in her mind. He had promised her so much more than she thought he might, and although the gardens were not the place to press anything further, Seraphina was certain they would soon find another occasion.

Laying her fingers across her lips, she smiled behind her hands, a joy rising from deep within her. She was overwhelmed with the astonishment of one who finds herself in exactly the place that she had long hoped to be. Her eyes wandered across the high-and-ancient walls of Blackhaven, the patina of stone worn in places from time and weather, hundreds of years of protection imbued in their very strength. When she had arrived here she had found the castle forbidding and hostile. Now all she could see was the beauty of it.

Chapter Six

23 December

Voices brought Seraphina from her room early the next afternoon to be confronted directly by a large group of strangers in the salon at the foot of the stairs.

She recognised one of them as Lady Frobisher, an inveterate gossip and snoop and her heart sank accordingly. Lord Blackhaven did not look pleased at all as three young women leaned in towards him and amongst their company she saw exactly how he would be received in London. It would be with complete and utter delight, for his form was nothing at all like the fops that overran the social halls and ballrooms with their mincing ways and effeminate habits.

Nay, Trey Stanford with his night-black hair, amber eyes and danger would be like a panther amongst kittens. The

Titian-haired beauty next to him had her hand upon his arm. Proprietary and challenging!

'I should love you to come to our place for Christmas, my lord. Mama has made a great show of the decorations and our cook came highly recommended.'

'I think not, Lady Lydia.' His fingers unlinked her hand and he moved back.

The Frobisher matriarch, however, was having none of it. 'You said the same last year, my lord, and we heard that you had hardly celebrated the season. Besides, my daughters and I would be most happy to see you at our table with the children, of course.'

The girl she presumed to be Lydia coloured dramatically. There was not much of an age difference between them, but Seraphina felt a hundred years older. Not wishing to be caught in the awkward position of an uncertain exit, she came forwards. Helen Frobisher raised her monocle, peering up at her with a quizzical expression and Seraphina saw the exact moment she recognised her.

'Good God, Stanford. This gel on your staircase is the lost Moreton chit, is she not? What on earth is she doing here and in such awful clothes when the whole of London town is searching for her? Come down, gel, and let me see you better.'

The mouths of the three younger ladies behind were wide-open, eyes filled with shock as Seraphina moved to the last step. She was glad for the slight height that kept her above them all—it meant she did not have to meet their glances so directly.

'Why is she here, Blackhaven?' The older lady's voice had taken on a shrill tone, the flinted anger in her words mirrored in her eyes. 'If she is alone in your company, then she is exactly as her mother was—a whore who pretended to be a lady.'

'No, you have it most wrong.' Seraphina finally found her voice at such a brutal criticism. 'I am at Blackhaven Castle because—'

'Because she is my intended.' Trey Stanford finished the sentence for her as he strode forwards, taking her hand in his and pulling her close. 'Just this morning, Lady Seraphina has done me the honour of agreeing to become my wife.'

Seraphina felt the pressure in his fingers bearing down on her own. *Keep quiet*, they said, *and we may yet get through this*. Her heart was beating so fast at this unexpected new turn of events that she doubted speech could have come anyway.

'Your intended? There are rumours she is promised on the bequest of her father to Ralph Bonnington, the Earl of Cresswell, and now you say she is also your bride-to-be? If this is a trick, Stanford, you will pay for it. My Lydia was under the impression that it was her hand in marriage you had sought and to be so rudely compromised...'

The young woman in question began to sob, softly at

first, but then building, until the whole room was filled with her anguish.

Trey stepped forwards. 'I have been largely reclusive in Essex, Lady Frobisher, and I am sorry if you were under the impression that my one meeting with your family in town a month ago constituted anything like a proposal of such permanency. It was not my intention at all.'

'Lydia said there were other more clandestine arrangements made?'

The howling heightened.

'I see.' The woman pulled herself together and faced Seraphina straight on, the chagrin on her face because of her daughter's lies sharpening her query. 'I take it that you are without a chaperone?'

Seraphina was relieved when the Duke answered for her. 'My sister Margaret, Lady Westleigh, and her husband are in residence and she is a stickler for the correct.' His lie sounded eminently authoritarian, but short of demanding the presence of these others, Lady Frobisher had no way of accounting for the truth or otherwise.

'Then be careful, Stanford, that this betrothal is not as foolish as your last one and hope that the daughter of Elizabeth Moreton failed to inherit the wanderlust her mother was cursed with.'

The stillness in the Duke of Blackhaven was more menacing than any raised shout. 'You have said enough, Lady Frobisher. It would be wise if you went now before you say more.'

'Now listen here, my lord…' A man at the rear of the group had taken up the argument, his face florid with anger.

But the Duke was at the very end of patience. 'Get out.'

With a heavy click of her fan the woman turned, then thought better of it. 'I feel it to be my God-ordained duty to let the magistrate in Maldon know of this contretemps. If I were you, Stanford, I should keep all the silver ewers well out of sight before you, too, feel the heavy weight of the Moreton temperament descend upon you just as Cresswell did.'

With that they were gone, the door shut behind them and a servant Seraphina did not recognise standing at attention by the door.

Trey unlaced his grip on her hand in a quick movement and waved the man away, the tension in the room building as all the shouted insults of the woman were remembered. Finally, he spoke.

'Lady Frobisher will probably calm down once she has had the time to think things over. I doubt she will want to alert the magistrate.'

'How could she know anything about me?'

'The papers are full of the mystery of your disappearance from London and with you gone…'

He stopped as she looked up at him.

'With you gone anyone can say anything. And they have.'

'I see.' He had not mentioned the matter of her being his

intended at all. Rather he moved back and poured himself a drink from a decanter on a small desk. Brandy, Seraphina thought by the colour, so shocked that she had begun to shake. Trey Stanford swallowed his tipple in a single shot and poured another. This one he handed to her.

'I find a clear mind often only makes matters worse, Seraphina.' The first time he had ever used her Christian name and she liked the sound of it off his tongue. Upending the liquid just as he had, she coughed as the burn crawled down her throat.

'Lady Frobisher is a woman who could ruin your reputation in a heartbeat,' he said at length. 'And to find you here at Blackhaven without a chaperone would constitute a great scandal.'

She smiled, fortified by the effects of the drink, for if only everything could be so very easy.

'Oh, I think my reputation is already ruined, my lord.'

'Perhaps not. The world will be wary of the word of a man who is both a gambler and a heavy drinker. Although Ralph Bonnington might say you attacked him, he is without witnesses. Conjecture is all anyone has to work with.'

Seraphina had had enough. 'I can see no conjecture bigger than the false news of the betrothal you confided to the group who have just left, sir.'

He laughed at that. 'Surely you understand that a governess looking as you do would be fodder for endless debate. No one would believe you were here merely to watch over my children and you would never again be accepted back into the society you are used to.'

'I had no mind to go back, my lord.'

'Your mother said exactly the same thing to me after Terence died, but she was at odds to find another place to be at peace in, no matter how hard she tried to.'

This truth made her sad, but she could not leave it there. 'My parents' marriage was as false as you profess your own to have been and both ended badly. I should never agree to marriage unless there was love.'

'Indeed, those are my sentiments exactly.'

Such words confused her and a hope long missing from her life bounded into possibility. Was he saying he could love her? Did he mean to keep to the words given to Lady Frobisher because of such an emotion? She shook her head. A man like him would have the choice of any woman he wanted, one spotless of reputation and from a family well able to bring in a substantial dowry.

But what if it *was* she he desired? What if even for this small moment she might be his?

The clock on the mantel struck the hour of four and outside she could hear heavy rain against the window, melting the snow. The boys would be being readied for a bath by the night nurse and supper was more than three hours away.

Here, then, for this time she was cocooned in a room with a man who had stood up for her in front of strangers. No, more than that even—a man who had placed his own name on the line for hers, protective and honourable.

The kisses from yesterday still burnt into her lips and the drink she had taken made her bones feel languid and heavy.

Lord, she was so very beautiful, the blue of her eyes fanned by a pale grey ring and her nose sprinkled with freckles, true and straight. As beautiful outside as she was inside, the soft honesty of her words in the garden still rang in his brain. She had admitted her share of the depth of feeling between them and had told him directly that the kisses they had enjoyed in the gardens were a gift. Catherine would have allocated only blame and reproach, but Seraphina Moreton spoke of truth and love.

The pad of his thumb drew along her jaw carefully and up across her swollen top lip and her gaze did not falter as her lips came to meet him, sampling, pushing forwards.

He knew that he should pull away, but it was too late for that, too late for anything altruistic or honourable because he wanted Lady Seraphina Moreton as he had never wanted anyone else before in the whole of his life.

Helen Frobisher's false and perfidious assumptions were everything he hated in society. Lord, his wife had been a master at gossip and innuendo and the memories of those hurt by her sharp tongue were numerous. Seraphina, in contrast, was an innocent, crucified by all those about her who held a duty of protection and had neglected such obligation. As his hands tightened about her arms, his mouth came down upon hers.

Soft warmth met him in an equal measure, his lips slanting hard, seeking entry and finding it, no mind now for anything save the feel of loving, the promise making his heartbeat quicken. Aye, bodies had their own particular language and the feel of her skin, lustre smooth and unblemished, made him groan.

She was like rain after a long drought, moisture to fill all the dried and lost recesses of heart and soul. The words he had given to the Frobishers burned between them too, thrust into a kiss that was unequalled, a stack of papers on his desk falling around them as he inadvertently knocked them over, no sense in anything save that which nullified reason, the melding of two souls long left alone. He pressed in closer, his manhood swelling, all time and place lost as each sought the promise of more. He felt her shaking, moving, wanting, her fingers threaded through his hair as she drew him in, the honesty of her tender touch shattering the cold anger that had resided in him.

Released and unfettered.

When he pulled away he cradled her head against his chest. Protection had its own voice too, and it was not one that thought only of the heat of the moment. Seraphina neither deserved nor needed that.

'Lord, help me,' he said even as he meant not to, frustration cresting against pure and utter lust. The buds of her nipples showed hard against the perished blue velvet of her bodice and he softened his grasp.

'My sister and her husband should have been here by now.' Words of warning and intent. Words to take the sting from any perceived pressure and leave her with a choice she had long seemed bereft of. To do just as she wanted!

The blue of her eyes filled with question. 'The Moreton name does not hold the power it once did. She might hate me, this sister of yours, as much as the Frobishers. She might hear of the false promises you have made and believe that you meant them.'

The bitter taste of his last marriage rose up to silence the words that he should have given back in reply, but nothing came out. He should say that the promises were not pretended and that all he felt between them was real and true and right. But Catherine's poison had seeped in deep and there had been so many years of only regret.

Seraphina saw the shock reflected in his eyes, burning amber with a hint of something lost, the wound that marred half his cheek redder today than she had ever seen it.

He was a gentleman caught in the crossfire of society rules, one half of him wanting her too much and the other half not enough.

False promises? He made no move to deny them. She might have wept had he moved away altogether, but he did not, his grasp on her cast in steel.

Was it too soon to tell him that she would take such a lightly given troth and always honour it? If she gave him the words that hammered beneath every touch of skin and breath and heartbeat, what might happen?

I love you. I have always loved you. I shall love you for

*ever and ever until I take the last breath of life and then
beyond.*

Tears filled her eyes and ran down her cheeks unbidden. She did not brush them away or hide her face against his clothing. No, she looked at him with all that she felt, hoping it would be enough for him to understand, though when he set her apart she knew that he had not and the moment of honesty was lost.

'You are young, Seraphina, and I should not wish to rush you into something you might later regret.'

It seemed so very simple to place the onus of his withdrawal onto her because she could make no defence against such an argument. The ghost of Catherine Blackhaven floated around them, too; Seraphina could almost see her in the expensive braided velvets she favoured, her décolletage as low as permitted in her search for favour from all manner of men. Lord, how Trey Stanford must have hated that.

'I am not like your wife.' There, the words were out, bent into frankness and candour. Her parents' marriage, after all, had been one where the truth was sacrificed to as much duplicity as could be managed and Seraphina had no will to follow such a path. If the duke was going to abandon her, then he had to know exactly what it was he forsook.

Unexpectedly he smiled, the soft humour touching his eyes. 'Aye, Seraphina, that you are not and I am glad for it.'

His fingers trailed quietly against her cheek and she could feel the redness bloom down her throat beneath his fingers, but at the door someone hammered, loud against the quiet, unreal in the context of the room, an unwanted intrusion.

'It looks like we have company,' the Duke of Blackhaven said as he moved to the chair on the opposite side of his desk before calling an entrance. His man came in quickly, announcing the arrival of guests, and Lord and Lady Westleigh walked forwards.

Lady Margaret and Lord Gordon Westleigh were nothing at all like the couple Seraphina might have imagined. Instead of being tall, dark and beautiful like her brother, Margaret Blackhaven was short and rather stout, her mop of red hair pulled back into an ill-fashioned bun. Her husband looked like a copy of his wife, though his pate was balding, the few straggling hairs left carefully combed. Both smiled profusely and looked more than pleased to be at the end of their long and cold journey.

'It cannot possibly have been a year already since we were last here, Trey—' she began, cutting the sentence short as she became aware of Seraphina's presence in the room. The shout of children also distracted her as the three boys flew in, their arms around their aunt before she had the time to draw breath. The harassed-looking nurse followed them in.

'Aunty Margaret. Uncle Gordon. We were watching out for you.' Gareth's voice was filled with excitement.

'David said that you would not be here till the morrow.'

Terence added his piece and Margaret Westleigh's eyes widened, the look she gave her brother one of astonishment and delight.

'You can speak now, my love,' she asked, leaning down to give Trey's middle son a special cuddle.

'Miss Moorland made him,' Gareth rushed in. 'She brought Melusine to see us and the dog did a wee on the rug and Terence laughed and laughed and after that he could talk.'

'Miss Moorland?'

'Our governess. She looks after us and she finds Christmas trees. Papa kissed her under the mistletoe in the front room yesterday and he said that you and Uncle Gordon were not too old to learn to kiss either.'

'You said that, Trey?'

'I think Gareth has taken some liberty with the words I did utter.'

'But you admit that you kissed the governess in front of the children?' Trey's sister's hands went to her mouth as though her brother might indeed have taken leave of his senses, though when her eyes met Seraphina's they contracted with surprise and shock, astonishment running in an equal measure with intrigue.

Seeing his sister's consternation, Trey called forth the nurse and asked her to shepherd his children back to their rooms, promising his sons that once they were ready for bed their aunt would come up to read them a story. Within a moment the room was quiet again, an awkwardness standing in the place where high spirits had just lingered.

'You are the lost Lady Seraphina Moreton, are you not?' Margaret's voice was tight as she looked between them.

'Indeed she is,' the duke answered, 'and from your expression I can see you have also heard of Cresswell's ridiculous accusations.'

'Ridiculous?' Trey's sister's voice was almost shrill.

'They are ridiculous in the sense that no woman of any wisdom is going to lie there whilst Ralph Bonnington tries to rape her.'

'Cresswell is saying her father gave them the blessing they had both long sought. If one could believe Bonnington's point of view, then the imminent betrothal was more than mutual.'

'No, this is not true, Lady Westleigh. I had not met the earl before Papa brought him home to Moreton and left me with him unchaperoned.'

'You were left alone with a stranger by your own father?' The older woman's face went white.

'His gambling debts were piling up and he saw my hand in marriage as a way of remedying any debt.'

'Lord. So you have taken it upon yourself to shelter her from the law here at Blackhaven, Trey?'

'I am protecting her until we can repair to London and fight the claim.'

We!

The warmth of belonging suffused through Seraphina.

She knew the duke hated London and seldom went there, yet he was prepared to do exactly this for her—to go to the city fully exposed to the vagaries of hearsay and scandal to try to help her?

Seraphina expected Margaret to counter such a claim, but instead she, too, did something most surprising. She started to laugh, quietly at first and then with a great measure of mirth. When she had finally collected herself she began again to speak. 'I can garner support as well, brother. Ralph Bonnington has many more enemies than he has friends.'

'Bonnington is a bully and a tyrant.' Gordon had joined the fray now, his small eyes bulging with emotion. 'He challenged me in the club a few months ago for bumping against him when he had a drink in hand. With such behaviour it's a wonder he hasn't been taken to task well before now.'

'You ought to have hit him harder in London, Lady Seraphina,' Margaret added. 'Then we should not need to be worrying about him at all.'

Blackhaven smiled. 'If my family is anything to go by, we will be able to deal with Cresswell most satisfactorily, Seraphina. If the law does not hold him accountable then Margaret and Gordon shall.'

'But what of the promise my father made? He signed the banns to force the marriage.'

'A signature no judge of any repute would recognise.

God knows who allowed such a travesty to happen in the first place.'

Hope began to fill the dread inside Seraphina. With the lofty names of the high-born families at court behind her, things might well turn out to her advantage and the life she had imagined for herself might come to pass. But just what did she imagine now? Things had changed considerably and the social calendar of London palled against the beauty of Blackhaven and its master. She belonged here. She loved Trey Stanford and his children and the fact that she was becoming a valued part of castle life. She did not wish to leave Essex, not even for a day.

The loneliness that had always surrounded her was replaced with a joyful belonging.

If only he might love me back!

Catching Margaret Westleigh watching her closely, Seraphina hoped the woman had not seen what she was sure was written all over her face. A sibling insisting on her brother 'doing right' by her was the very last thing that she needed and she tried to school her expression into a polite indifference.

She also prayed that Lady Frobisher would not make good on her final threat to call in the local magistrate.

'Just let me have Christmas, Lord,' she whispered beneath her breath. 'Please just let me have something lovely to remember when all of this is gone.'

Chapter Seven

Seraphina spent the next hour with the children, leaving the Blackhaven guests to be entertained by the duke, and so she was surprised when just before supper Margaret Westleigh came to the nursery to find her.

'Might I come in and have a few words?' she asked softly as the boys were gathered up by the night nurse to be readied for their meal.

'Of course, my lady.'

Once seated on a small *chaise-longue* to one side of the windows Margaret looked a little ill at ease.

Trying to relax the tension, Seraphina began to speak. 'I realise that the situation of my being here like this is most distressing for you, Lady Westleigh, but I would like to say in my defence that I would never wish for any harm to come to your brother or to his sons…'

She petered out as Margaret held up one hand.

'*Distressing* is not the word I would use, Lady Seraphina. I might, however, chance the expression "happier than I have ever seen Trey look before in his life".'

Such an admission kept Seraphina speechless.

'My brother was married young to a woman who was both spiteful and selfish and any outer beauty she might have been blessed with was soon lost on all who came into contact with her. For the sake of the children he stayed married, for his wife always threatened to take his sons from him if he left. Such was Catherine's venom. When she died I breathed a sigh of relief and thanked God for the mercy. I am a religious woman, you understand, so such a prayer would not come lightly. My brother would never admit it, but I am sure he did the same.'

Rolling her fingers against each other, Margaret sat forwards. 'I tell you these things solely because you watch him like a woman with feelings much deeper than friendship, though if I am in any way overstepping the boundaries of propriety by mentioning such a thing, please stop me.'

When Seraphina did not she smiled, the brightness lighting up her whole face. 'In the past years I have observed Trey become a man who is cautious of life in a way he never was before, his self-imposed exile to Blackhaven taking him largely from the communion of others. Until now, when by his account he has told the Frobisher party that you are his fiancée and I am your supposed chaperone.'

'It was only said to save my reputation, I think, Lady Westleigh, and a way to stem the gossip because she had recognised me.'

'No, I disagree. My brother rarely does anything on a whim, Lady Seraphina, and I can assure you that after the debacle of his first marriage he would hardly be bandying such a troth around lightly unless there was much more than a grain of truth in it.'

An errant late-afternoon sunbeam slanted into the room, like a small harbinger, covering everything with gold. Sera watched the shadow of it on her hand and she smiled.

'So I have come to say that as a chaperone I would look the other way should you want to take the chance of knowing my brother…further. Christmas is the time for miracles, after all, and what greater miracle can there be but that of love? I should welcome you into our family with open arms, my dear, if you cherish him with even a fraction of the feelings that are on your face when you look at him.'

'You think he might return my feelings? He might love me as I love him?'

'Indeed I do, but unless you take him by surprise he might feel honour bound to never mention it.'

'By surprise?'

'Tomorrow is Christmas Eve, the day of hopefulness and promise. What better time than that to let him know exactly how it is you feel about him?'

Seraphina pleaded her absence from the evening meal and spent the best part of an hour soaking in a bath. Margaret Westleigh's talk about the loneliness of her brother had cemented something inside that had only been vague and undefined before.

If she did not act upon her feelings for the Duke of Blackhaven, she would lose the one man who needed her as much as she needed him. In love they would save each other. It was that simple.

Rising from the bath and drying herself, Seraphina released her hair from the tie that held it so that it fell long down her back, almost to the line of her hips, small wisps curled into ringlets. Men had commented on the colour of her tresses ever since she had first come out, and tonight she would use the pale flaxen-gold to its full effect.

With care she left the curl on show, fastening the openings as she donned her dark blue velvet gown. A burst of thunder outside had her turning to the threatening storm and smiling. Catherine Blackhaven's doing, no doubt, her last and futile attempt at keeping her husband under the spell of sorrow. Well, she would allow it no longer.

A few moments later she began to walk down the corridor towards his room.

Trey removed his boots and his cravat, untangled from the simple knot he had fashioned it into, before divesting himself of his waistcoat and his shirt. It had seemed a long night without Seraphina at his table, though his sister had said she was tired and had pleaded an early repose when he had asked after her absence.

Wiping back the length of his hair, he thought that he should cut it before it got too much longer, when a knock at the door took him from such musings. He had dismissed his butler for the evening and hoped that it was not Gordon come for one of his late night-time chats. All he wanted was to get into bed and go to sleep, his slumber of the past few nights severely lacking as his mind had mulled over all the things his body would like to do with the beautiful Lady Seraphina.

'Damn,' he murmured beneath his breath as he reached out for his shirt again. But the caller did not wait for permission to enter; as the door opened the one he was thinking about materialised, her old gown largely hidden by a fall of golden curls.

He could neither move nor speak. Lord, was he so tired he was now having visions? His swollen manhood pushed out against the fabric in his trousers and with no shirt on he knew that such a reaction would be well on show to all who looked.

And Seraphina Moreton was looking!

He made himself stand still, for the worry in her eyes was very real.

'I know, of course, that my presence in your chamber is most…most…'

As she floundered for the word he supplied it. 'Diverting?'

A rush of words followed, her voice brittle. 'Your sister spoke with me this evening about the wisdom of chasing one's dreams and her conversation was very convincing, though, of course, I should not wish to embarrass you by coming here and speaking of such things and—'

'Your hair is longer than I thought it might be.' His statement stopped the deluge of her words completely.

'It is?' He saw she swallowed, saw too that the knuckles on each hand were stretched into whiteness.

'I should have put it up, of course, but I needed to ask you something before bravery failed me altogether.'

'Then perhaps a brandy might help?'

His suggestion brought a quick nod and he crossed to the decanter on the table near the window and brought forth two glasses. His fingers shook and he swore beneath his breath, taking one deep swallow to steady himself before he handed the drink to her.

When she reached out for the fluted crystal glass the fall of her tresses inadvertently touched his hand and she did not look away. Rather, she smiled shyly, inciting a tug of lust to wash across him; like a schoolboy, he thought, neither composed nor calm. Her feet were bare. He saw this, too, as the fabric hiked up across one ankle.

Lord, the force of his want for her took the very breath from his body; catching at her arm, he held her lightly, allowing an escape.

'Be careful of what you offer, my love, for there are limits on any man's patience, especially dressed the way you are tonight.'

Seraphina could hear the anger beneath his observation and feel the tension in the way his fingers clamped around her wrist. Yet he did not frighten her at all with his naked chest and unbound hair, lying in all shades of black across his shoulders.

There were other scars there, too, over his ribs and his

upper arm. Deep scars denoting much hurt and agony. She reached out to touch his cheek, running her first finger softly across the mark, and he flinched.

'Who did this to you?'

'War,' he replied, barely above a whisper. 'I was hit on the heights above Corunna at about the same hour General Moore took his ball to the shoulder. They buried him there, in Spain, and I made it home to a wife who lay dying of a malady of the lungs after conducting an affair in the rain. After she passed away I swore that I should never again consort with beautiful women, yet here I am with the most beautiful one in all of the world.'

Such honesty almost made her weep. 'Your sister said that you were not a man to do things on a whim and the troth you gave to Lady Frobisher about our engagement would not have been given lightly. She also said that if I wanted to get to know you better she would, as a chaperone, feel predisposed to look the other way.'

As she finished the room spun quiet all about her, dust motes swirling in the light of candle around and around, waiting.

'What exactly is it that you are offering?'

'I am offering you my heart.' Her nipples stood proud in the cold air this far from the fire, as an unfamiliar ache formed. Deceit and artifice had ruined the Moreton family and she meant to find in honesty what Elizabeth and Seth had never been able to manage in dissimulation.

Love. It sang in the Christmas air like an aria, the old

tunes of festivity and hope full-blown in the possibility between them.

No limits set. Only choice.

'I have loved you for ever, you see.' She whispered it, like a promise, and could see in his throat the deep and steady beat as she brought up his hand and laid it over her breast. Seraphina closed her eyes momentarily when his fingers moved, seeking and knowing.

He was hers. The truth blazed like a flag of truce above resistance.

'Ahhh, Seraphina, my love. Margaret was right in all that she said...' His voice broke, the sound of one whose patience was all used up and he was aware of the hard ridge of his manhood between them.

Whole. It was her first thought as they stood, fitting into each other, the contours and shapes of muscle and bone perfectly in tune. She no longer felt alone as the orange glow from a late-banked fire touched them gently and the ache of it made her lift her glance to his.

He watched her, amber eyes predatory, the gold on the edge of sable alight with passion, drawing her in and telling her without words all that he was and would be for her. She felt his fingers move across the shape of her bottom, then up, taking a good knot of her hair in his grasp before his lips came down. Hard. Like a challenge, the soft ease in the room changing into fierceness. She liked the difference because it was what was welling up inside her, this raw and undisciplined need to have him take her, now in his chamber, hours of darkness before the breaking dawn.

She kissed him back, measure for measure, hungry for him, shaking with the want until she knew his taste. No longer careful or circumspect, but avid and voracious, her grip keeping his mouth in place as the breath she took was shared with his. Inseparable.

And when he lifted her into his arms, striding towards the bed, Seraphina simply turned her face into his shoulder to taste the salt on his skin.

God! He wanted her now, without even a modicum of foreplay, the long slender lines of her body doing things to his mind that he barely recognised. He tried to hold on to the sense of honour that should keep her virginity safe or at least gentled, but he couldn't control anything save the surge of craving that took him.

Seraphina was nothing like Catherine had been. She held no use for measured limits or sullen allowances. Nay, her honesty lay in response and in yielding, her breasts flattened against his and her fingernails scraping the skin on his neck, bringing him closer, her legs opening of their own accord.

Urgency was like a madness, he thought, each part of his body answering in the dark, for union and for touch, for the entwined length of her against him, spent into the bliss of a fragile joy.

It had been so long since he had last felt free, so many

damn years lived without the liberation of choice and pleasure that he was dizzy with the delight of it.

'You have given me back life,' he whispered, barely believing he had said the words drawn in blood across his heart, but such a debt needed to be both confessed and acknowledged.

Her smile was like the sun coming out from behind a thick band of winter cloud, warming him and absolving everything. Just now and just them, harmony tuned perfectly.

'Love me, Trey.'

'Ahh, sweetheart, that I do.'

Afterwards she lay in his arms, the moonlight slanting across the bed, silvered beams of pale, the old blue-velvet gown a puddle on the floor. She knew now what it was like to be loved well and long, the pain of the first time settling into only pleasure. The throb of memory made her move again as his finger came into wetness.

'I would not wish to hurt you?'

'You won't,' she replied, her hand pressing down even as she opened her legs for more.

Much later he took her again as she roused from sleep, the scent of Seraphina undeniable. This time she barely wakened as he turned her, a natural union of flesh that bore them both to the place of pleasure in the beaching waves of release.

No regrets or hesitation. No reluctance. He might have

stayed there within her had not the light of a new day crept up the glass of the window, signalling Christmas Eve.

Yet even then they again found the essence of each other, riding high on the peaks of ecstasy one more time before reality split them into two people and he lifted her into his arms in a blanket and returned her to the bedchamber that was only hers.

Seraphina woke alone, the ache of it winding her with its intensity as the import of all they had done brought the blood to her face. A fire had been banked and the room was warm—Trey's doing when he had carried her back at dawn.

She was no longer a virgin, yet she felt neither ruined nor afraid. For the first time in all her life she understood utterly that she was in the place she was meant to be. There was no question in any of it, no wondered truth.

Stretching her legs, she began to smile. Today was Christmas Eve and the gift of love shimmered brightly. Her fingers closed around the pearl at her neck and she whispered softly, 'I know now, Mama. I know how you could not have lived without him.'

Another gift, she thought, that of the acceptance of her mother's death. A great ease came. Her world had turned and wisdom had followed, the dark shadows of resentment softened into understanding.

Everyone was in the salon that housed the Christmas tree when she was finally dressed and came down an hour and a half later.

Her new gold-velvet gown shimmered in the light of a chandelier, lit at midday in the winter dullness, and the Brussels lace cascaded across the bodice in a perfect fit.

Everything stopped, voices, movement and music, as the faces around the tree noticed her presence. Then the boys whooped with delight, Melusine barked at their excitement and Margaret and Gordon Westleigh watched with broad smiles on both of their faces.

But she looked towards none of them. Trey Stanford stood beside the window, like a god, she thought. Today he wore black broken only by a white cravat tied simply at his throat.

She had never seen him more beautiful.

'Seraphina.' He came forwards and took her hand, the joy in his eyes making him appear younger. 'You look… perfect in gold.'

'Mrs Thomas fashioned the gown for me.'

'Like an angel,' Gareth whispered from the place at her elbow, his small hand creeping into her own. 'Our angel.'

The other boys stood beside her now, too, and in the far corner of the room Melusine played with the remains of a broken paper chain.

Her life. Fine and true and real, the smells of a Christmas feast wafting in from the kitchens.

Trey's expression, however, grew serious, a heaviness suddenly about him that was worrying. 'I should like to ask you something before we go in to eat.' Tension coated his brow and a shot of panic lanced through Seraphina's stomach. So formal. So distant. Could he think their union a mistake?

He stepped back and went down on to one knee before her, his face raised to hers as his hand held out the narrow gold ring he always wore on his little finger.

'I should like to ask you, Seraphina, if you would do me the honour of becoming my wife.'

Tears pooled in Seraphina's eyes, tears of happiness and wonderment. 'Yes. Yes, I will.' She could not believe this was actually happening, even when Trey stood and took her left arm to place the band upon the third finger. It was too big.

'I promise to buy you a proper one as soon as we can journey to London to choose.'

'I love you.' She said the words to him directly, glad that everyone could hear and that the boys would know the true meaning of a marriage.

And then beneath the glow of the tree and amidst the cheers of congratulations she kissed him, no light kiss, either, but one that spoke of all the longing that yearned inside.

Perfect, she thought, as the embrace finished, and the sun broke through the latticed windows and flooded the room with light.

Epilogue

Blackhaven Castle
Christmas Eve 1813

'Let's call her Eve,' Trey said as his daughter was wrapped in soft blankets, her face red with the energy required for birth as she gave a loud and lusty cry. Small tufts of pale hair sprouted from her head, curling in whorls of moisture.

'Eve Elizabeth Stanford,' Seraphina returned and held the baby to her breast, her dark eyes the exact same copy of her father's.

A year since Trey had asked her to marry him, nine months since she had fallen pregnant and six since the debacle of Ralph Bonnington had been thrown out of a London court.

'The boys were hoping for a sister. They have said it time and time again.'

'And you, my love. What did you hope for?' She reached for her husband's hand, liking the way his fingers wound around her own as they always did.

'That you would deliver safely, that was all I wanted. But a daughter...' She saw his eyes fasten on the rosebud lips and the flaxen hair. 'Now a daughter such as this one is likely to run me ragged when she is older.' He stopped and began to laugh.

'When you came to Blackhaven in the eye of a storm, I thought that the boys would eat you up for breakfast, but they did not. You were the one who changed us instead and made us a family again. Six now,' he added and bent down to lay a kiss on the forehead of his daughter before his lips came to her own.

'Ahh, Seraphina, if you had not come...'

She shushed him. 'I would have found you somehow.'

'I believe that you would have, my darling.' The darkness that had cloaked him was gone now, his velvet eyes raking across her face in love.

'Are you ready for the others? They have been waiting most impatiently outside.'

'Of course.'

He opened the door to their chamber and a flood of happy excited people streamed through. The boys came first, subdued a little in the unfamiliar face of birth, then came Margaret and Gordon with their many grown-up children, Melusine barking at their feet. Mrs Thomas had returned as well, her help with the birth invaluable, and bringing up the rear came three local women with whom Seraphina had become firm friends.

A life, she thought, as all looked at the newest Stanford. Connections and community. Outside the world was white and the wind hurled itself headlong against the castle.

Aye, Christmas indeed was the season of miracle and surprise....

* * * * *

Governess to
Christmas Bride

Annie Burrows

Annie Burrows has been making up stories for her own amusement since she first went to school. Her love of books meant she had to do a degree in English literature. She still wants the heroines of her stories to wear beautiful floaty dresses and triumph over all that life can throw at them. But when she got married she discovered that finding a hero is an essential ingredient to arriving at happy ever after. Annie welcomes readers to contact her through her website www.annie-burrows.co.uk.

In loving memory of my dear Godmother,
Aunty Peggy. I shall miss my Christmas card
from you this year.

Chapter One

It was when he heard the sound of children playing, some-where just beyond the belt of trees, that Lord Chepstow suddenly recalled why he'd had a niggling suspicion he ought to think twice about accepting the invitation to spend Christmas at the home of Lord and Lady Budworth.

Pippa's former school friend, Miss Honeysuckle Miller, worked here as a governess.

Honeysuckle—hah! If ever a girl was less aptly named, he'd yet to meet her. The name Honeysuckle conjured up images of sweetly scented warm summer evenings, and delicate, clinging blossoms. But Pippa's friend was sharp and prickly. The last few times he'd seen her, she'd given him the impression she was looking down her bespectacled nose at him, which was no mean feat, considering the top of her head barely reached the bottom of his chin.

Oh, yes, he could just see Miss Miller as a governess.

While Pippa had blossomed, year by year, growing into a lovely young woman it had been a pleasure to launch into society, Miss Miller had hardened into a veritable gorgon.

Yet he pulled Diamond up, allowing the rest of the party to canter on without him. Though he was at a loss to understand why, Pippa still regarded Miss Miller as her best friend. It made no difference that they now inhabited very different spheres. They wrote to each other regularly. And once Pippa discovered he'd stayed here, she would think it very odd if he hadn't, at the very least, enquired after Honeysuckle's health.

As well to get it over with as soon as possible. In fact, he could not think of a better time to renew their acquaintance. While he was mounted on Diamond—the most recent, and by far the showiest addition to his stables—surely she could not help admiring him, just a little, when he cut such a dashing figure?

He'd always been at a loss to comprehend that disapproving way she'd taken to looking at him, not when he'd never had any trouble charming any other female. He shook his head. It was absurd that it should matter, but he would infinitely prefer this one brief meeting to occur while he was on horseback, and she on foot, so that he could maintain the illusion of being the one looking down.

Anyway, even if she did find something of which to disapprove, she would not be able to be rude to one of her employer's guests, not surrounded by so many little witnesses. A smile played about his lips at the prospect of having Miss Miller, for once, at a distinct disadvantage.

As he turned Diamond's head to urge him towards the group of children he could now pick out, through the branches, he heard another of the riders break away from the group and approach.

'Where are you going, Lord Chepstow?'

He glanced over his shoulder to see Lady Springfield urging her pretty little roan mare after him.

'Just going to take a look at the children,' he said, tolerating her intrusive question only because Lady Springfield was scarce out of the schoolroom herself. 'Or rather, their governess. Got a notion she's an acquaintance of my sister's. They boarded at the same school. Ought to pay my respects, since I'm here.'

Lady Springfield pulled a face. 'Oh, governesses. A dreadfully boring breed.'

His smile faded. Even though he'd just been thinking far less charitable thoughts towards Miss Miller himself, it was quite different to hear a person who knew nothing whatever about her utter such a disparaging remark.

'Miss Miller is by no means boring,' he said firmly. No, what Miss Miller was, was awkward. On her first visit to one of his homes he'd assumed she was shy, and perhaps a little in awe of her friend's big brother, since she'd been unable to utter a single word without turning bright red.

Subsequent visits had made him revise his opinion. Eventually he'd asked Pippa outright why on earth she would keep on bringing such a sullen, joyless creature into his house. *'Why couldn't you bring a pretty, amiable girl to stay, just once?'*—instead of one who grew steadily more withdrawn and less easy on the eye with every passing year.

To his astonishment Pippa had squared her shoulders, taken a deep breath and, with the air of a martyr about to go to the stake, declared, 'It does not matter to me what she looks like. She's my best friend. If it was not for her, I do not know how I would cope with school.'

He'd accepted that could be true. Pippa was not all that bright. The Miller girl had probably helped her with her work. He could see her as one of those dull but diligent scholars who excelled at whatever task their teacher set. He still had a set of watercolours she'd done whilst staying with him one year, hanging in the bedroom she'd used. They looked so like the leaves of the bushes she'd copied, they could have gone into a book.

Besides, the girls had both started at Moulsham Lodge about the same time, having both just lost their parents. That, too, must have created a bond. Strong enough for Pippa to want Miss Miller at her side during her Season. She'd been quite downcast when the girl refused, saying she could not afford it. So downcast that he'd very generously offered to meet all her expenses.

He looked towards the belt of trees. He had actually quite admired her for refusing to let him frank her. Whatever the source of friendship between the girls, avarice played no part on Miss Miller's side. Which was a rare quality to find in a female in a society where self-interest was generally predominant.

And while Pippa had taken her place in society, Miss Miller had been obliged to take a job as an unpaid teacher at the school where they'd both spent their girlhood, just to secure a roof over her head.

'Do you know,' he observed to Lady Springfield, 'I find it impossible to despise any woman, gently born, who finds herself obliged to work for a living.'

He didn't suppose a spoilt, pampered creature like Lady Springfield would understand, but getting Miss Miller this post had been the cleverest and kindest thing Pippa had probably ever done. She'd somehow managed to persuade her husband to use his connections to find her friend a paid position, which was how she'd wound up here, looking after Lord Budworth's brood.

Lady Springfield raised her delicately plucked brows. 'But we surely do not need to go out of our way to socialise with them?'

It was a touch unsettling to find that he disapproved of sentiments he'd held not two minutes earlier. He hadn't intended to so much as dismount from his horse or waste more than a moment or two in getting an unpleasant obligation over with.

But he had decided to do the right thing, no matter how grudgingly, and was not about to change his mind because some chit barely out of the schoolroom disapproved.

'We?' He smiled sardonically, turned his back on her and spurred Diamond through the thicket. He was going to pay his respects to a friend of his sister's.

She could do as she liked.

He checked the moment he broke through into the clearing where a group of children of varying ages were charging around, ransacking the shrubbery for seasonal foliage with the aid of two youngish undergardeners. They all looked as though they were having a wonderful time.

Miss Miller was sitting to one side, all bundled up against the cold in an ill-assorted collection of shawls, gloves and overcoat, topped off with the most unflattering bonnet he'd ever seen perched upon a woman's head.

'Good God. Miss Miller, what on earth do you look like, perched on that tree stump?' He couldn't help it. The entire scene was so very far from anything he could have imagined her presiding over that he burst out laughing.

She got to her feet. The light reflecting off her spectacles made it impossible to make out her eyes very clearly. But he would wager she was giving him one of her gorgon glares.

From behind him, Lady Springfield's voice rang out, clear as a bell. 'A gnome! I do declare she looks just like a gnome.'

Miss Miller stiffened. She said nothing, but a tide of red surged into her cheeks.

'Lady Springfield,' he said reprovingly, turning his head to frown at her.

He might have known it would be no easy matter to shake her off. She was due to make her debut in a month or two, and he was about the youngest and most eligible bachelor present at this house party. Last night, at dinner, it had amused him to let her practise her entire repertoire of eyelash batting, coy glances, fan fluttering and hair twirling upon him.

He wished now he had given her a sharp set down. He wished he could do so now. It was incredibly unkind of her to mock a person who had not the luxury of answering back.

It was not his place to reprove a lady publicly, but when she drew level with him, he said in an undertone, 'That was not kind.'

'No, I suppose not.' She shrugged, flicking a derisive glance in Miss Miller's direction. And then added in a voice loud enough for everyone to hear, 'She cannot help what she looks like, after all.'

The sneaky little cat. She'd made it sound as though he'd made another derogatory remark about Miss Miller, rather than attempting to remind Lady Springfield what she owed to her position.

At that point Miss Miller dropped them both a perfunctory curtsy.

'Lord Chepstow,' she said in a voice dripping with scorn, as though she held him entirely to blame for Lady Springfield's behaviour. And expected nothing else.

And wouldn't you just know it, but there was absolutely

no advantage in being mounted on a magnificent stallion after all. He might not have been the one to call her a gnome, but it had been because he had laughed at her that Lady Springfield had felt free to let fly with that poisoned barb.

At that point Diamond sidled and tossed his head, as if to say, *That fellow up on my back is nothing to do with me. I am very well bred. Shall I toss him into the dirt for you?*

'So *this* is your little governess,' Lady Springfield said with scorn while he fought to bring Diamond back under control.

'She is not *my* governess. She works for Lord and Lady Budworth...'

'Oh, how very droll,' she simpered, the look of scorn vanishing as she turned her face to him.

By heaven, she was an example of everything he most detested in society women. She did not see him as a real person at all, any more than she saw Miss Miller as a person with feelings that could be hurt. No, when she looked at him, she saw a matrimonial prize to be won at all costs. But what man in his right mind would ever want to get leg-shackled to a creature who could change her face as rapidly as that?

Not that there had ever been any chance of anything developing between them. He had left London precisely to avoid falling into the matrimonial trap. One of his friends, Havelock, had developed pressing personal circumstances that obliged him to marry quickly. And while he hadn't minded sitting in the club, helping the poor fellow compile a list of characteristics to look out for in a potential bride, he had no intention of being there when he embarked upon his quest.

It didn't do to stay too close to a man who was so intent on putting his neck in a noose. Ten to one the ladies would take his brotherly support as a sign he was ready to go down the same route. And from what he heard, some of them could be pretty ruthless once they saw a man as legitimate prey.

Naturally, he would have to marry and produce an heir, eventually. But nobody but a really dull dog, or a man with a set of problems as dire as the ones Havelock was facing, would dream of hampering himself with a wife and children before his thirtieth birthday.

Especially not to a woman who could speak of another lady as spitefully as that. It had been like…watching someone kicking a kitten.

'Well, you have done what you set out to do,' said Lady Springfield, all smiles. 'We ought not to intrude upon her lesson, or whatever it is she thinks she is doing out here.' She wheeled her horse away as though she had complete confidence that he would follow.

He shot one irritated glance in the direction Lady Springfield had gone, then turned his full attention back to Miss Miller. He might not actually like her, but she was still Pippa's friend and, as such, deserving of his respect.

'Miss Miller, I…'

She lifted her chin. 'Well?'

'Ah...' Something about her proud carriage made him feel as though he ought to sit up straight and...attempt to measure up to her expectations.

How did she do that? With one hard look, she made him aware he had let not only her, but also himself, down.

He touched his riding crop to his hat in salute and made good his escape. Later, once she had recovered from this encounter, he would seek her out and devote at least an hour to actually examining her working conditions and really enquiring after her health.

And while he was at it, he could make it quite clear he thoroughly deplored the way Lady Springfield had behaved.

Chapter Two

And so, during the lull that always occurred after luncheon, when it was too early to think about changing for dinner, Lord Chepstow startled one of the footmen by asking for directions to the schoolroom.

He wasn't looking forward to the encounter. He owed Miss Miller something very like an apology. And he wasn't used to having to explain himself to anyone. Yet he couldn't let it rest. He'd gone to that clearing anticipating the prospect of having the odds stacked in his favour. It had taken Lady Springfield to show him exactly how unsporting such behaviour really was. And he hated having even appeared to have participated.

He paused on the landing outside the schoolroom, somewhat surprised to hear, yet again, what sounded like a pack of children thoroughly enjoying themselves. He pushed open the door and stood quite still for a few moments, his brows raised. He would have expected Miss Miller to have the children all sat in neat rows at tidy desks, their heads bent over some books, while she prowled up and down, swishing a cane. Instead of which, a brace of boys were kneeling on a rug in front of a cheerfully blazing fire, roasting…chestnuts, he supposed, on coal shovels. Just to one side, on a mound of cushions, were two girls, peeling them, blowing on them and passing them out to an assortment of little ones.

There was greenery all over the place. In buckets, and on tables in various stages of assembly. And it smelled wonderful. Not just the pine, but the roasting chestnuts and damp clothing airing out after a day spent outdoors.

Though it looked a bit chaotic, it was probably a child's version of paradise.

Miss Miller had been expecting Jane, with a tray of hot chocolate for the children, when the door opened. Lord Chepstow was the very last person she had ever expected to see up here, so very far from his natural habitat. It could only mean he was bored and looking for some distraction.

She braced herself for the impending confrontation, sensing it would be as painful as their last.

Two years it had been since she'd last seen him, and the first chance he got, he mocked her!

Just because she was short and couldn't afford new clothing, let alone the latest fashions, wealthy, privileged people like Lord Chepstow and that haughty girl he'd been riding with thought they could treat her as if she was in some way a lesser being.

She firmed her mouth against the worst aspect of it all: the discovery he still had the power to hurt her. She had convinced herself she was cured of that particular complaint. But all it had taken was to know he was in the house and the feelings she'd had since she'd been a schoolgirl came surging painfully back to life. That morning, when she'd heard other riders pass by, all her senses had gone on the alert, because she'd been so certain he would be out there amongst them. He loved riding. And he always looked particularly attractive on horseback. There was something about the way he governed those massive beasts, with such little apparent effort, which made her very aware of his vitality. His strength.

She'd strained her ears to pick out the sound of his voice, amongst all the others. And when she had, her heart had started galloping, her hands had trembled, all because she'd hoped she might catch a glimpse of him through the trees.

And then he'd burst through the brake on a magnificent black stallion, dressed just as she'd known he would be in clothes that were both elegant, yet cut to permit him the freedom of movement his love of sporting pursuits demanded.

Something had happened in the region of her heart when she'd noted that he was still wearing his hair a touch too long, meaning he would be constantly having to flick the blond fringe out of his laughing blue eyes.

And then he'd crushed her by simply taking one look at her and laughing at her. Tacitly agreeing with that beautiful girl when she'd said she looked like a gnome.

Oh, she'd always known what he thought of her. She'd seen it in his dismissive looks, even before she'd overheard him complaining to Pippa that it was about time she brought a prettier, more amusing companion home to stay during the holidays: *'Instead of which you seem to have let the dumpiest, dowdiest, dullest girl latch onto you.'*

And to think that the girls in her school had sighed with envy whenever they'd heard she was to spend another holiday with the parlour boarder, Pippa Preston.

They had no idea of what torture it had been. She had tried to explain that it was not a pleasure to reside in the same house as a gorgeous man who, when he did actually notice her, looked upon her as though she were some sort of strange specimen of…insect, pinned on a card. She'd almost been able to make them understand, when she'd reminded them how it felt to stand with their noses pressed to the baker's window, inhaling the scent of all the delicious goods on offer, all the while knowing they would never be able to taste them, since the majority of the pupils at Moulsham Lodge had not two farthings to rub together.

And she was doing it again. While he was looking round the room with a perplexed expression on his face, like an explorer venturing into hitherto uncharted waters, she was taking the opportunity to gaze her fill at him.

It had to stop.

'Lord Chepstow.'

He started and turned in her direction, but he did not see her until she stood up from the table at which she had been sitting, trimming branches to fashion into garlands.

He bowed and flashed her one of those dazzling smiles that was designed to turn the legs of any woman in the vicinity to jelly.

Well, *she* wasn't going to melt. It would only encourage him to laugh at her even harder.

'What are you doing up here?' She was so tense her voice came out rather shrill. But at least it was better than letting him know what effect he was really having on her. Even if she could quantify it, which would be virtually impossible, since there were so many contradictory emotions surging through her all at the same time. Although uppermost at the moment was irritation with herself for longing to have a man so very far out of her league actually see her as a woman, rather than a figure of fun.

'What do you want?'

He kept his smile in place only with considerable effort. He was not accustomed to having a woman behave as though she did not want him anywhere near her.

But then, she did have cause for being a touch upset with him. He would make allowances. For *her*. Just this once.

'I have come to, well…' he flicked his fringe out of his eyes '…to offer you an apology.'

'What?'

He wasn't at all sure he was gratified by her frank surprise.

'I said,' he repeated a little irritably, 'that I am sorry I—'

'Called her a gnome!' One of the little boys by the fireplace was squirming round on his heels, a delighted grin on his face.

His brows knit in a frown. Not only had he *not* been the one to make such a nasty remark, but it now appeared that in doing so, Lady Springfield had undermined Miss Miller's authority.

It was a good job he'd come up here. He could redress the balance—though heaven alone knew why he felt so protective towards a woman who looked as though she resented his very presence in her schoolroom.

'It is not at all the thing to call a lady unflattering names,' he said to the boy, then paused. 'I was out of line,' he said, deciding to keep Lady Springfield out of it. If he was too frank, it would call Lady Springfield's character into question, which would negate the impact of the point he wanted to make. But he shot Miss Miller a look, hoping she would be able discern his intention.

'I knew Miss Miller when she was quite a young girl, you see. And today, having not seen her for several years, I slipped back into speaking to her in a…in a sort of teasing manner.'

But the boy, who had not taken his eyes off his shovel full of chestnuts, remarked, 'She ain't a lady. She's a governess.'

'She is a lady by birth,' said Lord Chepstow firmly. All the girls at Moulsham Lodge had come from good families, one way or another. Even the poorer ones, like Miss Miller, who were obliged to help earn their keep by teaching the younger pupils or doing various household tasks.

'Besides, are not you a young gentleman? No matter what your opinions of a lady, it is not the gentlemanly thing to speak them aloud.'

The boy shrugged. His companion sniggered. And Lord Chepstow felt a twinge of…something rather like concern. He was sure Pippa had said Miss Miller was employed to educate Lord Budworth's two girls. But she had a whole room full of children of all ages and both sexes. And these two, in particular, looked like total rascals.

'Surely your schoolmasters have taught you some manners at whatever school you normally attend? Or your tutors? I can remember being birched for speaking out of turn when I was your age.'

'Oh, but our Miss Miller would never, ever resort to using the birch,' piped up one of the little girls from the mound of cushions, 'no matter how naughty we are. She promised. And it is of parrot mount importance to keep promises. Isn't it, Miss Miller?'

The little boys looked at each other and grinned as they perceived that, along with that nugget of information, they had just received licence to do exactly as they pleased. He marched across to where Miss Miller was just visible behind a mound of greenery.

'Why are those boys here?' He asked it in an urgent undertone. And why had she made such a ridiculous promise to her charges? He would have thought, from the impression he retained of her, that she would have become a veritable dragon of a governess. But the little girl, who he assumed must be one of the Budworths, had spoken of her with real affection.

Just as Pippa always did.

'More to the point, why are *you* here?'

'I was invited—'

'I did not mean at Budworth Hall. Although I suppose I might have known you would prefer to go hunting than spend too much time with your family,' she said with a sneer. 'I meant, in the schoolroom.'

He winced. She obviously knew Pippa had invited him to spend the season with her oh-so-worthy, but oh-so-boring husband down in Kent. But Christmas was a time for making merry. And the last thing he wanted was to waste a week of his life enduring the company of a man who looked as though he was just itching to preach him a sermon on the value of abstinence, or chastity or any number of the virtues that robbed life of all its spice.

'I did not exactly choose to come here in preference to anywhere else,' he began. He'd just decided, after sitting up half the night helping Havelock compile his list, that it was high time he left the metropolis. 'I had several invitations from which I could have decided, but in the event, I picked one up at random, from the sideboard...'

'And just set out without bothering to inform your hosts you were about to grace them with your presence. It's all of a piece,' she huffed.

'Well,' he said, growing increasingly nettled, 'at least you cannot accuse me of *deliberately* choosing the Boxing Day hunt over the company of my sister, though I cannot deny I shall enjoy the sport on offer here. Nor do I care for the implication that I have ever failed in my duty to Pippa in the past.'

'What about the way you packed her off to school while she was still mourning the loss of your parents? Or the fact that you only managed to dash off one or two terse little notes, in any given year, when she *lived* for the hope of a letter from home…'

'I have never been much of a one for writing letters.' But Pippa had *lived* for them? Why had she not said? 'And what would I have put in them, anyway? What was there about my life I could have related to an innocent schoolgirl?'

That remark appeared to act upon her like pouring oil onto a flame.

'Hardly anything, to judge from the rumours that came to us about your…doings! And from the reluctance you demonstrated in accommodating her in any of your houses when you did deign to notice her existence.'

'That is most unfair. I put up with her bringing you to stay, didn't I? That should tell you something.'

She looked as though she was about to explode.

'It told us you were glad she had a companion to occupy her, so that you did not have to bother!'

'I did my best to amuse the *pair* of you. I took you to Gunter's for ices, and Vauxhall to see the fireworks…'

'That was only on the very last occasion I stayed with you, or rather, with Pippa, in the hotel rooms you had booked. Do you have any idea how excited she was when you wrote to say she would benefit from some time in Town before she had her Season? Or how bitterly disappointed when it was not you who came to meet us from the stage, but that woman you hired? During that entire month, you graced us with your magnificent presence a total of *four* times. And what a sacrifice you considered it! Oh, yes, you made us very aware of how much you wished you could have been doing something more amusing.'

Had he? He had thought he had concealed his boredom at having to accompany two such very young ladies to the various insipid events the duenna he'd hired had recommended, with considerable aplomb.

'If Pippa did not like the way things were, why did she not say so at the time? She has never complained. Not once.'

'It is not in her nature to complain. Pippa is the kind of girl who makes the best of everything. Besides, she idolises you,' she finished with a contemptuous curl to her lip.

'Whereas you clearly don't.' Because she thought he'd let Pippa down, which at least went some way towards explaining all those scowls. She'd clearly been harbouring a whole heap of imaginary grievances against him.

'Miss Miller,' he said rather tetchily, 'I came to make amends for the words I spoke to you this morning, not to rake over the coals of past errors. If, indeed, I made any.' Which he didn't really believe. If Pippa had not been happy, she would have told him, and he would have rectified the problem. 'And what do I find? A woman who is so overwhelmed by the number of children in her charge that she has become a shrew.'

She gasped as though he had struck her. And he found himself, once more, having to explain his position.

'Not that you can help it, I am sure. It is clearly too much for you, having all these extra children foisted on you. Especially those boys. Who are they?'

And why did it all bother him so much? Or at all?

He had never felt the least bit protective of any other female, except Pippa. He could remember his hackles raising in just this way whenever some unsavoury character had attempted to take advantage of his sister's innocent nature during her Season.

And suddenly it all made perfect sense. He'd only ever seen her before in company with Pippa. He identified her with his sister. And he couldn't help wondering how she would cope, faced with similar difficulties. After all, if their parents had been as improvident as Miss Miller's, Pippa could have ended up having to earn her own living.

This was some sort of…misguided brotherly concern he was experiencing.

'If you had the least scrap of intelligence you would realise these are the children of Lord and Lady Budworth's guests.'

Which reminded him she was not a bit like his sweet-natured sister.

'Yes, yes, that much is obvious,' he said witheringly. 'But why are they here? And why are there not more staff helping you mind them?'

'Since when,' she said, drawing herself up to her full height, which still did not make much of her visible over the greenery, 'did you care tuppence for servants, or how much work you make for them?'

'What? I—'

'Never! And the way you waltzed in here, without bothering to let anyone know you had decided to accept an invitation sent to you for all I know *weeks* ago, just goes to show you haven't changed a bit. You didn't care what problems turning up unexpectedly might cause the housekeeper or the maids who had to make up a room in the twinkling of an eye, not to mention the other staff who had to shift about to make room for the servants you brought with you—and you accuse the *other* guests of not considering the servants because they have consigned their children to my care for the duration of their stay?'

It looked as though she only paused then because she had run out of breath.

'You haven't changed much either,' he observed in a lazy drawl. 'Still as grumpy as you ever were. Quite unjustly, as it happens. It is true, I came here on a…whim, if you like, but I am most considerate of my own servants.'

'That's not what I remember. Your own housekeeper used to tell us tales of how you would disappear for weeks on end because you'd taken it into your head to…well, to sail off in a fishing boat so that you could find out what it felt like to be a smuggler, or some such ridiculous prank. And then as like as not you'd turn up with half a dozen guests she would be expected to put up and feed, and—'

'It is not the place of any of my servants to question my movements. And if they don't like their working conditions, they are free to leave my employ. But by and large, they don't, you know.'

'That is just because you turn on that smile of yours whenever one of them complains, I dare say, and…and grease their palms in the belief that your money can buy you out of *any* amount of trouble—'

'I think you have said quite enough, Miss Miller. I came up here in a spirit of goodwill. And I only spoke of your own position as a member of staff here because it seems to me that you are being taken advantage of. Surely you should not be in sole charge of so many children?'

'I am quite capable of minding any number of children. I have been doing so for years.'

'Girls, maybe. But not boys. And not boys who are used

to being kept in check by regular use of the birch. What on earth made you decide not to use it?'

'How dare you question my capability?' she snapped. 'And what business is it of yours how I run my own schoolroom?'

'As much as it is your business to question the way I live my life, or the relationship I have with my own sister, or my treatment of my own staff.'

She gasped. He was right!

She couldn't believe he'd provoked her into losing her temper like that. In front of the children, too. She always remained cool, calm and collected when in charge of children, no matter what the provocation.

But then no child could possibly be as provoking as Lord Chepstow.

'You need help,' he said firmly. 'You cannot possibly hope to control all these children.'

'I *was* controlling them very nicely before you strolled in.'

'That was before they discovered you will not beat them, no matter how naughty they are. There is nothing more appealing than taking down an authority figure without any real power. Only consider how much pleasure young men first on the town take in boxing the Watch.'

'Y...yes, I know.' It was galling to admit it, but he was right about that, too. She had no problem at all controlling any number of girls, of whatever age. She'd had plenty of experience during her time at Moulsham Lodge. But boys…well, she knew nothing about them at all. Jane, the second parlourmaid, who had lots of little brothers, had advised her to give them plenty of exercise and plenty of food. And so she had taken them outside and kept them there as long as she could, hoping they would burn off the staggering amount of energy they seemed to possess. So far, she had managed to keep them so busy they'd had no time to get into mischief.

But the look of glee that had passed between William and Thomas when Annabel had let slip that she never used the birch did not bode well.

'It is as well I am here, then.'

'Why?'

'Because,' he said irritably, 'I can keep an eye on them. Make sure they behave.'

'You?'

Why on earth would he do such a thing when she'd done nothing but shout at him from the moment he'd walked through the door? She felt terrible. If this was an example of turning the other cheek, then no wonder the Bible recommended it. It made her feel horribly guilty without him having to utter a single word of rebuke.

'I really can manage. Truly. You don't need to…' she began, only to stutter to a halt when he peeled off his jacket and rolled up his shirt sleeves.

She could not tear her eyes away from his forearms, which were corded with muscle and dusted with dark blond hair. So very strong. So very masculine.

So very…vexing. She couldn't stand here, drooling over the sight of his bare arms, when she was in charge of a room full of children.

Nor could she realistically beg him to cover himself up. It would be an admission that the sight of his skin did things to her that…were totally inappropriate for a lowly governess to feel for a viscount.

'I want some more!' One of the little ones was wailing, which drew her attention away from Lord Chepstow for long enough to notice that the chestnuts had all gone.

She clapped her hands to gain everyone's attention.

'Time to clean up,' she said. 'Jane will be arriving with some lovely hot chocolate any time now. Boys, will you sweep up the husks, and clear away the fire irons, while you two, Lotty and Honoria, clear a space on the table there for Jane to set out the drink. Annabel and Mary, would you please keep an eye on the little ones, so that—' There was a clatter of metal, and a bloodcurdling yell.

'Lord Chepstow. What do you think you are doing?' While her back had been turned to marshall the girls, he had got hold of a poker, which he was brandishing as though it were a sword. William was employing the tongs to fence with him, while Thomas was writhing on the hearthrug, clutching his shovel to his armpit and groaning.

'Defending the poop deck against boarders,' said Lord Chepstow, parrying a thrust from William's tongs. 'Take that!' He thrust his poker at the boy, who caught it neatly under his arm and collapsed onto the hearthrug next to his companion, by which she perceived everyone was supposed to understand he had slain both boys.

'Vile dogs,' he snarled, 'you are now my captives. Either walk the plank, or be prepared to swab the decks.'

From a pocket, he produced a red spotted handkerchief, which he tied over his head. And since he was already without a jacket, he immediately looked exactly like a pirate captain.

She watched, spellbound, as the boys, groaning piteously, picked up the brush and shovel and, on their knees, began to sweep up the chestnut husks, while Lord Chepstow stood over them, legs braced, hands on hips, threatening them with all manner of revolting punishments if they did not do dread Cap'n Cutthroat's bidding.

'Lord Chepstow,' she repeated sternly, advancing on him across the schoolroom, while the girls, rather than clearing anything away, giggled as they watched the performance.

'There be no Lord Chepstow here, me proud beauty,' he said in a most peculiar accent.

And felt as though he had been struck dumb when he turned to look at her. He couldn't reconcile the shapely sylph who was sashaying out from behind that table with the dumpy little creature who'd been huddled on that tree stump. Or the awkward little girl with her hair in braids who'd glowered at him over the breakfast cups. She was not wearing any kind of head covering today and had arranged her hair—oh, yes, very well then, her *braided* hair—into an intricate arrangement on the top of her head which put him in mind of a coronet.

And in the past she'd always worn such badly fitting dresses there had been no telling what shape she might have been underneath. There was no mistaking her shape now, though. The gown might be as unfashionable as anything he had ever seen her wearing, but that did her no disservice. It followed the natural contours of her body, nipping in at her neat little waistline before flaring out over generous hips.

He swept her a courtly bow, while he attempted to recover from the shock, and said, 'Cap'n Cutthroat, at your service.'

Then, to distract himself from the jolt of attraction he'd felt, he poked William in the back with the toe of his boot. 'Faster, you dog!'

'Lord Chepstow! That is no way to treat children.'

'These b'aint be no children,' he said, his accent growing even thicker. 'These be scurvy sea dogs, doomed to swab the decks of my ship for the next—'

'That is quite enough. I will not have you mistreating any child under my care...'

He leaned towards her, saying in an undertone, 'They're loving it. I've made a game of a chore they would have balked at, Miss Miller. You should be thanking me...'

She smelled of the greenery she had been handling. And soap. And woman. And the skin of her cheek was as soft as a peach. And she had a delicate little chin and a neck that seemed to go on for ever. And for some reason, the fact that her earlobes were bare of any adornment made him want to nip at them with his teeth.

'You are getting them over-excited,' she protested, 'when it has taken me all day to get them into a tractable state.'

Damn, but they weren't the only ones getting excited. He stepped back, raising his hands in a gesture of surrender.

She marched to the door. He found himself watching her hips swaying and her skirts swishing in time with her angry footsteps. And promptly decided he liked a woman to wear full skirts. There were such possibilities. She could hitch them up and go running after her charges, should the situation demand it.

And everyone would get a tantalising glimpse of ankles...probably calves and knees, too...

He brought himself up short. He had no business speculating about the shapeliness, or otherwise, of Miss Miller's legs.

'Get out,' she said sternly, flinging open the door.

'You don't mean that,' he said with his most disarming smile.

'No pirate captains allowed in my schoolroom.' She folded her arms and glared at him. 'Out!'

Earlier that day he had remarked on the tangible air of authority she bore. And now, with her hair as it was, she looked positively...queenly.

He shrugged. It did not matter how she established her authority over her subjects, only that she did so. And van-

quishing a pirate captain was as good a way as any to demonstrate who was in charge around here.

'If that be the law of this land,' he said in his best pirate
voice, 'then I must obey, my queen. Farewell, shipmates,'
he said, saluting the children as he strode to the door.

They waved back, but among the choruses of farewell,
he thought he heard her muttering, 'And good riddance,'
as she slammed the door behind him.

Chapter Three

~~~~~~~~~~~~~~~~~~~~~~~~~~~~~~~~~~~~~

Well, naturally he couldn't leave it at that. Lord Chepstow thrived on challenges and there was nothing at Budworth Hall that was anywhere near as challenging as Miss Miller's attitude towards him.

So, after dinner that night, instead of joining the ladies in the drawing room or going along with the men who were making their way to the billiard room, he headed straight up to the schoolroom.

He hadn't won Miss Miller over with his apology earlier. Nor his heroic efforts to keep the boys in line for her. She seemed to have stored up so many grievances towards him over the years that it would take some ingenuity to discover the way to win her round.

But then, as he mounted the stairs, it occurred to him that he'd never really attempted to do so before. He'd not thought her worth the effort. But he'd seen her in a new light today. In the two years since he'd last seen her, she'd metamorphosed into a shapely and quite startlingly attractive young woman—if you but ignored the spectacles.

Not only that, but she had character traits not often found in a female. She was intelligent, hard working, loyal to her friends, not motivated by greed… He came to a standstill. Had he just recited the first four items on Havelock's list? He shook his head in wonder. By that reckoning, Miss Miller would make his friend the ideal wife.

He frowned. No, by heaven, she wouldn't though. If Miss Miller had wanted a husband, she would have jumped at the chance to share a Season with Pippa.

He carried on climbing the stairs. Unlikely as it sounded, Miss Miller was a woman who would rather fend for herself than hand over control of her life to a man. In fact, she… Good God! What on earth had been going on since he'd last been up here?

The children were no longer in evidence, but they'd left behind a scene of…utter carnage. Boughs of pine and holly were strewn all over the schoolroom floor. Their buckets were overturned, the floorboards stained with the murky water that had seeped from them. The desks and chairs were strewn haphazardly around the room as though a giant had been playing spillikins with them.

And on the hearth, with a bucket of water at her side and a scrubbing brush in her hand, knelt Miss Miller.

She turned to see who had opened the door and, when

she recognised him, her whole face screwed up into the most ferocious scowl he'd ever seen her muster.

'Now what do you want? Is there nobody else in this entire household you would rather torment?'

She dunked her brush into the bucket with a splash and set to scrubbing the fire surround with vigour. It drew his eyes to the way her skirts moulded the stubborn little bottom pointing in his direction. His lips curved into a smile. If she had any idea how enticing those regular, rhythmic movements were, she would most certainly *not* be giving him such a treat.

He cleared his throat and dragged his mind out of the gutter.

'Miss Miller, it is most unfair of you to make such a cutting remark,' he said, feeling a bit like he did at the beginning of a fencing match, raising his sword in salute to his opponent.

In fact, if he stood here staring at her bottom for very much longer, he would be saluting her with something more tangible than an imaginary sword.

He turned round to shut the door behind him, incidentally shutting out the sight of her kneeling figure and the erotic possibilities that inviting posture had put into his brain.

'I know that I let some words slip from my mouth, earlier, before thinking what effect they might have had upon you, but you cannot deny I apologised and made amends.'

'You call this making amends?' She knelt up and waved

her scrubbing brush round to indicate the wreckage of the room, spraying a wide arc of dirty water across the hearth.

He was about to point out, in the spirit of a riposte, that she could hardly blame him for anything that had happened when he wasn't even there, when a telltale tremble to her lower lip slipped under his guard. She was not just angry. She was really upset. Almost on the verge of tears.

That was why she'd turned her back on him. She had not wanted him to see.

Any more than he had wanted her to see his burgeoning arousal.

'No horde of vandals,' she breathed, 'could have wrought more devastation upon ancient Rome than those…those little *beasts* did today.'

He knew she was talking about the boys. 'It was finding out you won't beat them, no matter what they do,' he said. Hands on hips, he gave the room a leisurely perusal. 'It must have acted upon them like a…' his gaze returned to her, to see her hunched over, one hand over her face, the other still clutching the brush, which was dripping water on to the hearthrug '…challenge,' he finished lamely.

'A challenge?' She raised her face to glare at him. 'You brush aside all their naughtiness as a…as a…' She flung the brush into the bucket with a splash. 'It was *you* who set them off with that stupid pirate game,' she said. 'After that, they turned every implement they could find into a weapon.'

The duel was on again. Thankfully. He much preferred

to see her with the energy to spar with him rather than slumped down in an attitude of defeat.

'I was at my wits' end by the time Jane—that's the second parlourmaid—came in with the drinks. I had run out of ideas to keep them at least in one corner of the room, so that they wouldn't accidentally hurt any of the little ones. But fortunately, or so I stupidly thought, she has lots of little brothers, so I asked her to find them something they would enjoy that would keep them quiet...'

'That was not a stupid idea. It was a very good idea...'

'No, it wasn't! She taught them how to make... Well, I don't know what you would call them, but I never knew paper could be put to such a disgusting use.' She waved at the hearth, which he now saw was peppered with spitballs.

His lips twitched.

'You find this amusing? Of course you do. Because at heart, you are just the same.' She scrambled to her feet, clenching her hands into fists as though gearing herself up to do battle.

'You saunter through life, untouched by care while legions of servants follow in your wake, cleaning up the mess you make...'

She'd said something of the same nature earlier regarding his treatment of servants. And since all his staff appeared perfectly content in his employ, it stood to reason that it was her own treatment, at the hands of her own employers, about which she was really talking.

'Miss Miller, you have already stated that the fact

that the boys learned to make spitballs was not my fault. You are—'

'But you do think it sport to ruin everything I've worked so hard for.' She stalked towards him, her whole body quivering with fury. 'I…h-hate Christmas! All it is is an excuse to pile more and more work on us so that you can have your stupid balls and parties, and…'

She was within striking distance. On a reflex, he caught hold of her clenched fists and drew them to his chest.

'Miss Miller, I don't think you know what you are saying. You are overtired and overwrought—'

'I know exactly what I'm saying,' she protested, but quickly turned her head to one side, as though she could not meet his eye. But it didn't appear to help her, because her shoulders sagged.

'How could I ever have been so deluded as to think I had any control over any aspect of my life? Not even this schoolroom. All it took was Christmas to burst in and shatter all my schedules, all my routine, into so much…chaos.'

Normally, whenever a woman began to make a litany of complaints, he would put on his hat and leave.

But then normally the woman doing the complaining would be a mistress, with whom he was already growing bored.

Instead of wanting to take to his heels, he found himself wishing he could do something to lift some of her burdens from her.

He put one arm about her shoulder, led her across to

one of the window seats and pushed her down onto the cushions.

The fact that she immediately turned her face away, removed her spectacles and, closing her eyes, pressed her face to the glass wrenched at him. She hated him seeing her like this. But she had used up every last ounce of her self-control.

He stepped back, racking his brains to think of something he could do for her. What was distressing her the most?

The state in which the boys had left her schoolroom.

'I'm dreading tomorrow,' she said in a weary voice, not even bothering to open her eyes. 'I was so grateful when Pippa got her husband to get this job for me. But I should have known from that interview...' She sighed heavily. 'When Lord Budworth told me he wanted someone who would keep his daughters in line and that I looked exactly the sort of woman who wouldn't stand any nonsense, I should have told him I would never, ever maltreat any child entrusted to my care. Instead, I stupidly thought that I would show him my way was better. I thought I could prove you don't need to beat children who can't do their sums or lock them in a cupboard for letting their attention wander during grammar. I thought I could be the kind of teacher I wished I could have had. The kind who listened and tried to understand, and found ways to help children overcome their difficulties, not beat them for failing to meet impossible standards.'

She could hear Lord Chepstow moving about the room.

Unsettled, she supposed, by hearing about a side of life in which he could have no interest. And trapped by his innate breeding into staying until he could come up with a legitimate excuse for leaving.

'You were locked in a cupboard?'

'I was not talking about me.' She sighed. 'I was bright enough to escape the worst sorts of punishment inflicted by teachers whose sole source of consolation seemed to be in making others more miserable than they were.'

But she had not had a happy childhood. He thought back to some of the things Pippa had said about her in the past and matched it up now to the fact that he always thought she looked as though she had forgotten how to smile.

And felt a flash of irritation with himself. She hadn't had anything much to smile about. He could have been kinder to her, rather than dismissing her as being dour and dull, and not worthy of a second look.

He *should* have looked. He would have seen, if he had bothered, what Pippa had always seen: that she was basically a kind person, struggling to survive in a harsh environment. Then he would not have been so surprised to find her prevailing over a band of happy, carefree children in the woods earlier.

'I don't even know why I'm talking to you at all.'

It was such a luxury to have someone in whom to confide. Someone she could trust. Oh, not because Lord Chepstow cared. In fact, the very opposite was true. It was because he *didn't* care, because there was nothing she could say that could possibly give him a lower opinion of her than he already had that freed her to speak the truth. She'd not dared let any of the staff here know how badly she was struggling. Who knew what they would do with the information that she was an impostor? That she didn't deserve to hold such a responsible position?

And the proof of that was that she was sitting here, complaining, when there was work to be done. Indulging in just one more weary sigh, she opened her eyes and put her spectacles back on.

'What are you doing?' While she'd been unburdening herself, he'd whisked through the room, righting over-turned chairs and pushing desks back into place. More or less.

'Well, even though I have never done the work of a housemaid before, I would have thought it was obvious I am making some attempt to set this room to rights.'

'You?'

'Why not?'

She briefly considered handing him a brush and shovel. Or the scrubbing brush. She would love to see him roll up his sleeves again...

She shook her head, impatient with herself.

'Because...you are just one of life's butterflies. You flit through life sipping at nectar wherever you happen to alight. You don't really care about...about anything.'

That was not true. He cared about a lot of things. Not that he was the type to go round making a lot of noise about it, like Pippa's self-righteous husband. But to liken him to a butterfly...well, that conjured up the image of a man who only thought about his clothes.

'I enjoy life. I make no apologies for that. I am impulsive, certainly—'

'Oh, so *that* is why you have come up here. It was some sort of...whim.'

The fact that she had pretty much hit the nail on the head made him determined to change the subject.

'More to the point, what is the likelihood of Lord or Lady Budworth coming up here? From what I have observed, I should think the chances pretty slim. So that they are never likely to know things got a little out of hand.'

'That's...that is true, actually.' She sat up a little straighter. 'Lord Budworth has only set foot in this schoolroom the once. And fortunately, at the time, the girls were both sitting at their desks, working on their letters.'

He bent to right an overturned chair. 'And by tomorrow morning you will have thought of some way to keep those...Vandals gainfully occupied. Boys are no worse than girls,' he said, suddenly determined to defend his entire sex. 'Just different. You have no experience with them, but I have never known you to fail at anything you put your mind to.'

'How do you know that? You have barely ever spoken to me.'

'Pippa never ceases to sing your praises,' he said drily, pushing a table back into almost exactly its original position. 'I expect the children are all a bit more lively than usual, with Christmas being so close. And I know you don't like Christmas now, but can you not remember what it felt like when you were a child?'

She flinched.

'Christmas was the worst, the very worst time of the year,' she said vehemently, 'because it…because, oh, everyone else in the town would be decking their homes with greenery and preparing to celebrate, but the tide of jollity would always sweep right past the doors of Moulsham Lodge, leaving its pupils stranded on our desolate little island. And it was always such a stark contrast to what I remembered from my…early years when Christmas *was* a time of warmth and jollity. That was what made it the worst day of the year. That was why I hated Christmas. It made me so painfully aware of all I'd lost.'

'You know,' he said casually, although he had been struck by a rather unsettling thought, 'Pippa never complained so much about the school. If it was really so dreadful…'

'Oh, well, she was a parlour boarder. Since you paid extra for her, she ate her suppers with the staff and other wealthy girls. And enjoyed all sorts of privileges denied to us charity cases.'

'I am sorry to hear your schooldays were so unhappy,' he said, though he was relieved to hear Pippa had not suffered in silence.

She sighed, removed her spectacles and rubbed at the bridge of her nose.

'How I wished there had been one teacher, just one, who would make some attempt to alleviate the drab uniformity of my life. Every child ought to know some happiness, don't you think? Even if she has been relegated to an institution. But they were all trapped in their own cycle of despair. I vowed I would never end up like them. I vowed if ever I had charge of children and I could celebrate Christmas how I wanted, I would make it a Christmas they would never forget. I wanted so much for it to be perfect. My first Christmas away from Moulsham Lodge and I have the freedom to do whatever I want with my rooms and their schedule. And I was going to organise games, and sing carols, and make garlands and...' She waved her hands at the greenery he had not yet made any attempt to sort into any kind of order. 'It's all ruined. They don't appreciate what I'm doing. They don't know what it's like to do without. They cannot imagine what it would feel like if their parents were to die and they were to find themselves suddenly transported to a place like Moulsham Lodge, where nobody gives a fig for their grief and loss. Where they are beaten for crying and punished for complaining—' She brought herself up short.

'I am sorry,' she said stiffly. 'You did not come up here to listen to this sort of talk.' Though she could not imagine what he had come up here for. Whatever it was, she would never know now. As soon as he decently could, he would beat a hasty retreat, thinking that he had never encountered such a pathetic creature in his life.

Dowdy, and dull and pathetic: that was her.

'Please, don't apologise. You have nothing to apologise for,' he said with a frown as she slumped back against the windowsill. What a grim childhood she'd had. Yet she hadn't let it make her bitter. Oh, she was not in the best of spirits at the moment, but if he knew anything about it, and he was beginning to think he did, once she had unburdened herself, she would throw herself right back into her quest to make the world a better place for children.

'I do,' she said. 'I don't deserve to have this job at all. I'm an impostor. A more experienced governess would have no trouble keeping those boys in line, no matter what time of year it was.'

It was a great pity she had not come to London for Pippa's Season. She was exactly the sort of woman who ought to have married and become a mother. She would make a damn sight better one than any of the society females downstairs who, once they'd whelped, had fobbed their offspring off on servants.

He'd watched the women at table earlier, gorging themselves on course after course of the lavish dinner the Budworths had laid on, knowing they'd dropped off their children at the front door along with their luggage, and thought of nothing from that moment forth but their own amusement. Dammit, you couldn't treat children like that. It was one of the reasons for avoiding the state of matrimony for as long as possible. He could not see himself ever dragging his own children halfway across the country to spend Christmas in the home of a stranger without so much as providing them with their own nurse, or maid or whatever to give them some sense of security.

And nor would Miss Miller.

'You know, I think you are being too hard on yourself.'

'What do you mean?'

'Well, in spite of—' He stopped short of telling her what kind of governess he had expected her to be. 'What I mean to say is, whenever I have seen you with the children, they all seem to be having a marvellous time.' He eyed the fire surround that was splattered with spitballs.

'Perhaps it is not in exactly the way you pictured them enjoying themselves, but they are having a…good experience of Christmas. Better than it would have been had you not been here.'

'Do you really think so?' What a lovely thing for him to say. Even though he could not possibly mean it. It was part of his charm, she supposed, to be always able to find exactly the right thing to say to a woman to make her feel…special.

'I do.'

She looked so wistful, so hopeful, so utterly…vulnerable that he wanted to go over and put his arms round her. Quite badly.

While he was still wondering how she would react should he give way to *that* particular impulse, she said, 'Thank you, Lord Chepstow. For listening to me. I do not know why you came up here,' she said, looking utterly perplexed, 'but…'

'Call it a whim, if you like,' he said, affecting indifference, though he didn't like the view she held of him. Any more than he liked the view he'd had of her. Who could blame her for being a tad…defensive, when she'd suffered so many misfortunes? Had known so little kindness?

He felt a strong surge of annoyance with her employers, and wished he could do something to improve her lot. Or at least, help her to enjoy the kind of Christmas she had always yearned for. It wasn't just children who deserved to enjoy Christmas. Governesses did, too. Especially ones who worked so hard to make it enjoyable for children who would otherwise have been neglected.

She might write him off as a…butterfly, but one thing he did know about, and that was how to have fun.

'Come for a walk with me tomorrow, when you have some free time.'

Oh, God. He felt so sorry for her, after listening to her whining and complaining, he'd asked her to go for a walk with him. But the last thing she wanted was his pity!

'Free time? I don't have any free time. I have the children from seven in the morning until seven at night. And my next half day off is not until January.'

'January!' No wonder she looked so worn down. And, worse, he would be long gone by the time she had her half day of leisure.

So he would just have to come up with some other way of bringing a little Christmas cheer into her life while he was still staying at Budworth Hall.

Chapter Four

There was somebody in the schoolroom.

Honeysuckle, who had been getting ready for bed, swung away from the mirror and stared hard at the door, her ears straining.

There it was again. The noise of a chair scraping across the boards, a desk lid rattling.

Her fingers clamped tight round the handle of her hairbrush.

She might have known one of those beastly boys would try to stage some kind of prank. Especially after the way Lord Chepstow had come to the schoolroom talking about gentlemanly behaviour and then encouraging them to *mis*behave. It was all of a piece. Men of his class grew up knowing they could wreak havoc, then stroll away without a backward glance. They didn't care who got hurt during their pursuit of pleasure. All those girls at Moulsham

Lodge, who were the natural daughters of peers who never, ever wanted any reminder of their existence, were proof of that.

Well, she might not have any say over what they did when they left, but she wasn't going to let them get away with wrecking what it had taken her all day to achieve. She seized the candle as she rose from the dressing-table stool and strode to the door that connected her private quarters to the schoolroom.

She flung open the door and, in her sternest voice, demanded, 'Just what do you think you are doing in here at this time of night?'

Then she froze.

'Lord Chepstow?' She had not seen him all day. To know he was somewhere about the place, avoiding her, had been like a weight she was dragging round with her, making every task she undertook need twice as much effort. She had turned down an offer he was never likely to repeat and he'd just bid her goodnight and gone away. And stayed away.

But now here he was, back in her schoolroom again, with a tray containing a bottle of wine and two glasses, which he'd just deposited on one of her desks.

'I'm bringing you a little Christmas cheer, Miss Miller,' he said. 'You work so hard to make it a happy time for the children. You ought to take a little time for yourself to enjoy the season, too. Come...' he held out his hand in invitation '...sit with me.'

She wanted to gush, *How kind of you my lord. Especially since I am so unworthy of your notice*, which made her annoyed with herself, and snap, 'I will do no such thing. I was about to go to bed.'

His eyes skimmed her figure, as though he'd only just noticed she was clad in a nightgown. He frowned. 'Why are you going to bed so early? This time last night, you were still bustling about—'

'This time last night,' she retorted, trying very hard not to dwell on the fact she was practically naked, 'I hadn't spent the entire day playing ball games and coming up with ever more inventive bribes to get the boys involved in decorating the schoolroom for Christmas.'

'And a splendid job you have done, too. It looks…like a fairy grotto.' In the space of one day, she'd transformed the schoolroom completely. The greenery was no longer heaped in random piles, but fashioned into swags and bunches, decorating every available surface, as well as hanging from unlikely-looking corners. Even the way the fire, banked down for the night, bathed the hearth in a crimson glow lent a touch of magic to the atmosphere.

'Come on.' He indicated the tray. 'I have cake, as well as wine. What harm will it do to sit for half an hour?'

On their own? While she was completely naked under her nightgown? Was he mad?

No, just impervious to her as a woman. To him, she was just a…dreary drudge in need of cheering up.

'I am far too tired to entertain you, Lord Chepstow,'

she said wearily. 'Can't you find someone downstairs to talk to?'

'Not about Pippa,' he said, playing his trump card. 'After what you said earlier about me not writing letters, it occurred to me that I may have been somewhat remiss. She does love getting letters. I only have to recall how she would squeal with pleasure whenever one came from you. It used to puzzle me, because surely she was the one with all the news, since she was the one having a Season? I could not imagine what you might have to say that would be of such interest to her. But then again, *I* have no idea what to say that might be of interest to her, either. Could you not help me compose something suitable, while we share a glass of wine?'

'If it will prevent you from mentioning all those things I told you last night, in confidence,' she grumbled. 'I really don't want her to find out that I feel as though I got the job under false pretences. Or that I'm struggling to cope with the additional demands of his lordship's guests. I would feel as if…as if I'm letting her down.'

She took a step closer to the desk where he was sitting, her brow wrinkled as though she was so intent on making her point, her feet had moved closer to him without her volition.

'And her husband. He gave Lord Budworth his personal recommendation, just because Pippa asked him to…'

She still looked a touch reluctant to come closer, but if he was any judge of things, concern about what he might put in a letter was now overriding her embarrassment at being caught in her night attire.

'She will be interested to read my impressions of how you are faring in your first paid post, though. Perhaps,' he said, 'I could relate the tale of how your kingdom was invaded by pirates and how you managed to put all their energy to good use. Because I have to say, I am intrigued myself as to how you got them involved in making so many decorations.'

'Oh, well, it was something *you* said, actually.' She looked as though the fact something he had said had been of help had astonished her.

'About them enjoying things in their own way. I realised that fighting them over those revolting paper pellets was a waste of time. Instead, I bargained with them. I said that if they made a garland of their own, they could then cover it in, um, *snow*, with my blessing. *After* they had helped to nail up all the garlands the girls had made, too, of course...'

'Glad to be of service.' He chuckled, noting that a good proportion of the garlands were covered in 'snow'. 'I am sure she would be highly entertained by that sort of tale,' he said, pulling a sheet of paper from a desk drawer and reaching for a pen.

'Now,' he said, 'where to start?'

Since it was obvious she wasn't going to be rid of him until he'd done what he came for, she pulled up a chair and sat as far from him as she thought she could get away with, without revealing how uncomfortable she felt. For he was acting as though it was perfectly normal to sit and have a conversation by firelight with a woman who was dressed only in a nightgown.

Knowing what she did of his history, no doubt it was.

She pinched her lips together in disapproval.

'What, by the by,' he said, eyeing the hairbrush she'd forgotten she was still holding, 'what were you intending to do with that? Spank me? From the look on your face you would dearly love to. Though…I thought you had vowed never to beat *any* boy, no matter how naughty he'd been.'

Immediately, he wished he had not said that. Not that he'd ever been much of a one for those sorts of bedroom games, but for some peculiar reason the thought of bending over one of the desks and letting her chastise him to her heart's content had sent blood rushing straight to his groin.

'As if anything I could do,' she said, settling her candle down on the desk, 'could have any effect upon you.'

'You might be surprised,' he said, shifting in his seat to ease the tightness of his breeches. 'I am surprised myself, to be honest.' He studied her with a puzzled frown. Her nightgown covered her from throat to ankles, not touching any part of her body in between, yet just knowing she was probably naked underneath it made him recall how very shapely she actually was.

'Perhaps it's your hair,' he said musingly. 'Because, you know, it looks very…enticing, unbound like that.'

Self-consciously she reached up with her free hand and

pushed the mass that had slithered over her shoulder back into place.

She had been on the point of braiding it when she'd heard him blundering about in the schoolroom. She had not had it cut for years, except to trim the ends. It reached right down to her waist.

'And without your spectacles…' He looked deep into her eyes. 'Your eyes are brown.'

'My eyes are brown all the time.' She tried to retain a strict tone of voice, but the intent way he was studying her was making her feel all soft and melting inside. It was thinking about all those other cosy fireside chats he'd had with all the other women in his past. The ones who'd also only been wearing…whatever it was that women of loose morals wore to bed.

She felt her cheeks heat. Whatever they wore, she was certain it was nothing as unflattering as the yards and yards of flannel currently swathing her from top to toe. He would want his mistresses adorned in scraps of lace and silk, not bundled up in a garment designed to keep the sole occupant of a chaste bed warm during the long, lonely nights.

She wasn't sure if it was too dark for him to notice her blushes or not, but he was smiling as he poured them both a glass of wine.

As he held out one of the glasses to her, it suddenly occurred to her that by this time of night, the chances were he was not completely sober. In which case, coming up here to write a long-overdue letter to his sister and cheer up the poor dowdy, incompetent governess probably seemed like a perfectly logical thing to do.

Not that he needed to be foxed to act in an unconventional manner. When she thought of the things Pippa had told her he got up to when stone-cold sober just because he took some crackbrained notion in his head it would be *fun*...

'One glass, that is all, and then you must leave,' she told him firmly. 'It is all very well for you, but I have to get up early in the morning. I don't have the stamina to sit up half the night drinking as well.'

'Point taken,' he said, raising his glass to her in salute. 'Though I do think you might give me some credit for thinking of you. How often does anyone come up here to just sit and talk to you at the end of your working day?'

'N-never,' she stammered, taking the glass and raising it to her lips, suddenly assailed by a feeling of loneliness so strong she almost shivered.

'I suppose you think it is entirely my own fault,' she said gloomily. 'I have done nothing but snap at you every time you have come near me, when I think, upon reflection, that you really have been trying to...I don't know, be friendly.' She shot him a questioning look.

'In some ways,' he said slowly, 'I can understand why you have spoken as you have. To be frank,' he said, setting down his glass and looking her straight in the eye, 'nobody has ever made me question my behaviour the way you have done over the past two days. I was a touch irritated by your…cheek, at first.' He smiled ruefully, to show that the comment no longer held true. 'But when you held that mirror up to my actions, you showed me an image of myself I did not much care for.'

He reached out and took hold of her free hand. 'Miss Miller, you seem to think I abandoned Pippa when she was still grieving over the loss of our parents. Please, try to look at it from my point of view. I was hardly more than a boy myself. I knew nothing about how to look after a twelve-year-old girl. I really did think I was doing the best thing for Pippa by sending her to school, where she would be with girls her own age. When I interviewed Mrs Moulsham, she seemed like a motherly sort. And she assured me she would teach Pippa everything a young lady ought to know.'

'Mrs Moulsham was certainly a very astute business woman,' Honeysuckle agreed. He was holding her hand. He had reached out and taken hold of her hand. It was almost impossible to concentrate on what he'd said about Mrs Moulsham, rather than just delight in the feel of his strong, warm fingers enclosing hers.

'She *was* very good at telling prospective clients exactly what they wanted most to hear. And…Pippa…' Pippa had been painfully shy when she first came to school. Inside, she had not changed all that much, in spite of acquiring the kind of gloss that deflected most people's perception of her real nature.

'She was never one to speak out. It used to infuriate me, the way she would keep up that determinedly cheerful front every time we came to visit you, instead of telling you how lonely she was and how much she missed you...'

'Aha! So you were almost as cross with her as you were with me? And you do accept that I was doing my best?'

She could not think why it should matter to him so much, after all this time, but she was nothing if not honest.

'Yes. I admit that I was wrong to suspect you of being deliberately unkind to your sister. There were faults on both sides.'

'Then we can drink to that,' he said, raising his glass again.

'Drink to w-what, exactly?'

'Getting to know one another. Now that we have both admitted that we have misjudged each other in the past.'

She gave him a dubious look, but she did obediently raise her glass and take another sip of wine.

'I don't suppose I could get you to smile at me, could I? Just the once?'

'Wh...what? Why?'

'Well...' he leaned back in his chair, his eyes fixed on her mouth '...I have this philosophy of life, you see. That it is so short that we should take what pleasure we can, whenever we can. Even if it is just the satisfaction of coaxing a smile from a lovely woman who looks almost as though she's forgotten how.'

And then he totally shocked her by reaching out with his forefinger and tracing the outline of her mouth.

Even more shockingly, she sat stock-still and let him.

And then wished she had slapped his hand away, for now her lips tingled and wanted more than just the touch of his finger.

She couldn't help looking at his lips, which were curved into a very sensual smile.

She sucked in a sharp breath. And then another, because all of a sudden there didn't seem to be enough air in the room.

'Do you know what I think?' He leaned forwards until their faces were so close their breaths mingled.

'N-no.' She shook her head, inhaling the scent of Lord Chepstow. His sweet breath, his freshly laundered clothes, his spicy soap, and something else she could not identify, but which was probably just…him.

'I think, since it is Christmas, that you should let me kiss you.'

She gasped and shot to her feet, panicked at how very easy it would be to lean forwards and make his seductively murmured words into reality.

'You don't really want to kiss me,' she said, shaking her head as she backed away from him.

'Oh, but I do,' he said, getting to his feet and coming after her. 'Honeysuckle, take it from me, as one who has spent a great deal of time studying the topic of feminine attractiveness. Any man who could see you now would want to kiss you.'

She stopped mid-stride, his words astonishing enough to paralyse her. He took advantage of her immobility to come right up to her and place his hands on her waist.

Honeysuckle's heart was beating so fast now that he must be able to feel its echo through the palms of his hands. But if he did, it did not distract him from studying her face as though he had never seen her before. As though he really was thinking about kissing her.

She was sure he had not come up here with seduction on his mind. That he really had only been thinking about mending fences with her, because she was a friend of Pippa's. Or wanting to cheer her up, because she'd admitted to feeling so miserable yesterday.

So she was not afraid. That was not what was making her heart beat so fast. It was just that, well, it was like a dream coming true, having him look at her like that, as though she was worth showering with jewels and fine clothes, the way Pippa told her he always treated the current object of his interest.

Though he couldn't really, truly, be interested in her. It was probably the wine making him talk like this. Or perhaps he was bored, and hadn't been with a woman for a very long time…or perhaps he did not like the fact that she wouldn't behave as though the sun rose and set on him, the way every other woman of his acquaintance must surely do.

Perhaps he saw her earlier antagonism as a challenge to his masculinity.

'You ought to let me go,' she somehow found the strength to say, even though she was aching to press herself closer. 'You really should not kiss me.'

'Do you know, whenever someone tells me I ought to do something, I have the strongest urge to do the exact opposite?'

There was nothing more likely to induce him to go off on one of his madcap adventures than someone telling him the thing was impossible to achieve. And she knew that. So why had she thrown down the gauntlet?

'Y-you should not tease me,' she said, recognising the glint of devilment in his eye. 'Not like this. I'm not a little girl any more.'

'No, you are not.'

He leaned back a little, the better to make a leisurely perusal of her body. With his hands at her waist, he must be able to discern the outline of her figure, even though it was covered in the thick flannel gown.

'You have grown up into a very attractive woman. You have a delectable body. Even that hideous nightgown you are wearing cannot completely disguise it. And your hair...' He raised one hand to run his fingers through its length. 'It is the kind of hair a man likes to see spread across his pillow.'

His pillow. She could see herself lying back and letting him spread it across his pillow with those long, capable fingers. Looking at her just like this, as though his next move was going to be to remove her nightgown and run his fingers over every single inch of her naked body.

'You are cold,' he said, misinterpreting her convulsive shiver of longing. 'It is freezing up here and you have nothing on your feet. It was selfish of me to keep you talking like this. Tell you what,' he said, sliding one arm round her waist and pulling her close. 'Kiss me goodnight,' he said, his voice dropping to a husky whisper that sent another shiver right through her, 'and then I'll let you get back to your bed.'

'That is an outrageous request to make.' She was saying the right words, but they were coming out all low and breathy. Nothing at all like the stern rebuke they ought to be. But the longer she kept arguing, the longer he was likely to hold her close to him like this.

'I don't think so.' He raised one hand, and cupped her cheek. He ran one thumb over her lower lip. 'A girl as pretty as you ought to be kissed. Especially at Christmas.'

'P-pretty?' Nobody had ever told her she was pretty before. Not that she cared what anyone else thought. The point was, Lord Chepstow was telling her *he* found her pretty. Even though he could not possibly mean it.

Good lord, flirting came as naturally to this man as breathing. Give him a spare hour and a woman who posed a bit of a challenge, and he would not rest until he'd made a conquest of her.

All she would have to do was admit she wanted him

to kiss her more than she wanted her next meal and he would no doubt recoil in horror. So naturally she did no such thing. Instead, she raised the stakes.

'This is a schoolroom,' she pointed out, even pulling away slightly to make him hold her a little tighter. 'It would be completely inappropriate,' she said, unsure whether she was talking about kissing in a schoolroom or her deliberately provocative behaviour. 'It's not even as if there is a kissing ball up here...'

'I have no need of a kissing ball,' he said scornfully.

His eyes were fixed upon her mouth. And she couldn't pretend this wasn't exactly what she wanted one second longer. Her lips parted on a yearning sigh.

He lowered his head towards hers. 'I am quite capable of kissing a pretty woman without any other stimulus whatever. And did I not warn you that if someone tells me something is inappropriate, I want to do it all the more?'

Yes, which was exactly why she'd reminded him. But if she was only ever to be kissed once in her life, she wanted it to be this man that did the kissing. Besides, he'd been the one to point out that life was short and pleasure was for snatching, wherever it was to be found. The chance to taste the ultimate delight of Lord Chepstow's lips was just as ephemeral as the ice cream he'd bought her that day at Gunter's. He might not be sober, he might be only reacting to the challenge he thought she represented, but if she did not taste him now, the moment would melt away, never to return.

And so she raised her arms, and put them about his neck.

'A C-Christmas kiss? Just one, and then you will let me go?'

He smiled the smile of a victor. Then fulfilled every dream she'd ever had since the first hour she'd met him by swooping down and placing his lips over hers.

She groaned with pleasure. It was as though she had broken into the cake shop while nobody was looking and had grabbed an armful of all the most expensive of those mouth-watering treats. And he did taste good. Sweet. She supposed it was the wine he had been drinking. But even better, she could feel the heat of his body through the soft folds of her nightgown. The press of his hands sliding up her ribcage.

'Good lord,' he said, breaking the kiss and looking down at her as though he'd never seen her before. 'I always thought whoever named you had got it completely wrong. But your lips are the sweetest thing I have ever tasted.'

Years of repressed longings swept away her natural caution.

She pulled his face back down to hers and pressed her lips feverishly against his.

She half expected him to reject her inexpert attempt to kiss him back. But far from seeming repulsed by her eagerness, he emitted a groan of his own and clasped her tighter. To her utter delight, he took charge of the kiss, parting her lips and thrusting his tongue inside her mouth. It sent hot shivers coursing all the way through her body. She wasn't quite sure what to do with her mouth, apart from yielding to his exploration of it, but at least she no longer had to resist the temptation to push that silky fringe from his forehead as he bent over her. His hands were roaming all over her body, so he could not possibly object to her running her fingers through the delightfully soft texture of his hair.

Lord Chepstow could not recall ever experiencing anything quite as inflammatory as her mixture of innocence and eagerness. For once, he did not make the calculated moves of an expert seducer of women, just gave in to the demands of his body, letting his hands roam where they would, until the urge to grab her bottom and hold her hard so that he could grind himself against her soft yielding flesh grew too strong to resist. But doing that only made him want to yank up her nightgown and touch bare skin. Rip open those buttons and taste the breasts he could feel pressing into his chest.

'My God,' he grated, tearing his mouth free and resting his forehead against hers. 'We have to stop before I...'

She wasn't the kind of woman you could just fling down on a hearthrug and use to slake the lust roaring through him. He should not have started this. But he'd thought any kiss they might share would have been sweet, not hot as Hades and twice as sinful.

'If I'd known you could kiss like that, I...'

'What? What would you have done?'

Her lovely dream shattered and came crashing down around their ears. He was too fond of his liberty to be tied into any relationship he could not step away from the moment he grew bored. Nor was he so lost to all sense of decency that he would take a friend of his sister's as his mistress. She stepped back, pushing his arms away from her.

And just as she did so, a small sound from the doorway to the schoolroom caught her attention.

She could just make out the silhouette of a female, though the candle she held aloft threw her face into deep shadow.

Lord Chepstow had noticed nothing. He was intent upon her, following her as she backed towards her room, re-placing his hands on her waist every time she batted them away.

'No, no, don't pretend to be cross with me,' he said. 'There is no point. Not now I have discovered the truth. You don't really dislike me at all, do you? All those frowns, all that scolding—it was all a bluff to disguise the fact that, deep down, you want me so much you don't know what to do with yourself.'

'How dare you speak to me like that?' And smile like that. His cocky grin made her fingers itch to slap the ex-pression from his face.

'Because you just kissed me with your whole body, not just your mouth. I don't think anyone has ever kissed me with such passion.'

The light flickered and faded, indicating that the female, whoever she was, had gone. But it did not alter the fact that she must have seen them in each other's arms. As if Lord Chepstow discovering the intensity of her feelings for him was not mortifying enough.

'You won't ever be able to fool me by putting on that prim, governessy voice again. It is just a front. Underneath, you are a passionate creature.'

'No,' she murmured, anxiously scanning the gaping doorway.

'Yes, you are. You have just never had anyone to share your passion with before. But it's all there. You are just dying to shower someone with all the love that is bottled up inside you…'

Was he suggesting she let him be the person to shower with her love? Was this all a prelude to suggesting she let him teach her all about passion? She was not so innocent that she did not know exactly what it was that had been pressing into her belly a moment ago.

'I'll show you passion,' she said grimly and did exactly what he'd suggested earlier. She whacked him hard on the backs of his hands with her hairbrush. And then, when he'd let her go with a surprised yelp, she darted backwards into her bedroom and shut the door firmly in his face—before she yielded to the almost overwhelming temptation to seize him by the lapels and drag him inside with her.

From the other side of the door, she could hear his low, throaty chuckle.

She sprang away from the door as though it had turned

red hot. She felt betrayed. She'd got carried away and let him kiss her—no, had kissed him. With her whole body.

And heart.

And now he was standing there, laughing at her. She wrapped her arms round her waist, tears stinging her eyes.

'Honeysuckle?'

He heaved a sigh. The door shivered, as though he was leaning against it.

'Oh, hell. I was completely out of line, wasn't I?'

He should not have teased her into that kiss. He shouldn't even have come up here, when he knew full well they would be alone. A man should never be alone with a lady of good birth. It just wasn't done. Normally, he would not have walked into a situation a woman could use to her advantage to trap him into marriage, but...

He sucked in a short, sharp breath as it struck him that if this had been London, and he had just kissed a débutante like that, society would consider he'd compromised her. Her reputation would have been ruined.

'I suppose at this point, as a gentleman, I ought to make amends by proposing marriage, but...'

Marriage. A state he'd been so determined to avoid he'd got as far away from Havelock, and the predatory females who stalked the fields he was intent on entering, as possible.

He would have to get married one day, of course, to make sure there were sons to continue the line.

And he'd already come to the conclusion that Honeysuckle would make a wonderful mother.

Good grief, now he thought of it, she was also an orphan, which Havelock had declared would be a bonus, given the complicated state of his existing family affairs.

He'd further stated that he wouldn't care if his bride didn't have any money, since he was very comfortably circumstanced anyway.

And Honeysuckle was so poor she had to work for a living.

It was astonishing. The men in his club that night might as well have sat down and just written the name 'Honeysuckle Miller' when they'd collectively drawn up a list of all the attributes that would make a perfect wife. The perfect mother to the children it was their duty to sire.

He laid one palm flat against the door that separated them. Honeysuckle would give him sons to make him proud. They would be plucky, and clever and resourceful.

And, by God, but he would enjoy the getting of them.

Contrary to what Lady Springfield had said, he couldn't even see himself ever getting bored with Honeysuckle. Not the way he grew bored with his mistresses, anyway. A man looked for entirely different qualities in a wife than a mistress. A mistress was for…the moment. A wife was a woman with whom to build a future.

In the past, when he'd tried to imagine being tied to one woman for the rest of his life, he'd had to run a finger round his neckcloth, as though he could feel it tightening like a noose. But he did not feel trapped, or tricked or imprisoned at all. On the contrary, he felt curiously liberated.

Right up til the minute he'd left London, he'd been declaring he was happy living the way he did. But that was not the whole truth. Of late, he no longer felt quite comfortable visiting any of his properties outside London, knowing they were all desperately in need of a woman's touch and that pretty soon he would have to give serious consideration to finding that woman.

Well, now he'd found her—when he had not even been looking. There was not a woman anywhere who would be better at transforming his estates into homes where he could raise his children than Honeysuckle Miller.

Honeysuckle took another step away from the closed door that parted them as the silence from the other side went on and on. This was worse than his laughter. To her, that kiss had been like a taste of paradise. But he was regretting it already. Counting the cost of it. There could be no other explanation for all that silence. He'd reminded himself that as a gentleman he ought to propose after kissing her like that—but he hadn't. And he wouldn't. Men like him didn't marry penniless governesses. He might want her, in a certain way, but there was nothing he could do about that either. He couldn't take a friend of his sister's as his mistress.

'Do you know,' he suddenly said, brightly, 'it has just occurred to me that Havelock had the right idea? Or at least, he was thinking along the right lines. No man wants to be leg-shackled to a harpy, just because she comes from a good family, and has a lot of money. It is like…a bit like… the fact that I brought Brown Bess down here as well as Diamond. Diamond is a fine-looking creature and I enjoy showing off his paces, but when it comes to the hunt, I cannot do better than Brown Bess. She has the temperament to keep going all day. Will never let me down.'

She shook her head, slowly. Just how much had he had to drink tonight? Until now, he'd seemed fairly lucid, but this rambling way he was talking about his horses, and some friend of his who sounded as though he really *was* contemplating marriage, made her think again.

'Honeysuckle? What do you say?'

There was only one thing she could say.

'Go away!'

He chuckled. He'd taken her by surprise. Well, he'd taken himself by surprise. But when she thought it over, she'd come to the same conclusion as he had.

She slumped against the door as she heard him turn and stroll away. She was sure he had not meant to hurt her by taunting her with the impossibility of them ever marrying. He was just doing what he always did. Saying the first thing that came into his head without thinking about what he really meant.

She was stupid to feel so hurt because he'd spouted a lot of nonsense whilst in his cups. He probably would not even recall much of what he'd said, once he'd sobered up.

With any luck, he wouldn't even recall he'd come up here.

Oh, Lord, she hoped he wouldn't. It was bad enough that he'd brought up the topic of marriage at all, when she knew full well that men like Lord Chepstow did not marry penniless governesses. When he eventually settled down, it would be with some wealthy, titled, fashionable lady. No Brown Bess for him. He would demand a Diamond. A showy, expensive creature, who would be quite willing to turn a blind eye to his indiscretions. For there would be many.

Lord Chepstow craved variety. Constant stimulation. He would never be content to restrict himself to just one woman.

Whereas there would never be, had never been, any other man for her.

Chapter Five

'Well, have you nothing to say in your defence?'

Honeysuckle looked at Lady Budworth with a sinking heart.

She could not gainsay Lady Springfield, not while she was standing right there. Besides, she *had* been kissing Lord Chepstow and she *had* only been wearing her night-gown.

Useless to protest it had gone no further than kisses, or that she had not permitted him to set foot inside her bedroom. For if she were to deny that part of Lady Springfield's tale, it would be to call her a liar to her face. Lady Budworth would have to decide which of them was telling the truth.

And how likely was it that she would take the word of a lowly governess over that of an earl's daughter?

'Your silence is an admission of guilt,' said Lady Budworth. 'You will leave my employ at once.'

Honeysuckle felt the blood drain from her face.

'You will not return to your room,' Lady Budworth continued. 'I cannot have you walking through the schoolroom. My guests will not want their children exposed to the corrupting influence of a person such as yourself.'

'B-but am I not to be permitted to bid Annabel and Mary farewell?' She had grown very fond of them and, she thought, they of her.

Lady Budworth made a slashing motion with her hand. 'Absolutely not. The fact that you have abused your position of trust in my home by acting like a…like a…'

'Harlot?' Lady Springfield helpfully supplied with a malicious smile.

It was all Honeysuckle could do to keep her hands meekly folded at her waist, rather than curling them into angry little fists. How could Lady Springfield be getting so much pleasure from causing her to lose her job? What kind of person was she?

Leaving that aside, there were more practical matters to consider.

'Surely you cannot mean to turn me out without letting me pack my things?'

'I will have them sent on.'

'But I don't know where I shall be going. I have no-where…'

Her middle section clenched into a block of ice as the

full horror of her predicament sank in. She had no family. No close friends apart from Pippa. But how could she possibly go to his sister, telling a tale that would make him sound like a…like a rake! Well, he was a rake, but he drew the line at seducing innocent girls of good birth. Besides, if she ran to Pippa, her husband was bound to want to call Lord Chepstow to account. He might even insist that he marry her. And if Lord Chepstow had really wanted to do so, he would have asked her last night, not muttered something about his horses and sauntered away.

It would be completely unfair to make Lord Chepstow pay such a terrible price. *She* had been the one to give in to temptation. For once in her life, she'd snatched at the chance to taste an experience she had known full well to be wrong. If she really had dashed into that baker's shop when she'd been a schoolgirl and stolen one of those slices of gingerbread, they would have hauled her off to the constable for theft. Last night she had stolen a moment of illicit bliss in Lord Chepstow's arms. She could have stopped him, had she wanted to.

But she hadn't wanted to.

'Would you…would you at least let me have a character?'

Lady Budworth flung up her hands in exasperation.

'I cannot be fidgeted with details at this hour in the morning. I have not even had my chocolate. Oh…go downstairs to the housekeeper's room. It is her job to deal with this sort of thing. All I want is to never have to see your face again. It is most inconvenient of you to let me down like this, with a house full of guests,' she finished pettishly. 'Now who is going to mind the children?'

She should have thought of that before she'd summoned her to answer Lady Springfield's charges.

Or, better yet, told the spoiled, spiteful madam that she would look into the complaint discreetly, then interviewed her in private, to ascertain the full truth of the matter.

But no. Lady Springfield had pretended outrage on behalf of one of her younger sisters, and because she was a guest, a titled, wealthy guest, Lady Budworth had yielded to her demands.

Honeysuckle dipped a curtsy and headed for the door, her back ramrod straight. She would not give in to tears, or beg for mercy, or show any weakness whatever! Besides, she didn't feel like crying. She was too angry for tears. Once in her life, just once, she had misbehaved and not even all that badly. But then when had the world ever been a place where justice reigned? Poor people could face imprisonment for stealing a loaf of bread to keep from starving. But if you had wealth, and position, you could behave as badly as you liked and get away with it.

'Is something the matter?'

Honeysuckle came to herself to see Mrs Gulpher looking at her with concern. Somehow she'd reached the housekeeper's room without knowing quite how she'd got there.

'I have been dismissed,' she said, reaching out to steady

herself against the door frame. All of a sudden, her legs had gone quite weak. How was she going to survive?

'No! What on earth for?'

Mrs Gulpher took her by the arm and ushered her into the upper servants' sitting room.

The next hour passed in a daze. She told her tale to Mrs Gulpher, and the butler, Rothman, and though they were sympathetic, there was not very much either of them could actually do beyond offering her tea and advice.

The next thing she knew, she was walking down the driveway, with one small bag in her hand, which Mrs Gulpher had one of the maids pack for her, and the driving rain was stinging her face like a million needles.

Rothman had suggested she go to the vicarage and ask for refuge for a few days while he attempted to extract the wages owing from Lord Budworth, though she could not see him paying up. Why should he? He might consider her alleged conduct left him with no obligation towards her. And men of his class saw nothing wrong in withholding money owed to tradespeople like tailors, or butchers or... governesses. You only had to look at the papers and read the lists of all the people who went bankrupt every week.

He wouldn't care that without that money it was going to be hard for her to survive until she could find a new post. Which would take a very long time indeed if he did not provide her with a satisfactory character, either.

Her future looked bleak indeed. As bleak and harsh as

this December weather. Not only did she have no home, and no job, but precious few prospects, either.

Squaring her shoulders, she gripped her small overnight bag more tightly and marched into the wind, screwing her face up against the stinging rain—and the pain of losing everything, just when she'd been on the verge of really belonging. She had longed for somewhere she could call home for so long. She had never dared hope it would be the kind of place Pippa had found, with an adoring husband. She knew she wasn't pretty, no matter what fustian Lord Chepstow had spoken last night. Nor did she have a dowry to redress that lack of allure. The most she had hoped for was to find a place where her skills as an educator would be valued.

To have it all so cruelly snatched away, just when it had been within her grasp, was almost more than she could bear.

As she'd sat at Mrs Gulpher's table, sipping endless cups of hot, sweet tea, she'd discovered, much to her surprise, that the staff of Budworth Hall thought of her as one of them. They'd been, without exception, incensed that she was losing her job because one of the male guests had strayed into her territory and snatched a couple of kisses. Instead of laying any blame on her at all, they had asked what on earth Lady Springfield had been doing up there, so far away from the guest wing? The maids had packed her this overnight bag and promised to stow all the rest of her belongings safely in a trunk that a footman had volunteered to fetch down from storage.

And they had all said she had been such a good influence on the girls, she was bound to find another job in no time.

Jane had promised to spend her day in the schoolroom, making sure the children were properly looked after. And when Honeysuckle had raised the subject of their Christmas party, several other, younger members of the staff had assured her they would make sure the children would have a rollicking time of it.

In fact, they had all been so kind that she suddenly found herself blinking back tears. The way they had closed ranks round her, their instant assumption that she had done nothing wrong, the way they had all been so swift to castigate Lord Chepstow and Lady Springfield had been so… touching.

She had never guessed they thought so highly of her. How could she, when none of them had made any attempt to breach what Lord Chepstow derided as her shrewish nature?

Not that she was really as shrewish as all that, was she? Her throat closed up as she tried to suppress a sob. She'd just grown used to standing up for herself. She didn't quite know how to handle having so many people rallying round her like that. To discover that they regarded her as one of their own.

Just as she was being forced to leave.

The sob broke free. And then tears began to stream down her face. And before long, she knew she was going to have to stop and blow her nose; for the combination of stinging rain and bitter tears was making it run in a hideous fashion.

As she put her bag down to fumble in her pocket for a handkerchief, she realised she had already, somehow, reached the wall surrounding the churchyard. The lych gate wouldn't be a bad place to shelter from the worst of the wind while she attempted to compose herself. She simply couldn't march up to the vicarage in this state. Making a litany of complaints against her employers, railing at the injustice of it all, would not make her look like the kind of person Reverend Colleyhurst would want to take into his home. Especially since he relied very heavily on Lord Budworth's patronage.

After a few moments, during which she thought she would never be able to stop crying, it occurred to her that the whole thing was much harder to deal with because it was happening at Christmas.

For once again, it felt as though everyone else was preparing to feast and make merry, while she was out in the cold, friendless and alone.

She looked up the path to the church, seeking—well, she wasn't sure what. But her eyes came to rest on the nativity scene the villagers had set up next to the porch. It struck her that the Holy Family had been poor and homeless at

Christmas, too. There had been nowhere for Him to lay His head except a place intended for cattle.

At least she wasn't going to have to sleep in a stable, not if she knew the Reverend Colleyhurst, she sniffed. Nor was she a helpless babe.

She was a grown woman, with a strong will, a healthy body and a good education. She might have nothing else, but nobody would ever be able to take her education from her. Moulsham Lodge had been a harsh place, but she had learned a lot there.

To start with, she had learned that it was pointless yearning for things she could not have. It only made her more miserable. She'd learned that the strong trampled down the weak to get what they wanted, that the wealthy lived by a different set of rules from the poor.

And there was nothing an orphaned girl could do about it, but endure life just exactly as it was.

With one last shuddering sigh, one last sniff, she removed her spectacles and rubbed the lenses on the one dry corner of her handkerchief remaining.

So, she was on her own again. But she had known, from the moment those heartless trustees had deposited her in Moulsham Lodge, that she would have to make her own way in the world.

She was not, she decided, perching her spectacles back on her nose, going to sit here wallowing in self-pity. And though anger was much more energising—only consider how rapidly her legs had carried her thus far—it would not do to let it take over her life completely, either. She would only end up bitter and twisted, like the teachers at Moulsham Lodge.

Besides, if she could go back and do things differently, would she? If she had known this would be the result, would she have found the resolve to virtuously spurn Lord Chepstow?

And never have known what it felt like, to be in his arms?

Oh, no. For once she agreed wholeheartedly with Lord Chepstow's philosophy. This life was the only one she had. She could not be sorry that, if only for a few seconds, she'd discovered what it felt like to be a desirable woman. A woman desired by the man she adored. Nobody would ever be able to take *that* away from her. She sat for a few moments, reliving the feel of his body pressed against hers from shoulder to knee. Of his hands clutching her so close there was no mistaking how much he was enjoying the encounter, too. She committed his scent to memory, and his taste, and the silky texture of his hair as she ran her fingers through it.

And then she blew her nose one last time, got to her feet, picked up her bag and crossed the village green to the vicarage.

Chapter Six

Lord Chepstow was grinning to himself as he made his way up to the schoolroom after lunch. When he'd got up that morning, his first instinct had been to go straight there and spend the entire day coaxing Honeysuckle into accepting his proposal. But after the heat of the kisses they'd shared the night before, he knew he was going to find it damned difficult to keep his hands off her. Not that he cared what a pack of someone else's children might think of him kissing their governess into submission. But he had an inkling that Honeysuckle would find his ardour embarrassing. Which would make her angry. And he didn't want her angry, he wanted her to melt for him again, as she had begun to do last night.

Lord, but it had felt marvellous when she'd kissed him back with such passion. He'd never, ever felt such a sense of—triumph, yes, that was it. As if he'd won some kind of battle. Because she had not set out to entrap him, like so many women did. Rather, she'd done all she could to resist. Her own longings, as much as his.

His grin widened. He had breached her defences, but by now, if he knew anything about her, she would have retreated into her defensive shell once more. Just as she'd retreated into her bedroom, when what had flared between them had become too passionate for her to handle.

Not that he minded. On the contrary, he was relishing the prospect of breaching her barriers all over again. Her natural reticence brought out the hunter in him. The fact that he was certain to catch her in the end did not make the pursuit of Honeysuckle Miller any less satisfying. It was all as it should be. The man pursued. The woman surrendered.

Though there was nothing predatory about his pursuit. He had realised, when he woke this morning, that he wanted to spend the rest of his life making up for all she'd had to do without so far by showering her with gifts. Jewellery, clothes...whatever her heart desired.

How could he ever have thought she was plain? With her hair rippling down to her waist, her body all shrouded in white, the night before she'd looked so damned desirable he could scarcely remember his own name, let alone why he'd gone up to the schoolroom.

She had to marry him. She needed him to take her away from this life of drudgery and treat her as she deserved to be treated.

Not that she would be likely to accede to any demand

she abandon the children and leave Budworth Hall right away, even though he'd had more than enough of the place. Not only was he beginning to seriously dislike his hosts for the way they had treated Honeysuckle, but he was also devilishly bored with the set of people staying here.

But Honeysuckle would not regard his wishes as of—he grinned—*parrot mount* importance. No, her priority would be to make sure there was someone else to care for the children before she would consider handing in her notice.

He paused on the landing, wondering why he did not mind the fact he was not first on her list of priorities. It didn't take him more than a moment to work out that her loyalty to the children in her care, her determination to do her best for them, no matter what it cost, whether they appreciated her sacrifices or not was one of the things he admired about her most. If she could just leave them behind without suffering a pang, she wouldn't be…Honeysuckle.

A tender smile played about his mouth as he thought of the one sure way to win her compliance. No matter how much she wanted to argue with him, the moment he took her in his arms, she melted like ice in the sun, which made him feel very…manly. As though, having conquered Honeysuckle, he was now capable of achieving just about anything.

Even spending the New Year with Pippa and her boring baronet. For that was what he would have to do, now that he'd decided to make Honeysuckle his wife. It would take a little while to organise a wedding. And Pippa's house was the obvious place to take her while they sorted out all the details. He'd instantly dismissed any notion of procuring a special licence and marrying her quietly. It might look as though there was something suspect about their union, as though he was not completely sure that she was the woman he wanted. So he was going to organise a grand wedding and show her off. Start as he meant to go on. Nothing was to be too good for Honeysuckle. And no expense spared.

And Pippa was the one person he could trust to stand by her through it all. In fact, Pippa would be absolutely thrilled to be able to call Honeysuckle her sister.

He walked the remaining few steps to the schoolroom door, savouring the prospect of making a grand entrance, whisking Honeysuckle away from her life of drudgery and showering her with all the things she'd had to go without. And seeing her look at him as though he was her hero.

Puffing out his chest, he pushed open the door and strode in.

'Miss Miller,' he began, for the sake of the children and her sensibilities. Though part of him still wanted to cry *Darling*, sweep her into his arms and cover her face with kisses, it would be prudent to moderate his behaviour.

'Miss Miller is not here,' said the servant, who appeared to be in nominal charge of the pack of children whose faces were beginning to look familiar.

'Oh? Where is she, then?'

One of the little girls, who'd been sitting on the servant's knee looking rather sullen, began to cry. Or, to judge by her mottled complexion, started to cry again.

'She's been dismissed,' said the servant.

'Dismissed?'

Another little girl peeled away from the rumpus taking place at one end of the room to come and put her arms protectively around, to judge by their identical dress, her younger sister.

'For misconduct,' said the servant, glowering at him.

'Misconduct?' It made no sense. What on earth could Honeysuckle have possibly done to result in her dismissal? She was so utterly devoted to the children he could not imagine her doing anything that would jeopardise their welfare.

'And it's Christmas,' wailed the first little girl. 'She was going to give us a party. Our first proper Christmas party.'

'We shall still have our party,' said the older sister. 'Jane promised. Didn't you, Jane?'

The servant nodded. 'Here,' she said, reaching into her pocket and withdrawing a bulging paper bag. 'Share these out, will you? I need to have a talk with this…' she paused, and a sneer crept into her voice '…*gentleman.*'

The little girl who'd looked so inconsolable stopped crying when presented with the bag of toffee. She took it over to the hearthrug and, as the others gathered round her, making her the centre of attention, brightened up considerably.

The moment the girls were fully occupied the servant whirled round and glared at him.

'She has nowhere to go, did you know that? Or care? She set off walking down the drive with just as much as she could carry in one small bag, with no idea what is to become of her.'

A chill struck him in the gut.

'She has already left Budworth Hall? Then I must go after her. Find her.'

He was about to make for the door, when the servant intercepted him. 'You've done enough already. You leave her alone, do you hear?'

'Me? What have I done?' he protested.

'You know very well,' said the servant indignantly. '*Everyone* knows what went on up here last night, thanks to that hussy Lady Springfield. You ought to be ashamed of yourself—sneaking up here last night and…and toying with our Miss Miller.'

'I did not sneak,' he said, completely shocked by having a member of the lower orders rebuking him, though in some ways her heated defence of Honeysuckle made him warm to her. And though he would not normally bother to explain himself to a servant, he found himself doing exactly that.

'Miss Miller is a friend of my sister's. We have known each other for years. Since she told me she had no time off during the length of my stay here, I had no choice but to visit her in her schoolroom. And I most certainly did not *toy* with her. I have done nothing of which I need be ashamed…'

He trailed off. To be completely honest, he'd known he ought not to have made so free with a woman who was well born. Wasn't that why he'd proposed to her?

And then he looked at the two girls, who were still quite subdued in spite of having cheeks bulging with toffee. And saw that the boys who had joined in with his game of pirates with such enthusiasm had taken a defensive stance at their side. All were looking at him as though he were a pantomime villain.

'Look, there seems to have been some sort of misunderstanding. Perhaps I should not have come up here so late last night, while Miss Miller was all alone, but nothing happened that…'

But now another aspect of the situation struck him. She was a servant here. He'd always despised the kind of men who preyed on vulnerable female members of household staff. Not that it had been anything like that, last night. But…to people who did not know about their life-long connection, it must have looked pretty damning.

'This is all completely ridiculous,' he said, spearing his fringe out of his eyes with agitated fingers. 'There was no need for her to leave. Even if she was dismissed, she should have just come to me…' But as soon as the words had left his mouth, he saw how impossible that would have been for Honeysuckle. She was too used to having to deal with all her problems by herself. She did not know him well enough yet to trust him. And she'd never had anyone she *could* trust, not in her whole life. First her parents had let her down by dying and leaving her so poorly provided for, then her guardians had demonstrated their indifference by leaving her to sink or swim in that school without doing more than paying the bills. His heart squeezed in his chest as he saw her assuming she would have to deal with the loss of her job alone, too.

'Oh, really?' said the servant, hands on hips. 'And what would you have done? Humiliated her even worse, no doubt. Men of your class always blame the woman. And it's always the woman who has to pay the price when you've had what you wanted.'

'I haven't had what I wanted,' he snapped. 'Not at all. In spite of what Lady Springfield might have said, all I did was kiss her a time or two. And ask her to marry me…'

'*You*,' the servant said, looking at him up and down with incredulity, 'asked *her* to marry you?'

'Why not?' It was one of the little girls with the bag of toffee. 'Miss Miller is the loveliest person in the whole world.'

'Yes, she is,' he agreed. 'Annabel, isn't it? And last night I realised—' about the time he'd been running through Havelock's list, and discovering she had every single virtue any of the fellows in his club had written on it '—that there is no woman on earth who would make me a better wife.'

The little girl sighed and looked at him as though he was now the romantic lead, rather than the villain of the piece.

'Well, if'n you really do mean to marry her,' said the servant, her face softening, 'then you couldn't do no worse than start looking for her at the vicarage. She meant to ask the reverend if he would kindly take her in, just while Mr Rothman tries to get the wages she's owed out of his lordship.'

'Do you mean to tell me that they threw her out without her wages?'

The servant shot a meaningful glance at the children, implying reluctance to speak ill of their parent in their hearing. But she added, in an undertone, 'Nor a character, neither.'

He was half inclined to head straight down to Lord Budworth and tell him exactly what he thought of a man who'd throw a vulnerable woman out of doors without any means of support in the midst of winter.

But he'd already wasted enough time. Night fell early at this time of year. And he had to make sure that Honeysuckle was in a place of safety before it did.

Pray God he found her, before anything worse happened than…he groaned…than losing her job, her wages, her home.

Because of him.

She must be furious with him. And why not? He was furious with himself. If Pippa had been a governess, and some guest had invaded her schoolroom when she was only in her night attire and taken such liberties, he would thrash him to within an inch of his life.

Well, she could scold him as much as she liked. He would welcome anything she cared to throw at him when he found her, so long as he did find her.

For the prospect of never seeing her again was just too horrible to contemplate.

Chapter Seven

Honeysuckle paused in the doorway of the vicar's study, her tray balanced on her hip.

It was just as well she'd had such a broad, not to say unconventional, education. The Reverend Colleyhurst might not have taken her in had Mrs Moulsham not used her younger pupils as unpaid staff.

'Usually, Miss Miller, I would be only too glad to offer you shelter in your distressing circumstances,' he'd told her, 'but you see, my housekeeper is away visiting a sick member of her family and I am not sure when she will be able to return. In the meantime, I only have a cook left to me. And while I do not mind, as a bachelor, you know, living quite simply, there is nobody to prepare a room or...or anything else. You see how it is?'

And that was when she'd virtually begged him not to turn her away.

'The principal of the school I attended believed in training every pupil in all aspects of domestic service. I am quite capable of doing any household task, from blacking a grate to laundering fine linen. It would give me great comfort to repay your kindness in taking me in by working for my keep.'

He'd glanced across at his desk, which was buried under mounds of papers, tottering piles of books and the remnants of half-eaten meals.

A hopeful expression had replaced the harassed one he'd been wearing when she'd first knocked on his door.

'Well, I…well, that is…would you really?'

Since then, she'd lit a fire in the spare bedroom, found linen, set it to air, then gone to the kitchen where she'd donned an apron and washed all the dishes she'd found stacked in the scullery. She'd then returned to her room and made up the bed.

And now she was back downstairs, having heard him go out a few minutes ago. She meant to take advantage of his absence to set his study to rights.

She placed her tray on the sofa, for want of any other clear, horizontal surface, and went to the desk at which he worked on his sermons to clear away the cups and saucers. As she carried the first pile of crockery over to the tray, her hand shook so badly the remaining contents of one of the teacups slopped into the saucer. She took several deep breaths, willing herself to calm down. She had nothing to fear now. She was not outside in the cold.

It was just that it had suddenly seemed as if her position was as fragile as the bone-china cups she was stacking. One slip, and everything could shatter into pieces too small to ever be glued back together again.

Better stop handling delicate china, then. She would put the books back where they belonged instead and tidy the vicar's papers.

Reverend Colleyhurst, she soon discovered, had a unique system of arranging his books, by topic rather than alphabetically. But she welcomed the challenge of finding the right home for each one, since it kept her mind occupied with something other than her own predicament—and the disturbing tendency to wonder what Lord Chepstow was doing, right that minute. Was he out riding with the other guests? Eating luncheon? Playing billiards? The hardest thing of all was not to allow resentment to creep in and overshadow the wonderful memory she had of those rapturous moments in his arms. She wanted them to be a source of comfort in the years ahead. But whenever she thought of him going on his merry way, without even wondering what had become of her, the episode that had felt so glorious at the time stood in very real danger of getting twisted into something that would have the power to torture her for years to come.

Her lips compressed, she rammed the last book from the desk back where it belonged and climbed down from the stepstool. At least now her hands were quite steady. She was ready to tackle the crockery.

By the time Reverend Colleyhurst returned, she vowed, he would look upon her as a godsend rather than an obligation.

Tomorrow, while he was conducting the morning services, she would lift the rugs in this room and give them a good beating. She did not mind doing hard, physical work. Besides, if she was still at Budworth Hall, she would be working even harder, putting together a party for all the children.

A pang shot through her as she thought of them all, left to fend for themselves up in the schoolroom. She hoped Mrs Gulpher and Rothman would stick to their promises and allow Jane to step into her shoes. She wouldn't worry so much if she could be absolutely sure Jane was up there with them right now. Jane had plenty of experience with children, coming from such a large family. And, more importantly, she liked them. She often lingered after bringing up the nursery tea, though that was partly to avoid the tasks she was supposed to have been doing elsewhere. Poor Jane. She wasn't likely to last very much longer in domestic service. She had a fatal tendency to ignore orders from the upper staff if she thought there was something more important to do, and was cheeky enough to answer back when reprimanded.

Which meant she had a natural affinity with those boys. It had taken Lord Chepstow and that game of pirates he'd played with them to give *her* the key to understanding how to manage them. They had a natural aggression that was foreign to her nature, but they also had a code of honour that at least made them take their wrestling matches into a corner where they would not endanger the little ones. In the end, she'd found them every bit as lovable as the girls, in their own way.

She gave herself a mental shake and stacked the vicar's cups and saucers on the tray. *Nothing* of what might be going on at Budworth Hall now was any of her business. She had to stop thinking about them as though they were... family. To stop worrying about children who weren't her children.

To stop wondering what kind of governess Lord Budworth would hire next for his girls. For he would certainly want someone to keep them out of his way, so he could throw his lavish parties without having them underfoot. What if the next woman *was* prepared to use the birch?

She was just about to start dusting the crumbs from the vicar's desk when she heard someone knocking on the front door. It was only when the person pounded again, a bit harder, that it occurred to her that she ought to be the one to go and see who it was. The cook, who was the only other servant in the house, did not seem at all inclined to leave her kitchen. But then, the poor woman was far too busy to wash dishes, never mind deal with the kind of visitor who would bang so importunately on the door at this time of night on Christmas Eve. Besides, if it was the kind of visitor with whom she could deal, they would have been knocking on the back door.

Whoever it was, they were not going to go away. So she removed her apron, smoothed her hair and went into the hall.

It was a total shock to see Lord Chepstow standing on the top step, looking far from his normal, devil-may-care self.

But though he had not been very far from her thoughts all day, the sight of him broke down all the good intentions she'd had not to blame him for taking what she had so freely offered—and consequently shattering her whole world.

'How dare you show your face here?'

A face that looked, if she did not know better, as though he was experiencing profound relief from whatever worry had previously been creasing his forehead.

'Thank God I found you,' he said, stretching out his hands, as though to embrace her.

'Oh, no, you don't,' she snapped, stepping smartly backwards. 'Haven't you caused enough trouble? And don't even think of coming in here,' she protested, just a bit too late, for the moment she had stepped back to evade his embrace he darted past her and kicked the front door shut behind him.

'Not one step farther!' She held her arms wide, barring the passage into the house. 'I have no idea what whim has brought you here, but I have no intention of letting you spoil the niche I'm trying to carve for myself here, as you spoiled everything at Budworth Hall.'

'And I have no intention of leaving you here to become a drudge for someone else,' he said, leaning back against the front door and folding his arms across his chest. 'Go and fetch your things.'

'Fetch my things? Why should I fetch my things?'

'I should have thought that was obvious,' he said. 'I've come to collect you.'

'I am not,' she said coldly, 'going anywhere with you.'

'Well, I'm not leaving without you. Now,' he said, pushing himself away from the door, and taking a pace towards her, 'I can see you're angry with me. And you have every right to be. Dash it, I've been cursing myself all the way here for not just whisking you away at first light and leaving a note to tell 'em all we'd eloped.'

'Elo—e—what?'

While she stood there, gasping and spluttering, he strode past her, opening one door after another and peering inside.

'Vicar not in, I take it,' he said, going into the unoccupied study the moment he'd identified it.

'No,' she said, trotting after him in a state of complete bewilderment. In his typical fashion, he was already making himself at home, withdrawing his gloves and hat and tossing his coat over the back of the vicar's fireside chair. 'He is over at the church, officiating at a wedding.'

'A wedding? How convenient! Let us both go over there, too, and he can marry us while he's at it.'

'What? What are you saying? Are you out of your mind?'

He said not a word, but, to set the seal on her confusion, grasped her by the elbows, tugged her into the room, somehow managing to shut the door upon them without her ascertaining how he'd done so, and then made as though he was going to kiss her.

She only just came to her senses in time to turn her head, so that his parted lips landed hotly on her cheek.

But the mere brush of his lips on her face sent a shaft of shameful longing coursing right through her. She trembled with the force of it. And the feel of his hands upon her arms, coupled with that smile...that smile...as though he had not a care in the world...

Anger and pride came to her rescue. 'You are insufferable!' A little late for her liking, she raised her hands to his chest and tried to push him away.

'Is it not bad enough that your antics have made me lose my livelihood? Do you intend to make the vicar turn me out for being a harlot, too? What have I ever done to make you torment me so?'

'I am not tormenting you. Unless you think being married to me would be torment,' he said, and, since she still held her head stiffly averted, made the most of the opportunity to nibble at her earlobe.

'Stop that!' she tried to rebuke him sternly, but her words came out in a kind of plaintive whisper, her anger mysteriously ebbing as torrents of delight poured through her.

'And stop talking about getting married. We cannot possibly—'

'Of course not!' He slapped his forehead with the palm of his hand, giving her the chance to evade his grasp.

Somehow, she did manage to take just one, rather wobbly, step backwards, where she fetched up against the door with a thump.

'No licence,' he said and smiled at her.

The apparent tenderness of that smile made her long to fling herself back into his arms. She darted across the room instead, taking refuge behind the solid bulwark of the vicar's desk. He was just too tempting. A few more seconds of him nibbling on her ear like that and she did not know what he might have persuaded her into doing. Or thinking. The sensations he could evoke in her body were just so powerful that her mind was having serious trouble staying anywhere near lucid.

'Well, never mind,' he carried on cheerfully. 'A hole-and-corner wedding down here was not what I intended, anyway. It just occurred to me that it would be fun to turn up at Pippa's with you on my arm and introduce you as my bride. But this is why you are perfect for me.' He beamed at her. 'You will always remember all those practical little details that slip my mind when I get the urge to embark on a new adventure. Lord, but I'm going to have such a lot to tell Havelock about the impact helping him make that list of wifely qualities has had on my life.'

She shook her head slowly, wondering if he'd gone completely mad. Or perhaps she was the one who'd lost her mind. Was that why nothing he said made any sense?

'I suppose I can see,' she said, trying to puzzle out his bewildering behaviour for herself, 'that when you found out that I lost my job because of what you did last night, you now feel you ought to make amends. But really, talking about marrying me is carrying your penance a bit too far...'

He marched up to the desk, a frown on his brow. 'Don't you remember? I proposed to you last night. Or did you not hear? Of course. You'd gone into your room. Well, that accounts for it,' he said, his face clearing. He walked round the desk to where she was standing, his hands outstretched.

'Oh, I heard you clear enough,' she said, skipping sideways, to keep the furniture safely betwixt them. She needed to maintain the physical barrier of a substantial amount of oak between them, since she'd already discovered that her willpower was no protection at all once he began to employ his lips upon any part of her person.

'Naturally I did not think you meant anything by it. Nor even that you would recall what you'd said, once you'd sobered up.'

He clutched at his heart, as though she'd wounded him. 'Unkind! How can you so malign me, when I have laid my heart at your feet, pursued you on horseback over frozen terrain...'

'Don't give me that! You like horses. You were prating on about them last night, if you recall, right after you said that as a *gentleman* you *supposed* you *ought* to propose.'

'Oh. Ah,' he said, shamefaced. 'I admit, I made a mull of it. But then it was the first time I have ever proposed, you know. But I absolutely refute the allegation that I was not thinking clearly,' he continued when she took a breath to make another point. 'I had only had a couple of glasses of wine with my dinner. Even skipped the port, so I could come up to your schoolroom and spend what remained of the evening with you. The only thing with which I was intoxicated…' he smiled salaciously, and inched sideways to the corner of the desk '…was what I tasted on your lips.'

Her cheeks heating, Honeysuckle inched to the corner diagonally opposite.

'That kiss…' He sighed. 'I can see you remember it, too. Was it your first kiss? Oh, please tell me that it was. For I never want any other man to taste those lips. To discover that you can kiss like that…'

'H-how dare you! If you were a gentleman, you w-would not remind me of…that…lapse of good conduct.'

'Well, that's exactly why you ought to marry me, sweet Honeysuckle. You can remind me every day of how I ought to behave. You can reform me.' He darted suddenly round the desk, making a grab for her, which she was only just nimble enough to evade.

'Hah!' she panted. 'That attempt to manhandle me just proves that you are beyond redemption.'

'I am quite sure,' he said, stalking her slowly round the desk while she kept on steadily retreating, 'that your vicar would argue that nobody is beyond redemption. I am sure he preaches that every sinner who repents may enter the gates of paradise.'

'Exactly! You would have to repent and you never do!'

'Now that's not true. You have challenged me and made me question my behaviour in a way nobody else has ever done before. I'm not saying that you won't have your work cut out, reforming me. But if only I had you around to point out where I am going wrong, *all* the time...'

'That's not the kind of wife I would ever want to be,' she protested, stung at his description of the way he perceived her. 'Always nagging at you...'

'Oh, I am quite sure you would never have to nag. I expect you have already learned in your career so far that, when handling naughty boys, a threat to withhold some treat,' he said, eyeing her mouth provocatively, 'is a sure-fire way to get him to do your bidding.'

'I don't have much experience with naughty boys. And anyway, you're not a boy. You are a fully grown man.'

'I always seem to grow even fuller around you,' he said suggestively. 'I dare say you couldn't help noticing that for yourself last night when you twined yourself round me like your namesake.'

'I'm sure I don't know what you mean,' she protested. 'And you ought not to be speaking of such things in the vicar's study, of all places.'

He clucked his tongue. 'And here was I, thinking you prided yourself on always being honest.'

Her cheeks felt hot. Her words had just proved she had

understood his allusion completely. But worse, his mock-reproof had struck deeply at her own conscience. Last night, as he'd pointed out, when she *had* been clinging to him like a vine, she had not only been aware of his aroused state, but had been thrilled to think that it was *her* kisses that had achieved such a dramatic effect upon his body.

He stabbed a finger at her as he made his next point. 'Admit it. I could have an improving effect upon you, too. You have longings and passions, for which you have never had an outlet before. You are all…buttoned up. As your husband, I shall have the right to unbutton you. The *pleasure* of unbuttoning you,' he said, his gaze straying to the front of her gown.

In her head, she could see his hand reaching across the desk and unbuttoning her bodice right now. Slipping those long, elegant fingers inside her clothing and caressing…

'Stop it!' She pressed her hand to her chest, inside which her heart was hammering wildly. 'This kind of talk is unseemly.' And unsettling. Not only was her heart pounding, but she was breathing harder. And there were sharp twinges of excitement in her tummy and her legs were turning to the consistency of jelly.

'Nothing is unseemly between a man and his wife.'

'I'm not your wife!'

'But you will be. You want to be. You will enjoy taking me in hand…'

He made a motion towards the front of his breeches. In spite of gasping with outrage, she could not help following the motion of his hand with her eyes. Nor noticing that he was, once again, um...*fully grown.*

'See how much influence you've had over me already. Mending my manners, planning on marrying and settling down, getting me all hot and bothered just from talking about kissing you...'

'You did not *plan* to marry and settle down,' she said, sidestepping his remark about getting hot and bothered, since she was so very hot and bothered herself. 'You never plan anything! A thought just pops into your head, and you go along with it. B-but I concede,' she said, darting round the desk suddenly, as she realised he had been inching his way closer whilst she had been temporarily fascinated by the impressive ridge that was pushing out the front of his breeches, 'that you are attempting to make amends for crossing the line last night. But please don't insult my intelligence by making it sound as though you were out looking for a wife and that you deliberately chose me when I know it was no such thing.'

'You are right. I never do plan anything. But now I have thought of it, I cannot think of anything I'd rather do than marry you. And I'm quite sure you would like being married to me.'

She had to make yet another strategic withdrawal when he attempted to inch closer. 'That is beside the point.'

'So you admit it—you do want me?' He took two large paces towards her. With a little yelp, she darted away, maintaining her distance. Her physical distance. But, oh, how hard it was getting not to let him seduce her with his words.

'Perhaps it is time I was completely honest with you,' she said, summoning all her courage. 'But don't blame me if you don't like what you are going to hear. I cannot, dare not, believe you are in earnest. P-perhaps you truly do believe, at this minute, you want to marry me. You have just admitted you have got carried along on one of those surges of enthusiasm you are always getting. But after a very brief time, it will wear off, and then where will that leave me? I...' She took a deep, shuddering breath. 'I want you, yes. I have always wanted you. Right from the first moment I saw you, when I was scarce old enough to recognise what that kind of wanting was.'

For a moment, they both stood stock-still, gazing at each other hungrily. She didn't think either one of them was breathing.

'What woman with eyes in her head would not want you? You are...' she waved her hand up and down, outlining his figure across the desk '...just gorgeous.'

He stood up straighter, grinning smugly.

'Except,' she said acidly, 'for your inability to give a rap about anything but your own pleasure.'

That wiped the self-satisfied smile from his face.

'What do you think it will be like for me, being hopelessly in love with a husband who is constitutionally unable to remain faithful? I will be miserable. No, worse than

that, broken! Can't you see, it will be much better for me
to remain single?'

'No. I cannot see that. You are condemning me without
giving me a fair hearing. Give me a chance, sweetheart—'

'Don't you sweetheart me! You have already caused me
to lose my job and my reputation. And what do you think
it felt like, having to leave with the few belongings I could
carry? And not even what I would have chosen to pack!
How far did you think I would get with what few shillings
I have in my purse?'

'You'd be surprised how far you can get with hardly any
coin at all, actually. I had a bet once, with a few fellows,
to see who could travel the farthest on only two guineas
and Wilbraham...'

It was the last straw. Could he take nothing seriously?
She had opened her heart to him, and all he could do by
way of response was to relate some tale about some bet
he had made.

With a howl of rage, she reached for the nearest solid object that came to hand and shied it at him across the desk.

He ducked. It was only when the missile smashed
against one of the shelves, spraying black liquid all over
the books she'd just spent ages tidying, that she realised it
had been the Reverend Colleyhurst's inkwell.

She clapped her hands to her cheeks in horror.

'Oh, look what you've made me do, you provoking man!
I've probably ruined all those valuable books. And your
coat,' she wailed. 'Your beautiful coat!'

A good deal of ink had spattered Lord Chepstow's shoulder and the side of his face, and was dripping in great fat globs down his shirt front.

She knew, from the times she'd stayed in his home as a girl, how often Lord Chepstow visited his tailor and how large were the bills the man sent to him. The cost of replacing what she had just ruined would wipe out any earnings she might have made, had she remained a governess, for years and years.

She stared at him in horror. Not only at her inability to pay for the damage she'd done, but at her loss of control. She *never* lost control. At least, she never had, until the advent of Lord Chepstow into her life this last time.

It felt as though an abyss was yawning at her feet. She had comprehensively insulted Lord Chepstow. Turned down his marriage proposal in the most unflattering terms. And, as if that was not enough, had ruined a whole set of his expensive clothing.

In short, she must have persuaded him that marrying her would be a fatal mistake. He would leave now. And she would never see him again.

She was the biggest idiot alive. Against all the odds, he'd pursued her with the notion of making amends by offering to marry her. And what had she done?

Oh, what had she done?

Lord Chepstow was looking down the front of his coat, an expression of complete shock on his face. And then he raised his eyes to hers.

She buried her face in her hands. She could not bear to see those laughing eyes of his turn upon her in coldness. But what else could she expect? She had said such unforgivable things, even before she'd thrown the inkwell at his head.

But being Lord Chepstow, he did the very last thing anyone could have expected.

He burst out laughing.

She gave a little sob of relief and dared to look at him then. Wasn't that just like him—to see the funny side of a situation that most men would have found infuriating?

Her heart turned over in her chest. He might be the most impulsive, self-indulgent creature in existence, but there was not a mean bone in his body.

'Do you know, before I came here I vowed I would take whatever you chose to throw at me. But I never d-dreamed...' he chortled '...that it would be an inkwell.'

'You aren't cross?'

'How can I be cross?' He rounded the desk, seized her hands and tugged her towards him. 'You just admitted you want to marry me.'

'Did you not hear a word I said?'

'I heard you say you were hopelessly in love with me,' he said, pulling her so close that when a drop of ink fell from his fringe it dripped on to her spectacles.

'But I'm so afraid you will get bored with me. You will take up with your opera dancers again and it will break my heart...'

He removed her spectacles with a rueful smile.

'How could I possibly ever grow bored with you?'

'B-because I am so dull and...'

'Dull? You? Not a bit of it.' He reached into his pocket and drew out a handkerchief. 'Every time I stepped into your schoolroom something new and unexpected about you took me completely by surprise. I have only just started to discover the woman you are, underneath all that governessy starch you hide behind. It will take at least the rest of my life to understand you completely.'

'There is nothing to understand. I love routine and order. And you,' she said despairingly, 'you crave adventure.'

'No,' he said thoughtfully as he wiped the lens clean. 'I don't crave it. This is how it is, sweetheart,' he said, sliding the spectacles back onto her nose and putting his arms round her. 'When my parents died so unexpectedly, the shock of it made me see what a precarious business life is. And then, you know, I was left in sole charge of an immense fortune. I could not see any point in being frugal with it, or living carefully, not when death could snatch it all away from me without a moment's notice. I just wanted to live life to the full, squeeze every last drop of sensation from each and every hour, so that, if it did all come to an abrupt end, I would never regret not having got the most out of it. But I have never taken my pleasure at the expense of another's happiness. What makes you think I would be unkind enough to take up with another woman, if I was lucky enough to have you to wife?'

'I am sure you would never *mean* to be unkind, but…'

She gazed up into his eyes and saw nothing but complete sincerity. She felt a little bubble of hope rising. After all, he was claiming those jumbled words he'd uttered about marriage last night had really been his idea of a proposal—a genuine proposal—when she had been assuming all day that he would have laughed the whole thing off in the same way he'd laughed off the hurting of the inkwell. And he hadn't noticed Lady Springfield, so he hadn't talked about marriage because he'd felt coerced. Could he be in earnest?

Dare she believe in him?

But still… 'The thought of living as you do scares me,' she admitted. 'I don't want adventure or experience. I just want to feel…'

'Secure,' he said, nodding. 'When you lost your parents, it had the opposite effect upon you, didn't it, to what it had on me? Because along with your parents, you lost your security. And you have been desperately searching for it ever since. You try to make yourself feel safe by constantly warning yourself not to rely on anyone else. You don't ever let anyone get close enough to hurt you.'

'Th-that is…exactly what I do,' she said in astonishment. 'But how could you know that? How do you understand it, when I have never told anyone…?'

'Because I'm not an idiot. I might behave in what you think is an idiotish manner at times, but I have a brain in my head. And when I choose to use it, I make some damned good choices. An idiot would have run through his fortune entirely, having it handed over to him the way I did, at such a young age and with no serious checks in place. But I didn't. Oh, yes, I know you think I am an extravagant creature, but I have never…well, actually, I did outrun the constable just once or twice, at the very first,' he admitted with a frown.

'But then I remembered I was responsible for Pippa. I made very sure that her portion would always be safe. You might not think I was the ideal brother to her, but I never played fast and loose with her fortune. On the contrary, I invested it so wisely that by the time it came to her Season, she had a very healthy dowry to bring to her marriage. I've more than tripled my own fortune, too. Hah! Stunned you to silence at last!'

'Yes, I…don't know what to say…'

She gazed up at him dizzily. Her whole perception of him was turning upside down.

'Just say you'll marry me. You will never have to worry about a thing, ever again. I will keep you safe. Your security will be in bearing my name.'

'S-safe,' she repeated in a daze.

'And free to discover yourself in a way you never have been before,' he said in a silky smooth voice. 'Come on, Honeysuckle, yield to temptation. I know you want to.'

She did want to…and not just because he was holding her in his arms. She had been alone for so long and he was saying she could finally belong to someone, in a way that far exceeded anything she had dared to let herself hope for.

Now that she knew him better, she was beginning to believe she really might be able to trust in him.

'You make it sound so simple, but—'

'I don't want to listen to any more arguments,' he said, realising he'd got as far as he could by that method. It was time to apply the sort of persuasion he knew she would not be able to resist.

Clasping her tightly, he kissed her for all he was worth.

He met with no resistance.

In fact, the moment his mouth met hers, she flung her arms about his neck and kissed him back. And just like the night before, it felt as though they were both going up in flames.

He had never felt so immediately, painfully aroused in his life. He had to get her horizontal. Somewhere in the room there had to be a sofa, or, if not, it would have to be the hearthrug. How could she think he would ever grow bored with this? This instant, total conflagration that consumed everything in its path as it surged through them both?

He broke free from her greedy mouth just long enough to draw a quick breath and scan the room.

'No,' she moaned and speared her fingers into his hair, dragging his face back down to hers.

But he'd located what he needed. There was a sofa, albeit one with a tea tray inexplicably nestling amongst its cushions.

He backed her ruthlessly in its direction, while she went

frantic, tunnelling her fingers under his waistcoat and yanking his shirt from his breeches, as though she would die if she didn't get her hands on bare flesh.

He sympathised. Totally. With a groan, he swept her up into his arms, just long enough to get her legs up off the floor, then they landed on the sofa in a tangle of limbs to the sound of shattering crockery as he elbowed the tea tray aside.

Then he set about the buttons down the front of her gown. He had to free what felt like hundreds of little jet padlocks from their chains before he could push the material aside and get his hands on what he longed to feel: the soft mounds of her breasts, crowned with satisfyingly stiff nipples. Just the right size to fit into his palms. Though what he wanted, what he really wanted, was to taste them.

She whimpered when he started trailing kisses across her jaw and down her neck. When he pressed his lips just so, beneath her ear, her whole body arched up into him. He teased her there a little longer, then continued to his chosen destination, pushing her chemise aside…

She gasped, and shoved hard at his shoulders.

Damn, he hadn't thought she would resist him, not at this point…

But then he heard it, too—the sound of footsteps in the hall, coming steadily closer.

'It's the vicar!' Honeysuckle shrieked, rolling out from underneath him, scrambling to her feet and making for the far side of the room.

How on earth could she have heard the front door open and close, when all he'd been aware of was the thunder of his own heart beating?

He sat up and pushed his ink-sticky fringe out of his eyes.

He'd done some pretty outrageous things in his time, but he'd never been so swept away by passion that he'd almost ravished a virgin on a vicar's sofa.

The virgin in question was shakily fastening her buttons up in all the wrong loops, whilst staring at the study door with an expression of complete panic.

And the wave of tenderness that swept through him explained it all: the fiery passion, the feeling of everything falling into place after he'd made that muddled proposal to her, the horror he'd experienced when he thought she might be in danger and, worse, the dread that he might never find her. That he might have to face the rest of his life alone.

Without her.

'Honeysuckle,' he said, 'I have fallen completely, head over heels in love with you.'

Chapter Eight

Her fingers stalled.

She was only dimly aware of the vicar coming to a shocked standstill on the threshold. What filled her vision was Lord Chepstow, sprawled on the sofa, looking at her with a slightly stunned expression.

'What the…what has…what is…?'

Lord Chepstow blinked, as though the Reverend's spluttered outrage had awoken him from a spell. He got to his feet.

'I hope you will offer us your congratulations, Reverend,' he said with not the slightest trace of embarrassment, though he was tucking his shirt into his breeches. She didn't know whether to resent his sheer nerve, or admire his insouciance.

'Miss Miller has just agreed to marry me,' he said, doing up the waistcoat her own fingers must have unbuttoned while her mind had abdicated responsibility for their actions.

Reverend Colleyhurst, who had been gazing round at the wreckage of his study, lingering over the smashed crockery on the carpet and the inkstains splattered all over his bookshelves, bleated faintly, 'Congratulations.'

'As you can see,' said Lord Chepstow, making for Honeysuckle's side, 'she put up some very strenuous resistance to my proposal to begin with. But as you may also perceive,' he said, drawing attention to the inkstains down his own clothing, then hers, which she realised in sudden horror must be a mirror image, considering the way she had plastered herself to him like a sheet of blotting paper, 'eventually I persuaded her to see reason. I shall, of course, reimburse you for all the breakages that occurred during what must be one of the longest and hardest-contested duels of will any man has ever had to fight in the name of love.'

With a smile that verged on the borders of smug, he set about refastening the buttons of her gown in the correct loops, causing her cheeks to flush hotly. Her only consolation was that the vicar looked as flustered as she felt.

'Might I suggest,' put in the vicar, hesitantly, 'that the procuring of a special licence would be in order?'

'Well, I had planned on giving her a lavish society wedding. But it might be better not to make her wait too long. Miss Miller is a woman of such strong passions, I fear she can hardly keep her hands off me, one way or another.'

'Ooh, you—'

He cut off any protestation she might have voiced by

swooping down and kissing her. Only once she was clinging to his waistcoat lapels, rather than trying to fight him
off, did he break the kiss.

'But then I cannot keep my hands off her either.'

That admission effectively dealt with any lingering
shreds of resentment that kiss had not already dispatched.

And then, just as she felt as though her knees might not
hold her up a moment longer, he swept her into his arms.

'Good day, Reverend,' he said, striding past the red-
faced vicar.

She buried her face in his neck, both to hide her blushes
and to savour the moment. She'd never thought of him as
masterful before, but he was shouldering open the door
and marching down the hallway with her as though he
was a conquering warrior and she the prize he'd snatched
from the battlefield.

Only the bitter cold that assailed her when he opened the
front door brought her back to some degree of rationality.

'My lord, you have left your coat and hat behind.'

He smiled fondly at her. 'Taking care of me already, just
like a proper, loving wife.' He dropped a brief kiss on her
mouth. 'But I shan't get cold with you in my arms. And
do you think you could possibly start calling me Martin?'

'M-Martin.' She sighed as he mounted Brown Bess and
hauled her up on to his lap. 'Martin, this is madness. It
might come on to rain again…'

He frowned. 'Should have thought of that. Do *you* need
to go back and fetch a bonnet or something?'

How could she have been so idiotic as to shatter the romance of the moment by mentioning something as prosaic as the weather? She flung her arms round his neck and clung tightly.

'I have all I need, right here.'

'I feel exactly the same,' he replied with an approving smile. 'But for once I should like to consider the practicalities, just to demonstrate to you that I can. I know you had to leave all your possessions at Budworth Hall. If you like, we can ride up there and demand they restore what is rightfully yours.'

'The last thing I wish to do is ruin this lovely moment by starting an unpleasant scene with Lord and Lady Budworth. Besides, I do not own anything of any great value.'

'Yes. Much better to pop over to Paris and get you an entirely new wardrobe,' he said with approval, and nudged Brown Bess into motion. 'Then you'll be all the crack when we go back to Town. If we do go back to Town. Do you want to go to London, or do you prefer the country?'

'I really don't care where we go, so long as we go together.'

He rewarded her confession with a kiss so heated it might have started snowing and she would not have noticed.

'And you said you were not adventurous,' he said when he broke off to let her breathe. 'I don't know another woman that would run off in the middle of the night without a coat or bonnet and not be insisting I buy her bride clothes *before* the wedding. Or saying she didn't care about where she lived, either. Do you know, I think you were born to be my wife.'

'When you hold me in your arms,' she admitted shyly, 'I feel as though…as though I've come home.' For the first time in her life, or at least since she'd been a very little girl, she finally felt as though she belonged.

'Right, then,' he said decisively. 'To Paris we shall go. Only, first, we shall have to make for the nearest town and procure a more fitting means of conveyance for my viscountess-to-be. Although…might be a tad awkward to get anything now. People have absurd ideas about travelling over Christmas. We might just have to—what is it?'

'Oh, n-nothing, really. It was just you mentioning Christmas. I dare say you would think I am just being silly…'

'Not you. If there is something bothering you, I am sure it is very far from silly. Tell me what it is and I will make it right.'

'Well,' she said, taking a deep breath, 'it is the children. On Christmas Day, I had planned—'

'A party! I went looking for you in the schoolroom and the children told me about it.'

He looked down at the troubled expression on her face and smiled ruefully.

'I want to give you the best Christmas you've ever known. My plan was to take you to bed, and keep you there all day, but…' he sighed and adopted a mournful expression '…if you would really prefer to attend a children's party, then…'

'A-actually, your plan sounds rather…interesting,' she said, biting her lower lip and shooting him a look from under her eyelashes that sent his pulse rate soaring.

'Perhaps,' he suggested with a twinkle in his eye, 'we could reach a compromise. I could let you out of bed, just for an hour or two, so that you can enjoy Christmas your way, providing you spend the rest of Christmas Day letting me enjoy it my way.'

'I think,' she said, sitting up to kiss his icy-cold cheek, 'recalling how much fun you had pretending to be a pirate, that you will enjoy my version of Christmas with the children very much.'

'Well, I can guarantee that you will enjoy my idea of how best to celebrate Christmas.' He kissed her. 'Very much.' He kissed her again. 'Indeed.' He let go of the reins so that he could hold her tight whilst kissing her again. Brown Bess shook her head, snorted, then carried on plodding steadily along the road.

'So, you are saying that we can both learn from each other, then?'

'Am I?' He looked at her dazedly for a while, before saying in a firmer tone, 'Absolutely. Do you know, I can hardly wait to have our own nursery full of children.'

Then, without warning, he retrieved the reins and pulled Brown Bess to a halt, looking troubled.

'Perhaps we should forgo the staying-in-bed part of Christmas. Who knows what might happen between now and the day that should be our wedding? I don't want to run the risk of leaving you pregnant and alone and…shamed.'

'I could never feel ashamed of bearing your child,' she protested, 'for it would have been conceived in love. The only thing I would regret, bitterly, is if we did not seize the opportunity we have, right now, to experience the fullness of love.'

'I thought you were supposed to be attempting to reform me,' he said. 'Instead, I seem to have corrupted you…'

'I told you, I have no intention of reforming you. I love you just as you are. And you are not corrupting me at all. Just encouraging me to…make the most of life.'

'Yes, but—'

She laid her finger across his lips, silencing him.

'I have spent years worrying and being careful. It is time for me to start living my life. With you. So stop arguing, my lord, else I shall have to be very, very strict with you.'

He sat up straighter, looking intrigued. 'What had you in mind? Have you packed your hairbrush?'

'What?' She looked perplexed. 'No. I left it behind at the vicararge, but never mind that. On second thoughts, it might be impossible for us to attend the children's party, anyway. Not without having some kind of a confrontation with Lord and Lady Budworth, which would completely ruin the day.'

'You forget you have now cast in your lot with an accomplished rake, my love. I have never had any trouble locating secretive ways into any property I have ever chosen to enter.'

She cuffed him lightly on the shoulder.

He dropped a kiss on her nose.

'Joking aside, I don't think it will be as difficult as all that. You know all the staff corridors and the back stairs from the time you worked there. And I don't believe any of the staff would betray our presence in the house, if you asked them not to. You have some loyal allies there, you know.'

'Yes, I found that out when I was dismissed. You wouldn't believe how kind they all were.'

'Yes, I would. You are so loving that you inspire kindness in others. But, Honeysuckle, you do know it will have to be farewell, tomorrow, to those children, no matter how fond of them you've grown?'

'Y-yes.' She looked sad for a moment or two, but then plucked herself up, and said, 'And as you said, it won't be long before I am looking after my own children.' She lay her hand upon his chest. 'Our children.'

He gave her a long look, then said, 'Knowing you, I don't think that will be enough. You will be sitting in the parlour drinking tea and wondering how many orphans there are out there, at the mercy of fate, and then you will start pestering me to sponsor a school for indigent young ladies…'

'Oh, what a wonderful idea!' Her face lit up. 'If we

could pay teachers a decent wage and make them happy with their terms of service, then they wouldn't be tempted to take out their frustrations on the children over whom they have authority. And we could make sure only to hire women who actually *like* children, who *want* to help them reach their full potential...'

'And you thought I might grow bored with you,' he said. 'I will never know what scheme for improving the lot of the poor you will be hatching next.'

'I beg pardon,' she said, abashed. 'It is just that it is so exciting to think that at last I might be able to do something to make a difference.'

'You don't need to beg pardon. I am glad you are excited about our future together. I am pretty excited about it myself.' He nuzzled her neck. 'If you know what I mean.'

Since she was sitting on his lap and could feel his erection pressing into her hip, she knew exactly what he meant.

'Let's not talk any more,' he said. 'No more planning. Let's just get started on this adventure and see what happens as it unfolds, shall we?'

'If you say so.'

'I do,' he said firmly. 'Trust me?'

'Absolutely.'

'Then hold on tight. Because I need to get you to the nearest inn, as quickly as possible, so we can start celebrating the best Christmas either of us has ever had.'

He dug his heels into Brown Bess's flanks and they shot off into the night.

Honeysuckle couldn't help giving a little squeal, but when Martin's strong arms tightened round her, her momentary flutter of nerves subsided. He wouldn't let her fall. Nor was she the kind of ninny who wouldn't do her level best to rise to any challenge this unpredictable, and utterly exciting, man might set her, now or in the future they would share.

She wrapped her arms round his waist and clung to him, relishing everything about the sensations of galloping through the night with the man she loved. The play of his muscles as he kept them both in the saddle, the breathtaking speed of their mount, even the cold wind stinging the cheek that wasn't pressed to his chest—all were equally wonderful.

She laughed out loud. Oh, but life with Martin would always be something of a wild ride.

When she had been growing up, catching glimpses of his life from time to time, she had seen his spontaneity as a selfish, dangerous way to live.

But now she knew better. When a man's heart was in the right place, how could he ever choose to do anything really wicked? He wouldn't. So all she had to do was hang on tight and enjoy the ride.

She flung back her head and laughed with sheer delight.

Oh, how good life was.

Now that she had let love into it.

* * * * *

Duchess by
Christmas

Marguerite Kaye

Born and educated in Scotland, **Marguerite Kaye** originally qualified as a lawyer but chose not to practise. Instead, she carved out a career in IT and studied history part-time, gaining a first-class honours and master's degree. A few decades after winning a children's national poetry competition, she decided to pursue her lifelong ambition to write and submitted her first historical romance to Mills & Boon. They accepted it and she's been writing ever since. You can contact Marguerite through her website at www.margueritekaye.com.

Chapter One

Derbyshire—December 1818

The hired gig that had conveyed them on the final leg of their long and arduous journey from Yorkshire trundled noisily over the stone hump-backed bridge which spanned the Blairmore River. Pushing back the hood of her red-wool cloak, pulling its comforting folds more tightly around her, for the cold was bitter, Regan Stuart peered anxiously ahead, eager for her first sight of Blairmore Hall in more than a dozen years.

'We used to climb these trees, Gabriel and I,' she informed the three children sharing the carriage with her, as they passed through a wooded copse, the bare branches silhouetted starkly against the watery winter sky.

Her two young half-brothers looked sceptical, but Regan's nine-year-old half-sister, Portia, gazed up at the mighty oaks in awe. 'They're huge,' she said. 'Weren't you scared?'

Regan laughed. 'A little, but I knew Gabriel wouldn't let me come to any harm.' Though the real reason she habitually rose to whatever challenge he dared her into taking on, she acknowledged to herself, was because she feared losing his respect more than she feared any potential danger. How she had idolised him in those distant childhood days.

'Can we climb the trees, Regan, can we?' Jack, her youngest sibling, piped up.

'We must ask his Grace's permission first,' she replied, wondering for the hundredth time why, quite out of the blue, the Duke of Blairmore had invited them to stay here at the hall over Christmas. Not that it wasn't a most welcome and generous offer, she thought, smiling at the three shining, excited young faces craning their necks to get a view of the huge manor house she had told them so much about.

The curved drive along which they were travelling was longer than she recalled. The ornamental pond with its extravagant Poseidon fountain, although drained for the winter, seemed much larger, too. As the gig turned the final sharp corner in the long drive and the Hall came into view, all three children gasped. 'Well, what do you think of it?' she asked. 'Is it as I described?'

'It's a castle,' Jack said.

'A fairy-tale palace,' Portia exclaimed.

'It's absolutely enormous,' Land declared.

They were all in the right of it. Blairmore Hall was built around two central courtyards with a turret at each corner linked by battlements. A huge portico complete with portcullis led to the banqueting hall, which formed the central nave. Though its origins were, like the gardens, Elizabethan, each successive duke had demolished, rebuilt, altered and enhanced, so that the resultant stately pile contained not only a warren of rooms, but a hotchpotch of styles. Despite this, or perhaps because of it, it possessed a unique charm, framed as it was by the rolling hills and cragged tors of the nearby Derbyshire Peaks.

'Will you show me the beautiful old clothes, like you promised?' Portia asked eagerly.

Regan smiled at the memory of the little shuttered room in the east tower where she had spent many happy hours dressing up in the finery of bygone days, the ornate gowns and wide-brimmed hats trimmed with ostrich feathers which were stored there in stout wooden trunks. She ruffled Portia's hair affectionately. 'Perhaps, if they are still there. It was a long time ago.' Though surely no one would throw out such exquisite antique garments.

As they bowled under the gatehouse into the lower courtyard, butterflies began to flutter in Regan's stomach. Before his death, her father had served as steward here for twenty years. Though she knew the Hall and its environs intimately, she had never before been accorded the status of guest. Circumstances had ensured she was a very different person from the gauche child who, with her recently widowed mother, had left Blairmore Hall to face an uncertain future. She wondered what else had changed in the intervening years.

A footman in the familiar claret-coloured livery held open the heavily studded door to the Hall while another helped them from the gig, and another supervised the removal of their meagre luggage. Entering the Hall through the flag-stoned reception area in the wake of yet another servant, who relieved them of their outerwear, even the normally voluble boys were stunned into silence by the sheer magnificence of the long gallery, which was, true to its name, over a hundred feet in length.

'His Grace asks that the young people remain here while he receives you alone,' the footman informed Regan.

Quickly reminding Land, Jack and Portia that they were to be on their very best behaviour, Regan, now so nervous that she had to clasp her hands together to stop them shaking, followed the servant along a wide, portrait-lined corridor, to the rear of the Hall and the most modern of the apartments. The running, skipping footsteps of the ghost of her childhood self rang out along the labyrinth of corridors. The dark oak-panelled walls echoed with her and Gabriel's laughter. The whole place was redolent with bittersweet memories. How carefree she had been. How very young. Twelve years! It was a lifetime ago.

The footman opened the door to the so-called small salon, and Regan stepped over the threshold. With its gold damask hangings, soft cream walls and straw-coloured sofas, it had been refurbished since last she saw it, though it still had space enough for ten couples to perform a set dance.

'Miss Stuart, your Grace.'

The door closed softly behind her, and the Duke of Blairmore, who had been staring out of the mullioned windows at the view of the Peaks, turned around. 'Regan.'

'Hello, Gabriel.' Regan swallowed hard. The man facing her across the room was the epitome of elegance in a tightly fitting cutaway coat of dark blue superfine with a high collar over a buff-coloured waistcoat. His equally tightly fitting knitted pantaloons showed off a pair of long, shapely legs. His Hessian boots shone with a mirror-like polish. His snowy-white neckcloth was tied into a most intricate-looking knot. He was much taller than she remembered. And broader. And infinitely more attractive.

The fluttering in Regan's stomach spread to her pulses as he covered the distance between them. Blue-black hair swept back from a high forehead. A strong nose, a cleft chin and a mouth that was frankly sensual. She knew she was staring, but she couldn't help it. It wasn't just a struggle to equate this devastating man with the youth she had known, it was impossible. She sank into a belated curtsy, horribly conscious of her grey-wool travelling gown, which no amount of new trimming could make anything less than careworn.

Gabriel helped her to her feet. 'Little Regan, is it really you?'

His voice was attractively deep. His eyes, which looked at her with detached amusement, were the same grey-blue colour she remembered. The touch of his hand sent a surprising little tingle up her fingers. She could feel a blush creeping over her pale cheeks. 'It's me, I assure you,' Regan said with a faint smile, 'though I barely recognised you.'

'It *has* been a long time,' Gabriel said, eyeing his visitor with some surprise. He held her at arm's length. 'Let me look at you properly.' Who would have thought that the wild little hoyden who had doggedly followed him like a shadow would turn into such a striking woman? The red hair which had, predictably, earned her the nickname Carrot Top, had darkened to luxurious auburn. The gangly child with all the awkwardness of a foal was now willowy slim. Though her high brow and rather long face were more intelligent-looking than beautiful, there was something about Regan Stuart that would make any man look twice. Was it her mouth, with that sensuous curve, such a contrast to her serious expression? Or those big hazel eyes? He remembered them gazing up at him imploringly, begging to be allowed to accompany him on his latest childhood escapade.

A curious silence prevailed as each took stock of the other, trying to reconcile their twelve-year-old memories with the very different reality confronting them. An extremely adult awareness thickened the air between them. Flustered, Regan pulled herself free just as Gabriel let her go.

'You really are quite transformed,' he said.

'As, indeed, are you.'

'Come, I don't know what we're doing standing here in the middle of the room,' Gabriel said briskly. 'Please make yourself comfortable by the fire. I had them bring tea.'

Gratefully focusing on the ritual, carefully measuring

out the leaves from the ornate silver caddy, pouring water into the pot from the little spirit boiler, setting out the delicate china cups embossed with scarlet-and-gold dragons, Regan managed to regain a little of her usual poise, though not all. She was acutely aware of Gabriel lounging opposite her, his long legs stretched out in front of him. He had very shapely legs. It was as well he did, for those pantaloons fitted him like a second skin. She wondered if he fenced. Or boxed, perhaps. She dragged her eyes away. 'Cream or lemon?'

'Cream. Lemon. I don't care. I hate tea.'

'Well, I must say, I'm thankful for it.' Regan passed him a cup, careful not to allow her fingers to touch his. 'I was so sorry to hear the news of your father's death. I sent my condolences to your mother.'

'Did you?' Gabriel frowned. 'I don't remember her mentioning it.'

'I don't expect she would. Your mother never did approve of your friendship with a mere steward's daughter.'

'I'm sorry,' Gabriel said automatically.

Regan shrugged. 'What for? I never made the mistake of equating her opinions with yours. In fact, you were disposed to take up a contrary position to her on almost any subject. Your father, too, if memory serves, but his death must have been a shock all the same.'

'As you rightly say, my relationship with my parents could never be described as close,' Gabriel said drily, 'but, yes, it was a shock none the less. Or more accurately, a shock to the system.'

'A strange way to put it.'

It was Gabriel's turn to shrug. 'It was five years ago. Water under the bridge.'

She felt rebuffed, though she knew she had no right to. Her notion that they would pick up where they had left off was not only naive, but frankly foolish. The man opposite her was not Gabriel, friend of her childhood, but the sixth Duke of Blairmore, a man of the world, assured, hugely attractive and essentially a stranger. A rather intimidating stranger. Her teaspoon tinkled against the delicate china, and she realised she was holding an empty cup, which was shaking slightly in her hand. The silence between them was almost palpable. Regan put her cup back on to the table. 'So, how does it feel to hold one of the most prestigious and respected titles in England?' she asked brightly.

'Onerous. Oppressive. I could go on, but I won't bore you.'

'You never did have time for the trappings of authority, did you?'

'I no longer have the option to dismiss them.' Gabriel's expression tightened. 'Authority and its trappings come with the territory, along with other, equally unwelcome responsibilities. My priorities are different now.'

Regan's smile faded. 'I only meant that when you were younger…'

'That was a long time ago, Regan.' Gabriel put down his untouched cup of tea and forced a smile. 'Did you notice the unicorn's horn has grown back,' he said, referring to the elaborate topiary creature that stood guard at the portcullis.

'The one and only time, I think, that I refused to accept one of your challenges.' Regan poured herself another cup of tea. 'What a fuss there was. And though all I did was stand guard while you lopped it off, Papa read me such a lecture.'

'You must miss him.'

She nodded. Gabriel had been away at school when her father had died. He had not written, and by the time he came home for the summer, she and her mother were gone from Blairmore; she had never heard from Gabriel again. The pain of his silence had taken a long time to fade.

She waited for him to comment on it, but either Gabriel did not recall his omission, or guilt kept him silent. Or perhaps he simply did not care. 'Your mother did not wear her weeds for long,' he said.

Regan stiffened. 'When Papa died, my paternal grandfather, Lord Dallilongart, wanted nothing to do with us, Papa being but a fourth son and I, his only child, a mere female. One cannot blame Mama for choosing to marry again. She was very fond of my stepfather. They had five happy years together.'

'It was a fever, I believe, which took them?'

'Yes, it swept the village. We nearly lost little Jack, too.' Once again she waited, but Gabriel obviously deemed the five years which had elapsed since that dreadful time was suffice to preclude commiserations. Regan put her teacup carefully back down on the table. 'Jack is my youngest brother.'

'And there are two other half-siblings also in your care, I understand?'

'Yes.' Gabriel's expression gave nothing away. He was making her nervous. Was he just making conversation or was he actually interested? 'Portia is nine, Land is eight and Jack is six,' Regan explained.

Gabriel frowned. 'Land?'

'Orlando. And Jack is actually Ajax.'

'Good grief!'

To her relief, Gabriel finally smiled. 'Mama's passion for the bard went a little overboard when it came to naming her children,' she said with a little laugh.

'You should be grateful you are not called Goneril,' Gabriel said, finding himself rather distracted by Regan's smile. Her mouth tilted up at the corners delightfully. She had an attractive laugh, soft and seductive, like satin brushing over skin. Regan, who was not at all the Regan he had expected. Had he made a mistake, asking her here? He had been so intent on making good his carefully constructed plan, he had not thought to question her likely reaction to it.

Almost as if she read his mind, Regan turned the conversation resolutely to the question which had been uppermost in hers since she received his invitation. 'I have to tell you, Gabriel, your letter came as a complete surprise. A very pleasant one, of course. I am very much aware of the honour you do us in inviting us to the Hall, especially at this time of year. What prompted you to get in touch after all this time?'

'As to that…' Gabriel hesitated. He had, he realised, simply assumed that Regan would agree to his proposal without question, just as she always had. But the Regan seated opposite him was clearly no longer the biddable waif he recalled—was, in fact, a very assured, surprisingly attractive woman whom, he suspected, had developed a mind very much her own. He got to his feet and took out his snuffbox, turning it over and over in his hand. 'The thing is, I need to get married,' he said abruptly.

Of all the reasons Regan had imagined, this one had never crossed her horizon. She was vastly relieved she had not the teacup in her hand or it would currently be smashed to a thousand pieces. There was a pounding in her ears, like the sea. 'You need to—you want to....' Her voice seemed to be coming from far away.

'I am nine-and-twenty, it is well past time I set up my nursery,' Gabriel said, still apparently fascinated by his snuffbox. 'These last five years since I inherited have been—well, there have been other pressing issues, but they are dealt with now. Producing an heir is my last obligation to the title. The time has come—I cannot forestall any longer.'

'Forestall? You make it sound like—you are talking as if you don't want to marry at all.'

Putting his snuffbox away unopened, Gabriel finally looked over at her. 'Frankly I don't, but nor do I have any option. If I must marry, I may as well make a decent fist of it, which is why I've drawn up a list of qualities.'

'A list of qualities?' Mindless repetition seemed all she

was capable of as Regan struggled to make sense of this bizarre turn in the conversation.

'Qualities I consider essential in a wife,' Gabriel replied, as if it were perfectly obvious.

'Good God.' Regan swallowed a hysterical desire to laugh. Was he serious? He looked serious. He *could* not be serious. 'What—may I ask what these qualities are?' she said faintly.

'Well, all the usual ones, obviously. Impeccable lineage—and it must come without any encumbrances, too. I don't want to have to support a troop of sisters, nor have to tow any dissolute brothers out of the River Tick. A spotless reputation goes without saying. As to accomplishments,' Gabriel continued, counting off each quality on his fingers, 'I confess, I don't much care whether she can paint a watercolour or play upon the pianoforte as long as she possesses some artistic talent befitting a duchess. She must also be presentable and biddable. I want a wife who will share my opinions, not contradict them. Which is the very reason I invited you here to the Hall.'

Regan felt as if the ground was tilting beneath her. Was he really implying what he seemed to be implying? She gripped the gilt arm of the sofa in an effort to anchor herself. 'I'm afraid I still don't quite understand.'

'The qualities I've mentioned are vital,' Gabriel said, 'but there is another which I consider to be of paramount importance in any wife of mine. One which is extremely difficult to evaluate.' He smiled encouragingly at her. 'You and the children are the perfect answer to my dilemma.'

Now she felt as if she were looking down a precipice from a great height. Dizzy. Completely disoriented. She took a deep breath. 'Gabriel, would you please tell me, in simple language, what it is you're asking of me?'

'Come, Regan, it's obvious. You of all people should recall what a lonely, miserable upbringing I had as the product of an advantageous match first arranged when my father was in short coats and my mother in swaddling. My father's interest in me began and ended with my arrival as the direct heir to the line. As to my mother's feelings for me—I doubt they ever existed.' Gabriel took his snuffbox back out of his pocket, looked at it blankly, and put it back. 'I have no desire to subject any child of mine to such a fate,' he said tersely, 'which is why I need you to help me choose. You and Portia and Jack and—er—Land.'

'Choose?' Realisation was finally beginning to dawn on Regan. *Thank the Lord she had not betrayed her utterly foolish assumption!*

'Between Lady Olivia Fortescue, Lady Sarah NiLaighin, and Lady Lucinda Fairbright. They will be joining us tomorrow for Christmas. They are each of them eminently suitable in every other way, and having the children here will give me the opportunity to assess first-hand their maternal qualities.'

'You mean that you have actually drawn up a short list of potential brides, a list of runners and riders, so to speak?'

'Well, I wouldn't put it like that precisely.'

'Then how would you put it?' Having been buffeted from one extreme of emotion to another in the space of the conversation, Regan was having difficulty in deciding which to give rein to—anger, mortification, hurt, disappointment, disbelief?

Gabriel sighed. 'It's quite simple. I need an heir, therefore I must marry. With such vivid first-hand experience of the abject misery an arranged marriage can inflict on all involved, especially the children, I will take every precaution to avoid a similar outcome. I wish my children to be raised by a woman who is not, like my own mother, completely lacking in any maternal instincts. What I want is a compatible woman with an aptitude for motherhood and a fondness for children; in order to establish that, I need a ready-made family. Your family.'

He looked expectantly at her, obviously feeling that he had now explained unequivocally how two and two made four, though to Regan what he was saying might as well have made one, or five hundred. She felt as if he had rounded up every single one of her hopes and expectations for this visit and cold-bloodedly destroyed them. 'So your invitation,' she said, swallowing hard, 'it was nothing to do with wanting to give us a lovely Christmas?'

'Well, of course I want the children to have a lovely time and they will,' Gabriel said. He had been leaning against the mantel; now he joined her on the sofa. 'All I ask in return is that they do so in the company of my other guests. I thought it best I claim them for distant relatives and you their governess—'

'Governess!' It was the absolute last and final straw. 'You want me to pretend to be a governess to my own siblings?'

'If I claim you as a relative, it would engender far too many questions. As a governess you will provoke no curiosity. Besides, if the ladies know you are related, they will behave quite differently towards the children—what have I said to upset you?'

'I'm not upset,' Regan said through gritted teeth.

'You are, I can tell. I always could tell. You have a little pulse that gives you away.'

'I do not. Where?'

Gabriel touched the fluttering just behind her ear lobe. 'It's right here. Can't you feel it?'

The shock of his fingers on her bare skin made them both freeze. Regan felt the giveaway pulse beating faster. Gabriel smelled of clean linen and lemon soap. Though he had shaved this morning, she could see a hint of bluish stubble on his jaw against the snowy white of his starched neckcloth. Blue-grey eyes met hazel. His knee was pressing against her leg. For a moment, she thought, as he leaned towards her—she thought—she didn't know what she thought! Then he moved away, dropped his hand, and she blinked, wondering if she had imagined it. Whatever it was.

'So you got us here under false pretences and expect us to lie for you.' Her voice sounded shaky. She clasped her hands together in her lap, struggling to maintain her usual equanimity.

'Not lie, pretend,' Gabriel said impatiently, confused by her hostile reaction to his proposal. 'The children will most likely have the time of their lives, acting as little lords and ladies.'

He was probably right, but Regan was not about to admit that. 'You've put me in an intolerable position.'

'When it comes to being placed in an intolerable position I brook no competition,' Gabriel said with a misguided attempt at humour. They stared at each other across this impasse. 'So you refuse to help me?'

Regan shook her head. 'Would that it were so simple. As I said, you've put me in an intolerable position. I must either agree to take part in your charade, which on principle I find objectionable, or deny the children the perfect Christmas I have promised them, which would be a monstrous thing to do.'

'I wish to make a marriage based on shared aspiration and mutual respect in order to secure the best upbringing for my children. I fail to see how that can offend your principles,' Gabriel snapped, for he was quite unused to having his judgement questioned and had not at all expected to have his motives interrogated, most especially not by Regan Stuart. 'You must not think I am entering into this *charade* lightly.'

'Which makes you sincere, but misguided. I cannot believe the Gabriel I once knew would allow doing his duty to hold such sway over him.'

'I'm not the Gabriel you once knew.'

'On that, if nothing else, we can agree.' Regan bit her lip. 'And I am not the Regan you clearly thought you knew. I ought not even to be considering taking part in such a subterfuge, to say nothing of embroiling the children. I ought to be turning on my heel and returning home this instant.'

'Ought? Which means you *are* considering it?'

'You give me no option.' Regan got to her feet and shook out the skirts of her travelling dress. 'I warn you, in return I shall expect you to ensure that the children have the most memorable Christmas possible.'

'If I have to import snow from the Arctic, I will do so. Then we have a bargain?'

'Yes, Gabriel,' Regan said, taking his outstretched hand, 'I suppose we have a bargain.'

His fingers tightened around hers as their eyes met and a little *frisson* shivered up her arm at the contact. She saw the surprise of it reflected in the lift of his eyebrows. He raised her hand to his lips, still holding her gaze. His mouth was warm on her skin. His lips lingered longer than they should, a second, two, five. She found herself taking a step closer to him. His kiss trailed along the length of her middle finger. A surge of heat flooded her, then the sound of approaching footsteps in the corridor make her jerk her hand away. The door opened to reveal a huddle of downcast children trailing in the regal wake of the formidable Duchess herself.

Chapter Two

Sweeping into the room, it was obvious that her Grace was not best pleased. But then, Regan thought to herself wryly, she never was. Tall, whip thin and aquiline, the Duchess was all glacially sharp edges with a tongue to match. Dressed, as was her unwavering habit, from head to toe in black velvet, she eyed Regan through the quizzing glass that she kept, by means of a black satin ribbon, around her neck. The glass, which had a single lens and had belonged to her late departed husband, magnified the Duchess's eye to saucer-like proportions.

'I gathered, from the mêlée, that you had arrived,' she said to Regan by way of greeting. 'I assume my son has informed you of your role. I do not concur with his methods, but it is the outcome that matters. If bringing a coterie of children to the Hall will aid that purpose, then I must resign myself to the upset,' she said, looking very far from resigned. 'You will, however, oblige me by restraining them more effectively than you have thus far, Miss Stuart. I do not know what possessed you to leave them unattended in the long gallery. It dates back to the sixteenth century, you know, but they seem to be under the impression that it is some sort of playground.'

Casting a despairing glance at Gabriel, Regan dropped a deep curtsy. 'My apologies, your Grace. They had been cooped up in the stagecoach for so long, I'm afraid, that...'

The quizzing glass dropped. 'You travelled here on the public stagecoach?'

The Duchess looked utterly appalled. As if, Regan thought, she had transported the children to the Hall by means of a chamberpot on wheels. 'Indeed we did, your Grace,' she replied with acid politeness, 'for we travel so rarely that it makes little sense for us to keep a carriage and six.'

'Four horses are more than sufficient,' her Grace said, eyeing Regan suspiciously. 'Unless one is royalty, six are undoubtedly vulgar.'

Choking back a hysterical little laugh, for the Duchess was every bit as terrifyingly ridiculous as she remembered, Regan looked to Gabriel for assistance.

He was frowning. She thought at first that her irreverence had offended him, until he spoke. 'That was remiss of me,' he said, addressing himself directly to her. 'I should have sent my own coach to collect you.'

'All the way to Yorkshire!' his mother exclaimed. 'Nonsense. Miss Stuart would not have liked to be obliged to us for such an additional and unnecessary outlay.'

'You forget yourself, your Grace. It is we who are obliged to Miss Stuart for her kind assistance in this matter,' Gabriel said curtly, doubly embarrassed by this evidence of his own thoughtlessness and his mother's blatant condescension. 'Please accept my apologies, Regan, you should not have been put to the inconvenience of making your own travel arrangements. Rest assured that I will facilitate your return journey.'

The Duchess once more employed her quizzing glass, surveying Regan from head to toe. 'You were a slip of a child when last we met, and forever leading my son into some scrape or other, as I recall. You have the look of your father about you now you've grown. He was a good man, so my husband informed me. It is a shame you take your colouring from your mother, though, that red hair is not at all the thing,' she said, looking at Regan's simply dressed auburn tresses as if they had committed some sort of social solecism.

'Regan's hair is not red, it is Titian,' Gabriel said, surprising himself as much as his audience. 'Though it may not be in vogue just now, I have to say that I much prefer it to any brunette or blonde,' he added, surprising himself again with the realisation that what he said happened to be true, despite the inescapable fact that his potential brides consisted of two dusky brunettes and one golden blonde. As a consequence, he quite failed to notice that this mildest of compliments was making its recipient blush. 'Now if you'll excuse us, your Grace,' he said, holding open the door for the Duchess, 'I wish to be introduced to Regan's brothers and sister. After all, I have just adopted them as my own.'

The Duchess fixed her son with a baleful stare. 'That, Gabriel, is not even faintly amusing.'

Gabriel bowed. 'I am relieved to hear it, ma'am. One would hate your Grace's hard-earned reputation as a bastion of gravity and sobriety to be tarnished by over-exposure to humour.'

The click of the door closing behind the formidable black-clad woman who had interrupted their breathless game of chase released Portia, Land and Jack from their unusually subdued state.

'Regan, that scary woman looked at us through a glass that made her eye look *this* big,' Jack said, stretching his little arms as wide as he could manage.

'Regan, I'm hungry.'

'Regan, when can we go to the maze?'

'Regan, I'm hungry, too.'

'And me.'

'You shall have your dinner shortly,' Regan said, ruffling Jack's hair, 'but you are forgetting your manners. Introduce yourselves to the Duke.'

Three pairs of very blue eyes peered up at Gabriel from varying heights. Two ungainly bows and one wobbly curtsy were made. The faces looked at him with awed expecta-tion. He felt like a prize exhibit in Bullock's museum or a show horse at Astley's Amphitheatre. He had no idea what sort of performance he was expected to put on. 'How do you do?' he said finally.

Portia giggled. Land and Jack nudged each other. Gabriel looked helplessly at Regan. Ignobly pleased to observe his discomfort, she made no move to assist him. The irony of the situation made her smile inwardly. Intent as he was on establishing the presence of maternal qualities, he appeared quite oblivious to the fact that he was distinctly lacking in the paternal equivalent.

'Your sister tells me you travelled here on the stage-coach,' Gabriel said stiffly, speaking down from his great height to the children as though he were preaching to a congregation.

'Jack was sick,' Portia volunteered.

'Sick as a dog,' Jack confirmed proudly. 'Three times.'

'Indeed,' Gabriel said, quite nonplussed by this information. 'Capital.'

'Sir.' Land tugged on Gabriel's sleeve, 'I mean, your Highness…'

'Your Grace,' Regan corrected, stifling a giggle.

'Gabriel will be quite acceptable.'

'May we please see the maze, Gabriel?'

She would dearly have loved to hear Gabriel's reply, for his face was a picture, but she would not take the risk of him giving any of the children a set-down. 'Perhaps tomorrow,' Regan said hastily. 'You must not bother his Grace at the moment. No doubt he has much more important business to attend to.'

'Indeed, tomorrow will be much more convenient,'

Gabriel said, clutching gratefully at this grudgingly offered straw, for the last hour had left him unaccountably
drained. 'I will leave you to settle in. Mrs McGlone will
show you to your quarters. I will send her to you directly.'

Regan watched the door close behind him with a sinking feeling. She had come here with such high hopes and
expectations, excited at the prospect of rediscovering an
old friendship, but Gabriel was evidently only interested in
her as a means to an end. So now, for the sake of the children, she was going to have to spend the next three weeks
pretending to be someone she was not in front of a trium-
virate of social butterflies, each of whom was desperate to
get her talons into a Duke. Not that butterflies had talons.
In fact, she was being extremely unfair; they were probably very nice. And beautiful. Blonde, no doubt, for it was
the fashion, even if Gabriel had said he preferred Titian
hair. Not that she cared what colour of hair he preferred.
Or what type of female.

Regan made a face. Whatever type of female they were,
they would not be interested in a mere governess. It was
not for a moment that she resented the title; governess was
a perfectly respectable position and a vocation she might
even have pursued herself had circumstances been different. No, it was not that, nor did she grudge the children
their treat, but it was just difficult, sometimes, to be the
one always having to make the sacrifices. She sighed. At
least they would all still have Christmas at the Hall to look
forward to. She must not be selfish. Tomorrow, she told

herself stoically, when she had had time to readjust her expectations, she would hopefully not feel quite so cheated.

Mrs McGlone, Gabriel's eminently practical housekeeper, had set aside an entire suite of rooms located far from the main guest chambers for Regan and the children's exclusive use. 'Where they'll be able to make as much noise as they like without you worrying that they'll be disturbing anyone,' she explained with a kindly smile. 'A lovely lady, your mother was, Miss Stuart. As you know, I used to write to her now and then, just to keep in touch. It was myself who gave his Grace your whereabouts—I hope you don't mind? Such a tragedy, her dying as she did, though it must be some comfort to have the little ones looking so like her. You must miss her dreadfully.'

Regan sniffed back a rare tear. 'I do. She always spoke most kindly of you, too. You used to let me stir the puddings for the Yule party in the old days, do you remember?'

'What I remember is you doing more eating than stirring,' Mrs McGlone said, her ample bosom quivering as she chuckled wheezily.

A cosy hour of reminiscing had restored Regan's spirits somewhat. Next morning, waking from a restful sleep, she was, she told herself, reconciled to the situation, if still a little disappointed. Walking with the children in the extensive gardens after breakfast, her spirits lifted further. Things were not as she had hoped, but they were certainly a lot better than the alternative—spending a frugal Christmas at home, alone with the children.

It was a bright December morning, though the distant clouds looked to be laden with snow. She was in the act of thinking that Mother Nature looked as if she was going to keep Gabriel's promise for him, when the man himself came striding across the lawn to meet them. He was dressed less formally today, in a frockcoat and tight buckskin breeches with top boots. He was hatless as well as gloveless, his hair slightly rumpled, and Regan's heart gave a funny little skip. A funny, foolish little skip. It was so unfair of him to be so very attractive. Gabriel, she reminded herself sternly, was not in the least bit interested in her.

'Are you on your way to the maze?' he said by way of greeting. 'You won't mind if I accompany you? I thought it would be prudent to give the children a chance to get acquainted with me before my guests arrive.'

'Prudent? And here was I, thinking you had a desire for my company, your Grace.'

'How serendipitous it is, then, to be able to combine the two.'

She ignored that. 'I have not explained the situation to them, deeming it best that it should come from you.'

He cast her a harassed look but, gathering the children around him at the entrance to the maze, he embarked on a rather complicated explanation of the situation. Jack, Land and Portia craned their necks up at the imposing giant, too awed and confused to comment. 'So, what do you think?' Gabriel finished, nonplussed by their lack of reaction.

'I think you're too tall,' Jack said. 'My neck hurts.'

'That's why he's called your High-ness,' Land whispered, earning himself a reproving look from Regan and making his brother and sister giggle.

Remembering, of a sudden, how much he had hated having his father loom over him in just such an intimidating manner, Gabriel cursed his own insensitivity and dropped to his knees beside them. 'There, I'm now your Low-ness. Is that better?' To his relief, all three children nodded shyly.

'Yes, but please, your Grace…'

'Gabriel. Please, call me Gabriel.'

'Please, Gabriel, we don't understand the point of this game, do we?' Portia said, seeking confirmation from her siblings, who nodded vigorously.

'Oh. Well, it's a game where you all pretend to be different people, even Regan.'

'Like when she used to pretend to be a Duchess?' Portia asked.

'Did she now?' Gabriel looked at Regan quizzically.

'Yes, in the big tower where there are boxes and boxes of clothes. She said—'

'Never mind that,' Regan said, blushing. 'It's not that kind of dressing-up game, more of a secret game.'

'We like secrets,' Jack declared.

Gabriel cast Regan a grateful look. 'I used to like secrets, too, when I was your age,' he said, remembering as he furrowed his brow and tried to place himself in Jack's shoes, that he had also been fond of very tall tales. Beginning his explanation anew, suitably simplified, embroidered and exaggerated, he was rewarded with three children extremely eager to take on their new roles.

'And now,' he said with immense satisfaction as he got to his feet, 'I think the three of you should see who can get to the centre of the maze first. I will award a prize to the winner. Your sister and I will watch from the top terrace up there. Which,' he continued *sotto voce* to Regan, tucking her hand in his arm, 'is also far enough away to offer some respite from the excited screaming that will inevitably follow.'

'You really are—'

'Ruthless, selfish, manipulative,' Gabriel said with a grin. 'I prefer *persuasive* myself. You're not going to tell me that you'd rather spend the next hour pretending to be lost in a yew hedge that you know like the back of your hand?'

'No, your Grace, not when I can spend the time in your exalted company.'

Her smile was teasing, but Gabriel frowned. 'Is that how I seem to you, high-handed, imperious?'

'No, but you have a sort of certainty—I expect it comes with the position you hold—that your way of looking at things is the only correct way.'

'You seem to possess a similar brand of certainty,' Gabriel replied. 'Perhaps it, too, is a result of having unwelcome responsibility thrust upon you.'

'I don't think of the children in that way.'

Gabriel looked sceptical. The gravel crunched under their feet as they walked. Their breath made clouds in the crisp air. Below them, Portia, Land and Jack's laughter echoed as their own had once done. 'I can't pretend it's been easy, nor that it is what I would have chosen for myself,' Regan said. 'Our circumstances, since Mama and the children's papa died, have been—well, let us just say that it is a good thing that none of us has a taste for luxury.'

'You may not have been able to provide your siblings with much in the way of material wealth, Regan, but they have other, more valuable riches in abundance. You love them and it is clear they adore you in return. I envy you all, more than I can say. All the estates in England cannot buy such a precious commodity.' Gabriel distractedly kicked a small pebble on the path. 'My apologies,' he said gruffly. 'I did not intend the conversation to stray into such deep waters.'

He guided them towards a wooden bench, wiping it with his kerchief before motioning Regan to sit down beside him. 'I never did offer you my condolences when your father died,' he said awkwardly.

'No, you didn't.'

'It was remiss of me.'

'Yes,' Regan said simply, 'it was.'

'I hoped you might still be here when I came home for the holidays.'

'So did I, but as your father pointed out at the time, Blairmore Hall requires a steward, and the new steward had a right to the steward's house. The house I was born in. The house Mama came to as a bride. So we were forced to leave somewhat—somewhat precipitately.'

'I should have written.' Her clear-sighted gaze was making him uncomfortable. The Regan of those days would never have looked at him so. He was finding it almost impossible to believe that the Regan he once knew had metamorphosed into this poised, assured and unsettlingly desirable woman. 'I was—it wasn't the same here without you,' Gabriel admitted reluctantly.

For a moment, just a moment, he allowed her a glimpse of the lonely child he had been—the loneliness he'd kept so well disguised that her younger self hadn't even noticed. The loneliness that must be at the root of his burning desire to raise his children in a loving family environment. Regan's heart wrenched, but she could not bring herself to comment on such a very private subject. A triumphant shriek heralded Land's arrival at the centre of the maze. She smiled. 'Do you remember the time you forced me to climb the statue of Poseidon in the fountain?'

'Forced? You make me sound as if I was some sort of youthful despot.'

'Deity rather than dictator, if you must know,' she admitted, twisting her hands together in her lap. 'I missed you, too, when we went, and Blairmore Hall. Terribly.' She flushed. Her skirts were brushing against his coat-tails. His buckskins were as tightly fitting as his pantaloons had been last night, showing his excellent legs. She dragged her eyes away, realising a fraction too late that they had been lingering where they should not ever have been looking. Her gaze snagged on his, and it happened just like yesterday. A change in the air. A tension. The expectation of something. Her breathing became erratic.

Gabriel touched her cheek with his gloved hand. 'Are you happy, Regan?'

'Why should I not be?' she said, trying desperately to ignore whatever it was that was happening. 'Are you?' she countered, annoyed at the way her voice sounded: breathless and tremulous.

'I hope to be.' *Did he?* He knew well enough what it was to be unhappy. Did he truly believe that this companionate marriage he planned, the family he hoped it would produce, would invoke the opposite emotion? He had assumed it would, but now Regan had posed the actual question, he found he had no satisfactory answer. He was not inclined to dwell on that. Anyway, there were other, far more pressing things to think about. Like the fact that Regan smelled of fresh air and some light, flowery scent. Her skin was creamy white, save for a faint smattering of freckles on her nose. Her lashes were long and thick, the same dark auburn as her hair. A lock of it had escaped its pins. He brushed it back. Such a vulnerable spot, this softest of skin behind the ear. Such a delightful one. The shock of contact sent a *frisson* of awareness down his spine.

Regan couldn't seem to move, though Gabriel was improperly close. She felt as if she were rooted to the spot, as if held by some magnetic force. His touch was heating her skin, making it burn from the contrast with the cold winter air. She intended to push him away, but instead found her hands resting on his chest. She could feel his heart beating. 'What would you have done,' she said, her voice no more than a whisper, 'if I had refused to go along with your proposition?'

'I don't know,' he admitted frankly, 'I hadn't considered it.' Her mouth, Gabriel decided—it was her mouth that gave her that air of sensuality. The plump curve of her full bottom lip, like an invitation, such a contrast to the rest of her. 'I'm glad you did, though,' he said, touching the wool of her cloak, running his hands up her arms. Desire clutched at him, hot and sharp and insistent, shocking in its strength, more shocking in its source, for this was Regan, Regan Stuart, he reminded himself. It made no difference.

'Gabriel.' There was a glitter in his eyes, a look of barely contained hunger that made her nervous. Like being too close to a tiger. His thumbs were stroking her shoulders. Did he know he was doing it? 'Gabriel…'

'Regan.' He was quite definitely not going to kiss her. Even though he wanted, urgently, inexplicably, to kiss her. Kissing Regan Stuart was categorically not part of his grand design. He would content himself with the merest brush of the lips. His were cool, hers soft. Her mouth seemed to fit his perfectly. She did not resist. He wrapped his arms around her and settled his mouth on hers.

For a few heady moments Regan succumbed. Never, ever, had any man taken such a liberty. Never had a man held her so close that she could feel his body pressing into hers. A hard, muscled body it was, so different from her own slender frame. So solid. She would feel safe, had she not felt so utterly unsafe. She closed her eyes, lost in the sensation of his lips on hers, his hands on her back. It was delightful. Exciting. And utterly wrong.

She wrenched herself free. 'Gabriel! What do you think you are doing?'

'I don't know,' he replied, staring at her in consternation. 'Why didn't you stop me?'

Regan touched her fingers to her lips. Her first real kiss. She should be shocked beyond measure, and she was, but she felt, too, a guilty sort of elation. 'I don't know,' she said, too stunned to offer anything other than brutal honesty.

'I beg your pardon,' Gabriel said stiffly. 'Rest assured, it will not happen again.'

'No? I mean, no, of course not.'

He could not understand what had come over him. Especially not now, with the imminent arrival of his three guests. Though when he tried, it was surprisingly difficult to conjure up the image of any one of them, imminent or not. 'A mistake,' Gabriel said, more to himself than Regan, 'an inappropriate echo of our previous fondness, nothing more.'

'Yes.' It was plausible. As an explanation, she was willing to try to force it to fit, because what had happened, delightful as it had felt, was undoubtedly wrong. For a myriad of reasons.

'Yes,' Gabriel said firmly, getting to his feet. 'I best get back to the Hall.'

'What about the prize?'

He looked at her blankly. 'What prize?'

'You promised the children a prize for reaching the centre of the maze, Gabriel—surely you have not forgotten?'

He had, but he was not about to admit it. 'I promised a prize and a prize they shall have.' But what? What did young children like? 'Pony rides,' he exclaimed triumphantly. 'They will like that. You always did, I recall.'

'Yes,' Regan said doubtfully, 'but do you actually have any ponies suitable for them?'

'Absolutely,' Gabriel said with conviction, for it must surely be an easy enough thing to track down three docile ponies on an estate the size of Blairmore. Or so he fervently hoped his groom would inform him. He helped Regan to her feet, but did not let go of her hand. 'They shall have pony rides. I don't go back on my promises, Regan.'

'No,' she said, telling herself that she had reason to be very glad of that as she watched him stride purposefully off.

Chapter Three

Later that day, when the children had returned, tired but exhilarated, from their pony ride, they all watched from the vantage point of the turret as the new guests arrived in their carriages. Lady Olivia was blonde, Lady Sarah and Lady Lucinda brunettes, Regan noted. So much for Gabriel's claim that he preferred Titian hair! So much also for his claim that they were simply presentable. Each of the well-born, impeccably turned out young ladies was quite beautiful. Each emerged from her carriage with a maid carrying her jewellery box and dressing case. Each lady had at least one trunk and one portmanteau. Each wore a highly fashionable swansdown muff and an elaborate carriage dress with matching pelisse. Their boots were of kid, as were their gloves. They had rosebud mouths and peach-perfect complexions. They were dainty, delicate and lovely.

'They look like princesses,' Portia whispered, her eyes

wide as she gazed down at the last arrival, whose travelling dress was of cherry velvet trimmed with sable.

'They do indeed,' Regan agreed, fighting back an unaccustomed gust of envy. 'Three princesses. It's a shame for them there is only one prince.'

It was not like her to rail against circumstances, but as the day progressed, a raft of unfamiliar emotions combined to put Regan in a most unusually intemperate mood. Try as she might, she could not help resenting having to play the role of governess, which would effectively prevent her mixing with the other guests. Did Gabriel not realise how much she'd been looking forward to some adult company? Clearly not, any more than he realised the turmoil his kiss had caused. *An inappropriate echo of our previous fondness*, he'd called it, but the more she thought about it, the less sense it made. Whatever *fondness* Gabriel had had for her when they were younger had been youthful affection, nothing more. Whatever it was that had led to their kiss was something completely new and completely adult, and he had been completely unwilling to acknowledge it.

'And rightly so,' Regan muttered to herself as she donned her evening gown, for she had been bid to present the children in the blue salon prior to dinner. 'He has no business kissing me when he is upon the brink of becoming betrothed to another woman. Any more than I can have any business kissing him, though why that fact slipped both our minds,' she said despairingly, fixing a tortoiseshell comb into her hair, 'I have absolutely no idea.' Further, she found the fact she seemed unable to stop herself from reliving the whole event with the most shocking relish quite mortifying. But still, the telltale blush stole over her throat as she recalled the tingling, bubbling fizz of excitement as his lips fastened on to hers.

Her first kiss, and it had been from Gabriel, of all people. Who was, she was certain, quite used to kissing and therefore most unlikely to be sharing her confused and contrary emotions. Regan picked up her evening gloves. Silk, not kid, and her only pair. Not that it mattered, for as a governess she would be expected to dine alone in her room. So much for her fond imaginings of parties and gaiety and dancing. With a sigh, she dropped her reflection a little curtsy. 'Neither pretty enough nor quite wretched enough to be Monsieur Perrault's Cinderella, but I know how she felt,' she said, summoning a smile and calling to Portia to help button her gloves.

In the blue drawing room, the Duchess was discoursing on the Hall's history, while Gabriel tried to recall the excellent qualities that set these particular ladies above the others he had discounted from his matrimonial stakes.

He was not having much success. Despite being faced with three undoubted diamonds of the first water, each, without doubt, nourishing in her corseted bosom the hope of becoming the sixth Duchess of Blairmore, he was feeling rather less than inspired and rather more than usually distracted. His mind kept straying back to the memory of Regan. Of the feel of her lips on his. Her body pressed against his. That surge of desire that shot through him when she twined her arms around him. For what felt like the hundredth time that day, he forced himself to obliterate the image, to turn his attention to his carefully selected guests, but he felt like a man with no appetite faced with a groaning banquet. His enthusiasm for the task ahead was almost non-existent, despite the fact that the ladies ensconced in his drawing room were without doubt the pick of the crop.

He supposed he should be grateful that his mother had persuaded *their* mothers to release them unchaperoned. He could not understand her enthusiasm for matrimony, given how very little pleasure she herself had derived from family life. Had she been unhappy or was she simply incapable of feeling, emotionally desiccated? Strange that he had never before thought to ask himself such a simple question. Was it also strange that he had not asked the same question of himself?

Regan seemed to think so. Regan's presence here was raising all sorts of uncomfortable questions. Raising all sorts of distracting feelings, too. No one could ever accuse Regan of being emotionally desiccated—she was the exact opposite, whatever that was. How he envied that easy, warm relationship she had with her brothers and sister. Was he capable of forging something similar with his own children? For that, he realised with a start, mattered even more to him than that the children's mother should do the same. Was it *that* which would make him happy? Were his priorities then all askew?

Dammit, he was tying himself in knots. Regan was tying

him in knots! He must remember how straightforward it had all seemed before she came here. Five years of struggle it had been, to repair the damage of his father's ruinous legacy, and now things at Blairmore were finally on an even keel. He had worked too hard to let anyone divert him from completing this final duty, to ensure that his own legacy was sound. That is what would make him happy. He must remember that! He must put Regan Stuart and her uncomfortable questions and her disturbingly beguiling presence from his mind.

The door opened and Regan came into the room, her three siblings clutching at her skirts, and Gabriel was immediately entranced. Her gown, to his experienced eye, was not of this Season's design, nor even of last, but the emerald-silk overdress with the simple cream petticoat complemented her elegant form and emphasised the fiery lights in her hair.

'Your Grace.' Regan sank into a deep curtsy. Gabriel looked very ducal in his formal evening clothes. Black coat. Black waistcoat. Black silk breeches. Black shoes. His starched cravat emphasised the clean line of his jaw, the little cleft of his chin. A diamond pin winked in the neckcloth's snowy falls. The merest touch of his hand on her glove. His eyes were more grey than blue tonight. She held herself rigidly, reluctant to meet his gaze for fear of giving away her emotions. 'I brought the children, as you requested.'

Her voice sounded odd. Aware that the Ladies Sarah, Olivia and Lucinda were looking at him expectantly,

Gabriel ushered his supposed kin across the room. 'I would like to introduce you to some young relatives of mine who will be sharing Christmas with us here at the Hall. Distant relatives,' he added quickly, for he could almost see each lady mentally reviewing his family tree. 'Very distant, in fact. Portia, Orlando and Ajax. Though the boys are known as Land and Jack,' he added swiftly.

'Such original names,' said Lady Sarah.

'From Shakespeare, if I'm not mistaken,' Lady Olivia said.

'Indeed,' Lady Lucinda whispered.

'And this is Miss Stuart, their governess. The children are, sadly, orphans.'

'How unfortunate,' Lady Sarah said.

'Poor little mites,' said Lady Lucinda.

'Tragic,' said Lady Olivia, determined not to be outdone.

Gabriel patted Jack's head enthusiastically in what he hoped was a paternal manner. Jack made a harrumphing noise and tried to wriggle free. Gabriel pulled him firmly back to his side. 'It is my earnest hope that you make them feel welcome,' he said with one of his most charming smiles, as his grip tightened on Jack's shoulder. 'At this special time of year, it is so important that we try to make them feel part of our temporary little family, do you not think?'

'I sincerely hope we are to be spared the warm glow of familial joy at mealtimes,' the Duchess said acerbically, rather spoiling the effect of her son's heart-warming plea. 'Children have no place at the dinner table.'

'I could not agree more, your Grace,' Lady Sarah said fervently. 'My sisters and I were not permitted to sup with my parents until we were sixteen. Mama, you must know, believes that children should be seen and not heard.'

'And you, Lady Sarah,' Gabriel asked, 'what do you believe?'

Realising that she had made some sort of *faux pas*, though having no clue as to what it was, Lady Sarah looked down at her lap. 'I do not—that is Mama said—I am sure that whatever you say is best, your Grace.'

'Well I, for one, think it is a jolly idea to have children around,' Lady Olivia said astutely, smiling warmly at the children. 'I believe there is snow forecast. Such very Christmassy weather.'

'We are going to skate on the pond,' Jack informed her shyly.

'Excellent, I shall look forward to that,' Lady Olivia said, earning a look of approval from Gabriel.

Not to be outdone, Lady Lucinda joined in. 'I believe there is a skittle alley in the Hall. Perhaps if his Grace would condescend to teach us the rules?'

'We don't need the Duke for that,' Land scoffed, 'it's easy. Even girls can play. Regan said that when she was my age—' He broke off in confusion as Portia pinched him.

'Regan? Who is Regan?' Lady Lucinda looked confused.

The Duchess's imperious tone cut into the uncomfortable silence. 'Another character from the Bard's canon. If my memory is correct—and it always is—one well capable of assuming the mantle of deference in order to serve her own ends. Miss Stuart, you may take them away now, if you please.'

Her gimlet glare held in it a hint of malice that left Regan in no doubt as to her meaning. She dropped a very, very shallow curtsy. 'Indeed, your Grace, I think the children have had a surfeit of excitement for one day. We don't want to spoil them with too much attention, do we?' Turning her back quite deliberately on her hostess, she waited by the door as the children made their relieved bows and ushered her brood out without a backward glance.

When she emerged from settling the children, she found Gabriel waiting for her in the sitting room that connected with their bedchamber. Pacing the small space between the fireplace and the bow window, his face was like thunder. 'I'm sorry, that was unwarrantably rude of my mother.'

'She always did enjoy putting me in my place.'

'You are not a servant.'

'No, I'm a governess, which is worse, for it puts me neither above nor below stairs,' Regan said waspishly.

'For convenience's sake only. I think of you no differently from my other guests.'

Regan raised a disdainful eyebrow. 'Save for one crucial point. I am not in the running to become the next Duchess. Don't dissemble, Gabriel.'

He tugged at his neckcloth. 'I will not lie to you. I did not consider the implications when I asked you to pretend to be their governess, but you must believe me, it was never my intention to have you act the servant. I've made that quite clear to my mother—unequivocally clear, in fact,' he said firmly. He held out his hand to her. 'I've been thoughtless and I'm sorry for it. Will you forgive me?'

His frank admission, more than his apology, quite took the wind out of her sails. 'I suppose so.'

Gabriel grinned. 'I may have dared you into climbing trees that were too high, or riding a horse that was not yet properly schooled, but it was because I couldn't resist challenging you, Regan, not because I wished to demean you.'

'Why did you kiss me, Gabriel? Was that a challenge, too? Because I don't believe it was for the reason you said.'

'An inappropriate echo of our former fondness.' Gabriel shook his head. 'Embarrassing, pompous and complete balderdash. It had nothing to do with those long-off childhood days. I don't know why I kissed you, frankly. You've grown into an extremely attractive woman, Regan Stuart. Perhaps it's that simple,' he said with relief, for perhaps it was.

'I'm not. Compared to your ladies, I'm a complete frump.'

'You are quite wrong. Now, do not force me to pay you any more compliments, nor to delay dinner any further— and before you say anything, I have already informed my mother that a place is to be set for you. You may be perforce a governess, but you may still dine with us if I so choose.'

'If you are certain?'

'I am certain that I don't want to earn Lady Sarah's disapproval for being tardy. I suspect it would be enough to spoil any man's appetite.'

Regan was forced to laugh. 'Gabriel! You are talking about the woman who may become your wife.'

'Now that thought truly has ruined my appetite,' Gabriel muttered darkly.

Dinner was such a stilted affair that Regan began to wonder whether she would have been better served to have eaten alone in her quarters. Though Lady Olivia made a small effort to include her in the conversation, and Lady Lucinda, perhaps sensing Gabriel's approval, followed suit in a somewhat desultory manner, both ladies were obviously taken aback at their host's insistence that a mere governess join them at dinner, though they were far too well bred to show it. Lady Sarah, however, had no such qualms and followed the Duchess's glacial example of holding herself aloof to the extent that Regan began to feel that her very presence was contagious. Grateful as she was to Gabriel for ending her self-imposed exile, by the end of the meal Regan was even more grateful to be able to make her excuses and, citing the need to be up early for the children, retire without taking tea.

The next morning, with Portia, Land and Jack having been entrusted to their new best friend, Gabriel's head groom, Regan took the opportunity to pick a spray of winter foliage and set off on her own private pilgrimage. Wandering past the brew house, the old bakery, the still-rooms and cold stores that had been built for the original manor, she took the short path that led to the steward's house. Smoke billowed from the chimney. Clutching her cloak around her, for the first flakes of snow were beginning to fall, she leaned against a mossy wall and lost herself in the past.

'I thought I'd find you here.'

'Gabriel! You startled me, I was miles away.'

'Years, you mean. Has it changed much?'

'Very little.'

'Do you remember the time when your father caught us using his precious accounts table as a spinning top?'

Regan smiled. The table, made of sturdy oak, was circular and set on a rotating device that facilitated access to the alphabetised drawers. She had been sitting in the middle of it, with Gabriel whirling her round and round, when her father had come in. 'What a lecture he read us. You especially, I recall.'

'*"One day, the privilege of administering this most esteemed estate will fall to you, Master Gabriel. I trust by that time you will have learned to treat it with more respect."* I've never forgotten. He made me feel so unworthy, a much more effective punishment than anything my own father ever meted out. Beatings, I could easily forget. The disapproving and disappointed look on your father's face, never. I like to think he would approve of my actions since I inherited the title.'

'I was just on my way to visit his grave.'

'Shall I accompany you?'

'I'm sure you must have other things…'

'Oh, a thousand, but none more important. I won't come if you don't want me to.'

She tucked her hand into his arm. 'No, I'd like that. Thank you.'

They walked together in silence, their steps evenly matched, along the lane that followed the path of the Blairmore River, across the rustic wooden bridge, to the ornate gate which gave entry to the graveyard. Gabriel lifted the latch and ushered Regan through. It was quiet here; only the tumbling of the water over the rocks on the shallow riverbed disturbed the silence. The ducal crypt was a simple stone building with the crest over the door, rather like a small chapel. Around it, the graves of other family members were clustered, some dating back over two hundred years, the inscriptions eroded and worn smooth by the passage of time and the weather.

It was testament to the esteem in which her father had been held, Regan knew, that he was buried there, for it was a privilege accorded very few outside the immediate family.

'I'll wait here,' Gabriel said. 'Take as much time as you need.'

Twelve years since she had been here, but she picked her way without hesitation to the spot against the western wall where Papa lay. In the lonely days after he died, Regan had come here often. With Gabriel at school and Mama too taken up with her own cares, clearing the house that she had called her own, Regan had been largely left to her own devices. Setting the spray of greenery she had picked on the ground beside the stone, she knelt down on the cold ground. An immense sadness overwhelmed her, for how happy a family they had been, unwittingly thinking their life at Blairmore Hall would go on for ever. When they left, and her mother had remarried, she had been discouraged from mentioning their previous life, for her mother wanted to look to the future.

'I hope you do not blame her, Papa, as I did, at first,' Regan whispered, her fingers tracing his name on the cold stone. 'I thought she wanted me to forget you, but I realise now it was just her way of coping. Dear Papa, I hope you do not blame me either. I could not talk of you to Mama, but you were always in my thoughts, I promise you.'

At the gate, Gabriel watched her, caught up in a tangle of unfamiliar emotions. Had his father been more like Regan's, he would perhaps have realised how much his death would affect her. Though there was little he could have done other than write expressing his condolences, he felt guilty for not having performed even that small act of kindness. The loss of her mother had brought her a different kind of hardship. Duty and obligation—Regan understood those every bit as much as he did.

Strange coincidence that they had been similarly burdened in the last five years, she struggling to raise a family that was not hers, he struggling to repair the damage inflicted on the estate by a profligacy not his. It was true, such a struggle was isolating, but was he lonely, as Regan was?

Perhaps. Was it odd that he had not considered that a wife and family would remedy this condition? Most people would say so. Would Regan? There was no denying that he felt an inexplicable urge to confide in her. She would understand, he was sure of it. He had never craved understanding before, but he needed Regan to understand him, if only because it would stop her judging him harshly. It confused him that her opinion of him mattered so much. He was not used to being confused. It was an uncomfortable feeling and it was all Regan's fault.

Regan. She had none of the English peaches-and-cream beauty each of his potential brides had. Her attraction was in the serenity of her brow, the clear-sighted gaze of her big hazel eyes, the inviting curve of her mouth. It was in her expression rather than her features. There was, too, a hint of latent sensuality that whispered its soft desire to be woken. When he had kissed her, it had not so much been the touch of her lips, nor the feel of her slender body moulded to his, that had aroused him so. More the way she had looked at him, the way she had kissed him back. Her desire would match his. Fiery, like her hair. Like her temper. He still could not quite come to terms with the changes in her, so strong-willed and so ready with her opinions. Circumstances had moulded her, experience had shaped her. He knew all about that.

A longing for something he could not describe and did not want to name filled him as she made her way across the grass to him. 'I have to get back. I promised I'd show the ladies around the portrait gallery before luncheon,' he said, his voice sounding much more brusque than he intended.

'Then we had better make haste,' Regan said. 'Thank

you for coming with me this morning, Gabriel. It made a difficult task less onerous.'

'It was nothing, truly. I only wish I had done more to lessen your burden at the time.'

'As you said yesterday, water under the bridge. We should hurry—I won't have your mother accusing me of leading you astray yet again.'

Chapter Four

Despite his stated anxiousness to get back to the Hall, they walked slowly on the return journey, stopping to throw sticks over one side of the bridge, rushing to the other rail to watch their journey downstream. There were icicles hanging from the wooden struts. Gabriel tucked Regan's hand into his arm as they walked. 'Are you really happy with your lot in life?'

'You asked me that yesterday.'

'You didn't answer yesterday.'

She frowned. 'If pressed, I would say I am content rather than happy. I confess, there are times when doing one's duty is not quite the reward it ought to be.'

'With that, I can agree wholeheartedly.'

'This estate, the title—it must carry great responsibilities.'

'More than you can imagine.'

He was looking straight ahead, his face set into forbidding lines. Only yesterday, it would have been enough to discourage her from probing further, but something had subtly changed in the nature of their relationship. He was still essentially a stranger to her, but a stranger whose fate mattered. 'This marriage you are contemplating...I cannot help but think you will regret it.'

Gabriel sighed. 'I thought I had explained my reasons.'

'Explained, but not persuaded me of their validity. You are placing too much reliance on how the ladies relate to children. If you had seen how I was with children before I was obliged to learn, you would have thought me disastrous. Necessity is a wonderful teacher.'

'Not always. I have an example very close to home which proves that.'

Regan grimaced. 'True, but—has it never occurred to you that your parents were largely indifferent to you because they were so indifferent to each other? Such an ill-matched pair could never be happy.'

'Which is precisely the reason for how I am going about things. By taking care to select a wife who shares my own values, then I believe affection will in time grow between us.'

'Affection is such a trivial emotion compared to love, Gabriel. True love. Real love. The love that should exist between a man and his wife. And you have to remember, you will be a husband before you are a father. Wanting always to be with someone. Feeling incomplete without them. I believe—I *strongly* believe—that it must be the foundation stone for any marriage.' Regan stopped abruptly, conscious of having strayed far into very personal territory.

'Which romantic folly explains your own single state, presumably,' Gabriel said, made cruel by being made once more to question himself. 'Though more likely your siblings put paid to any such hopes.'

'Well, in that you are quite mistaken,' Regan retorted, hurt by his coldness. 'Not all men are so wary of *encumbrances* as you are! As a matter of fact, there was someone, only it did not transpire.'

'What happened?'

'Mr Elmsley is an eminently respectable, perfectly nice, kind man with a most respectable fortune, and he was happy to welcome Portia, Land and Jack into his home. Only—only I didn't love him.'

Gabriel's eyebrows shot up. 'In your circumstances, surely you cannot have considered *that* of such import?'

'I consider it *the* most important thing. Foolish as it may sound to you, I am not willing to sacrifice my own chance of lasting happiness just to provide the children with a father figure and a more comfortable home.'

'You also sacrificed the opportunity to have a family of your own.'

'My own children, if I am ever blessed with them, will be the product of love, not of duty. I, thank heaven, do not have your dynastic obligations.'

'And I, thank heaven, do not have your sentimental, illogical mind,' Gabriel threw at her. 'The very idea of basing a marriage on such a volatile emotion strikes me as foolish to the point of madness. Spent passion is more dangerous than indifference, it is a receipt for disaster.'

They had reached the gate to the Elizabethan terraces. Gabriel tilted up her chin with his finger, forcing her to meet his eyes. Grey more than blue, a hint of the temper he was straining to keep in check in the set of his mouth. 'I told you already, Regan, but I'll say it again, just so that there is no room for misunderstanding. I am taking the happiness of my future family very seriously.'

Regan pushed his hand away, determined not to let him intimidate her. 'But not your own, I note. I know you mean what you say, Gabriel, but I cannot agree with you.'

She made to walk away, but Gabriel caught her cloak and pulled her to him. 'It is you who are misguided, Regan, holding out for love. At least the qualities I seek actually exist.'

His body was hard against her own, tensed like a coiled spring. The same tension coiled in her, making her reckless. 'You are choosing duty over happiness, Gabriel. Security over love.'

'You mean passion.' Under her cloak, Gabriel's hand tightened on her waist. He knew he should not be doing this, knew it was dangerous, but could not seem to stop. He flattened his other hand on her back. He could feel the heat of her skin through the wool of her gown, the soft leather of his gloves.

'I mean love. Enduring love, which in turn makes passion endure.' She was speaking from the heart, about feelings so deep she had not ever put them into words, yet she felt no embarrassment, only a sense of urgency. It mattered somehow, though she did not know why. 'When one loves, truly loves, passion cannot be spent,' she said recklessly, wondering if she would ever find out the truth of such a bold statement. She couldn't breathe. Gabriel's touch was indecent. This conversation was most improper. Her reaction to it even more so, for though she knew she should end it, she did not want to.

'Passion is nature's chemistry, nothing more. The attraction of opposites, which first pulls, then repels. It is nature's whimsy to make that desire burn too bright, for it makes the extinguishing of the flame all the more bitter,' Gabriel said, taking sanctuary in cold, dispassionate logic, in an effort to explain the quite illogical effect Regan's kiss had had on him. Simple attraction, nothing more. Irrelevant, if temporarily distracting, as was the curve of her bottom at the base of her spine and the swell of her breasts through her dress.

'Love is not so ephemeral,' Regan replied. Gabriel's touch was making her hot and cold at the same time. A confusion of impulses made it impossible for her to move. 'Such passions as you are talking about are not love.'

'Basic instincts,' Gabriel insisted, 'that is all they are. That is what drove our kiss yesterday. Now that we understand it, we will be able to resist it.' He meant it, though his voice did not echo his conviction, for the heat of her, the heady perfume of her, her slender softness were making his senses reel, his groin ache.

'Resist?' She was sure he was going to kiss her again.

She was sure he was talking arrant nonsense. She had no idea what she thought, save that she wanted him to kiss her. She couldn't think of anything but his kissing her; she couldn't take her eyes from his mouth, willing it to claim hers, until he hesitated, and she remembered just as he did, and pulled away.

'The portrait gallery,' Gabriel said curtly.

'Where your Three Graces await.'

'My what?'

'It's how I think of them,' Regan said, looking away to disguise her blush. 'You had best hurry or you will be late.'

'Yes. Yes, I should not keep them waiting,' Gabriel agreed. It was not like him to run away. He was not running away! There was nothing to run away from. What he was doing was sticking to his plan.

'Basic instinct, he would have it this time,' Regan muttered to herself, pulling the long hood of her cloak over her hair as she watched him stride off. 'Which feels no more of an explanation than his talk of inappropriate echoes, but he was right about one thing, it should be resisted. A steward's daughter, no matter that she is the granddaughter of a viscount, could never be a match for the Duke of Blairmore, even if she was biddable and unencumbered and all the other things he wants. Not that I would, even if he wanted me. Gabriel Toward is as incapable of love as I am of being so hen-witted as to allow myself to fall in love with him.'

Satisfied with this little declaration, she went off in search of the children, guiltily aware that she had barely given them a second thought all morning.

* * *

Gabriel was nothing if not thorough. Duty might be a demanding master, but it at least had the merit of familiarity. Not bothering to summon his valet, he changed his buckskins for pantaloons and pulled on a clean white shirt, as he tried to reassemble the carefully constructed reasoning that had led him down this matrimonial path he was following.

'I need an heir,' he muttered to his reflection as he deftly folded and tied the length of starched white neckcloth into that most deceptively simple of knots, the Waterfall. 'I must therefore marry.' Another neat fold. 'I want my heir to be happy, as I was not. I must therefore ensure that his mother and I are as one in our ambitions for him.' He paused, trying to picture himself with this as-yet-unconceived child. Would he make a good father? An image of himself only this morning, pontificating to Portia, Land and Jack, made him wince. He didn't want to take a chance on necessity teaching him, as Regan said it would.

As he finished the last complex manoeuvre, which resulted in a perfect Waterfall, Gabriel grinned. There was no need for him to do so, when he had a ready-made family to learn from. Buttoning his striped waistcoat and shrugging himself into a dark-brown cutaway coat, he resolved to spend as much time with the children as possible, which would mean spending more time with Regan, but that was unavoidable. He could ignore her allure. He would stop himself from thinking about her. Her lips. Her taste. Her desirable body. He could stop. He could!

* * *

He spent the afternoon making a concerted attempt to become better acquainted with his Three Graces, as he now could not help thinking of them, to stop himself from wondering where Regan was and what she was doing and to stop himself from comparing their responses to what he imagined would be hers. And, most of all, to stop himself from wishing that he had kissed her again. Just once. Because the ache of *not* having kissed her was proving more difficult to bear than the guilt he would have suffered if he had.

His concentration was not what it should be. The Three Graces were not as diverting as they should be, considering he was set upon making one of them his wife. Though he encouraged them to voice their own opinions, they chose instead to seek his. He encouraged them all the more. Though Lady Sarah more often than not resorted to espousing her mama's or papa's views, Lady Lucinda surprised them all with a passionate defence of the Dutch school of painting over the English.

'And contrary to the plaque on this painting, I do not believe it is by Rembrandt,' she said, peering closely at a portrait of the fifth Earl, who had become the first Duke. 'See here? The hands are far too clumsily rendered. I believe you should more accurately have it labelled *from the school of.*'

'You are something of an expert on the matter,' Gabriel said.

He meant it as praise, but Lady Lucinda blushed with

mortification rather than with pleasure. 'I beg your pardon. I did not mean—I should not have questioned—I am sure that if you have labelled it as Rembrandt, then it must be.'

Gabriel turned his attention to Lady Olivia. Lady Olivia had perfectly arched brows. She had rather fine eyes, too, an unusual shade of blue that was more like turquoise. Further encouraged, she proved herself well-informed upon subjects as wide ranging as the shocking novel *Frankenstein*, and the possibility that Lord Liverpool might facilitate a return to the gold standard. Lady Olivia had a sense of humour, too, though at times—when she was speculating on the peculiarities of Shelley's domestic arrangements—he found her cruel rather than funny.

But this, Gabriel assured himself as he bathed before dinner, was a minor consideration. As was the fact that he found her just a little cold. As he shaved himself, not allowing his valet to do so, he tried to imagine kissing her and his razor nicked his cheek, for another pair of lips, and a pair of clear-sighted hazel eyes, swam into view instead. He tried, but Lady Olivia's mouth refused to take form and his body refused to be roused by the thought of hers. A minor consideration. Very minor. Almost of no import at all.

The weather deteriorated over the next few days. With snow now falling heavily, the Blairmore Hall party opted for skittles—most of the party, for the Duchess, when asked if she wished to take part, produced a basilisk stare that suggested she had been asked to act as a swineherd's laundry maid.

The skittle alley, a very grand affair, had been the work of the third Duke, reputed to have been a Jacobite, if the letter from Bonnie Prince Charlie himself held in the archives was to be believed. He had lent the Prince a sum of money, never repaid. 'And more likely used to fund his lavish lifestyle than to pay the wages of his rebel army,' Gabriel informed his guests. 'A taste he shared with my great-grandfather, as you can see,' he said, throwing open the doors to allow them to precede him.

The alley was constructed almost entirely of wood, with a hammer-beam ceiling embossed with the ducal crest, the walls clad in oak panelling and the skittle run itself, twenty-four-feet long, of highly polished mahogany. A long wooden chute ran the length of the run at an angle to allow the balls to be returned to the bowlers and benches were set down one wall for onlookers.

Only Land and Gabriel had played before. 'So we should play and everyone else should watch,' Land suggested excitedly.

'Land!' Regan cast him a reproving glance. 'Don't be so selfish.'

Her brother, his competitive hackles raised, looked mulish. 'I only meant—'

'You meant by way of a demonstration, didn't you, Land?' Gabriel interjected smoothly.

'Well, perhaps,' Land said grudgingly.

Gabriel handed him a ball. 'Since you are quite the expert, you may show us the way,' he said solemnly.

'That was adroitly done,' Regan said, as Land, his mood

soothed and puffed up with importance, began to demonstrate how to throw.

Gabriel shrugged. 'He was just a little over-excited.'

'He has a dreadful temper sometimes.'

'He's a very intelligent lad. He just gets impatient, that's all.'

'Remind you of anyone?' Regan said innocently, delighted when this comment was rewarded with a bark of laughter.

Volunteering, along with Lady Lucinda, to set up the ninepins, keep the scores on the large chalk board and return the balls through the chute, Regan had plenty of opportunity to observe Gabriel with the children. He no longer towered over them when he spoke to them, but automatically crouched down to their level. With shy Portia he was gentle, with exuberant Jack he was firm, but Land he talked to as an equal, consulting him gravely on the finer points of the game and encouraging him to demonstrate tricky shots. She hadn't noticed how much Land had changed these last few months. She'd noticed his temper becoming more volatile, she'd noticed that his trousers seemed to be always too short, but she hadn't realised the boy was taking his first tentative steps towards manhood.

A whoop of excitement from Lady Sarah, whose eye was as eagle-sharp as the Duchess's, startled Regan from her reverie.

'Sticker,' Land shouted, for every one of the pins had fallen over. 'We won.'

'A return, a return,' Portia, who had been playing on the other side, in Gabriel's team, called enthusiastically.

'I think it only fair that Lady Lucinda join in,' Lady Olivia said, with a malicious smile. 'Little Jack can take her place at the other end.'

'Oh, no!' Jack cried, tugging on Gabriel's sleeve. 'Please may I not play another game?'

'Yes, if you will let go of my coat, for you are creasing it,' Gabriel said, laughing. 'I shall take Lady Lucinda's place.'

To Regan, then, fell the job of setting up the pins, while Gabriel stood beside her, keeping the score and returning the balls. 'I have to say that I am, despite my reservations, rather enjoying myself,' he said.

'You are finding the ladies' company charming?'

'I was actually referring to the children,' Gabriel replied with a wry smile.

When he smiled at her like that, Regan's heart behaved in a most ridiculous fashion. When he smiled at her like that, she couldn't help wishing—thinking—things she should not!

They both watched while Land tried to adjust Lady Lucinda's aim. She bowled wide, scoring nought for the third time in a row, making Jack scowl, though Portia, Regan was touched to see, gave her a consoling hug. 'Lady Lucinda has been very kind to Portia,' she said, trying to distract herself.

'She has many admirable qualities,' Gabriel said. He turned away to chalk up Lady Sarah's second sticker. When he turned back to Regan, he was frowning. 'Truth be told, so too do Lady Olivia and Lady Sarah. I didn't expect this to be so difficult.'

Regan stooped down to set up the pins. The curve of her bottom visible through her gown was rather too delightful a view for him to eye with impunity. When he realised that his admiration was taking rather solid physical form, Gabriel quickly averted his gaze.

Another couple of throws passed before Regan could work up the courage to speak her mind. 'Gabriel, I think the reason you are finding it difficult is that you don't love any of them.'

'The reason I'm finding it difficult is that I'm being thorough. My method is sound.'

'Then why can you not make up your mind?'

'I can. I will,' Gabriel said, sounding horribly unconvinced.

'Have you tried to imagine any of them as the mother of your children?'

'That was rather the point of having Portia, Land and Jack here,' Gabriel said uncomfortably. In truth, he had tried, but had signally failed to conjure up an image of any of the Three Graces as the mother of his child.

'And yet you are still struggling to choose. Perhaps you should try kissing them,' Regan said exasperatedly.

Gabriel dropped the chalk he had been using to mark the board. 'I beg your pardon?'

'To help you decide, I mean. I'm sure none of them will object. Quite the contrary, I would imagine.'

'I cannot go around indiscriminately kissing young ladies.'

'A laudable aspiration and yet it did not prevent you from kissing me.'

'That was different. You're…'

'Not important?' Regan snapped. 'Not worthy of the same consideration?'

'That's not what I was going to say,' Gabriel said to her retreating back as Regan stormed from the skittle alley. 'What I was going to say,' he said morosely to the empty space where she had been, 'was that you, unlike them, are someone I actually want to kiss.'

Chapter Five

Though he told himself there was no point in attempting to explain, that it was futile to tell her what he had been about to say because there was no point in talking about something that wasn't going to happen, Gabriel left the skittle alley at the earliest opportunity and went in search of Regan. He finally found her in the old Elizabethan bake-house, which was used for storing hay. He'd remembered that she had often hidden there as a child when she wanted to be alone. He pushed closed the heavy door. She was sitting in the loft, her legs dangling over the edge, her chin resting on her hands.

Gabriel climbed up the ladder and sat down beside her. 'You do me an injustice, Regan. You quite misunderstood what I was trying to say.'

'Did I? Perhaps it is because you do not even know yourself what you are trying to say.'

He smiled ruefully. 'I probably deserve that.' He tugged at his neckcloth and a lock of blue-black hair fell over his brow. He closed the small gap between them and propped his chin up on his hands, resting his elbows on the cross beam as she did. His buckskin-clad leg brushed against her thigh. She was acutely aware of him and trying desperately not to be. 'Explain to me, Gabriel. I want to understand.'

'Five years ago, when my father died, I discovered he had gambled away the better part of the family coffers. The estate was in a parlous state. I couldn't believe it. My sole purpose in life, according to my father, was as heir to Blairmore, yet he had put the entire estate, the lives of hundreds of our people, in jeopardy. I have no idea why he did it—was he simply profligate or abjectly miserable? I don't know, but it made me realise how much Blairmore meant to me and it made me determined—even more determined—not to be like him. I have worked tirelessly since then to repair the damage. Blairmore is in as good heart now as it was when your father was alive.'

'I had no idea,' Regan said softly.

'Very few know how bad things were, not even my mother.'

'That must have been a terrible burden to bear.'

'Yes, but I have borne it and it's changed me, as your circumstances have changed you. My father saw Blairmore as an asset to be stripped. My mother sees it only as a status symbol. The one thing it never was, was a secure, loving family home.' He took her hand in his. 'I didn't quite appreciate—until you came here with the children—I didn't realise how much I wanted that, needed it. I don't just want an heir, I want my children to be happy, not damned bloody miserable as I was.'

Regan swallowed hard, for a lump had formed in her throat as he talked, so filled was she with admiration and pity. 'And what of your happiness?' she asked softly.

'That is what will make me happy, Regan, knowing they have what I never had. Do you see now?'

Love was the thing he had never had, she could see that now. Love, which he obviously thought himself incapable or undeserving of. That was the real legacy his parents had given him and there was nothing she could do about it. 'I can see that is what you truly believe,' she said sadly.

'I do.' Gabriel stroked her arm, running his fingers from her shoulder to her elbow and back again. They were sitting back from the guard rail now, propped against a hay bale. He pulled her head on to his shoulder. His fingers tangled in the heavy bun of hair at her nape. It was soft and silky. He breathed in deep of the scent of her and sighed.

He stroked her cheek. His thumb touched the curve of her mouth, trailed along the plump lower lip. 'I do,' Gabriel said, 'but what I don't understand is why, when I am so certain that I am right, can I not actually choose? Why is it, Regan, that when I am upon the brink of making the most important decision of my life, instead of thinking about kissing my future wife, all I can think about is kissing you?'

'Gabriel, I…' She couldn't breathe. She couldn't think. She was hot and cold and panicky. There was something she should do, something she should not.

'Night and day,' he said huskily, 'I think about your lips, your touch. And I know, I know it's the last thing I should be thinking about, but it consumes me, torments me.'

If only he had not been so honest. If only he had not confided in her. If only she had not been thinking the same thing. 'Oh, Gabriel.'

'Oh, God, Regan,' he said huskily, pulling her on top of him and kissing her hungrily.

It was different from the last time. Very different. More. His mouth fitted hers more perfectly. The taste of him, the cool, delicious taste of his lips on hers, made her want to melt. He kissed her slowly, carefully, tasting her. His fingers stroked her cheek, her ear, her neck. His hand pressed her back, moulding her to him. Hard chest. Her arms went around his neck. The crisp feel of his collar, the soft curl of his hair. She sighed, a strange little noise, like a whisper or a whimper. He teased her mouth open, ran his tongue along the inside of her lips.

Kissing. Behind her closed lids, the world was bathed in a golden glow of sunlight. Down they sank into the hay, his fingers still stroking her, his lips triggering delightfully unfamiliar sensations. His tongue touched hers and the melting feeling gave way to a sharper, more visceral sensation. He rolled her onto her back, pressing her into the hay. His kiss was velvet-dark now. She could feel his breath coming sharp and fast, like hers. She liked the feel of him, heavy on top of her. Reassuringly solid. His hands stroked down her arms, the curve of her waist, making her arch up under him. Behind her lids now it was fiery. Scarlet. Crimson.

His fingers stroked the swell of her breasts. She thought she might faint clean away, the sensation was so tantalisingly unbearable. Her hands clutched at his shoulders. The linen of her chemise felt rough on her nipples. She felt them swell and pucker. She touched his cheek, her fingers grazing on the shadow of stubble on his jaw. His tongue thrust deeper into her mouth, making her arch again, against the length of his body. Kisses were not enough. Straw tickling her cheek. She brushed it away. Opened her eyes. Met grey-blue, gazing deep into hers. Heavy-lidded. Slashes of colour across his cheekbones.

Gabriel sat up. Regan sat up. They gazed at each other, chests heaving. She had straw in her hair. His cravat was askew. Wanting, desire, passion, heated the space between them where words should be, a tangible thing, a jagged-edged thing, a glittering thing, a force so strong they almost succumbed again to its powerful lure. She leaned towards him. He leaned towards her. His hand on her neck. Hers on his jaw. Wanting. Her lips parted. He moaned. She jerked herself free.

'No.'

'No!'

Gabriel looked around him, at the platform upon which they had lain, the bales of hay, the rickety ladder, the skylight, dark with the shadow of snow clouds. 'I did not intend to—I did not mean…'

'No more did I,' Regan said, feverishly pulling straw from her hair.

They stared at each other. It was Gabriel who laughed

first. 'Godammit, Regan, I'm the sixth Duke of Blairmore. You are a respectable spinster of a Yorkshire parish and we are cavorting in a hay loft like—'

'A groom and a dairy maid,' she finished for him with a shaky laugh. 'It's not amusing. I'm not sure I even understand it.'

'There is nothing to understand. We are attracted to each other. Physically attracted. It is nothing more.'

Regan's smile faded along with the last tingling remnants of desire. What he meant was that he would not allow it to be anything more. Or, worse, that he was not capable of allowing it to become so. The harsh reality of his confession hit her with the force of an avalanche. Gabriel did not seek love because he did not believe in it. Truly did not believe himself capable of it. She had not, until this moment, taken his claim seriously. Now, she would be a fool indeed if she did not. 'I see,' she said.

He pressed her hand. 'Do you? It matters a great deal that you understand.'

'Does it? Then I do. I understand that you are set upon this course and I wish with all my heart that it will make you happy.'

'It will,' Gabriel said fervently.

Regan blinked back a tear. 'I hope, I truly hope, you are right.'

Gabriel tried to make good on his avowal. He tried to put her from his mind. He tried not to ponder the questions she raised, but he could not stop himself. He had not thought himself capable of feeling, yet he felt. *What* he felt, he didn't know, but it was powerful, insistent and would not be denied.

He had not thought his desires mattered, but they did. He not only wanted his children to be happy, he wanted happiness for himself. And what would make him happy? That was the most daunting question of all, for time and again, when he posed it, the image that flitted into his mind was that of Regan, and that was the most shocking thing of all. Because it made no sense at all. If it were true… But it could not be true, it *could* not.

Gabriel arose from his twisted sheets exhausted and frustrated. It was a beautiful day, after a sharp overnight frost. Skating, that would surely clear his head. Hard physical exercise. Clear, fresh air. That would be bound to do the trick.

'Though, sadly, Lady Sarah has declined to join us,' he informed the rest of the party, who had assembled at his request in the lower courtyard, one of the gardeners having confirmed that the lake was frozen quite solid. 'Apparently, she has a morbid fear of water on account of her uncle drowning at sea. She cannot bear to be near it, even in its frozen form.'

Jack digested this information, a frown furrowing his brow. 'She must be really smelly. I wish I didn't have to bathe, I hate it. I wish *I* had an uncle and *he* drowned at sea.'

'Well, it is your great misfortune that you haven't,' Gabriel said, scooping Jack up and hoisting him on his shoulders. 'Now then,' he said with a wink to Regan, 'are we going to stand around all day talking about dead uncles or are we going skating?'

'Skating!' the children squealed in unison.

'Should I perhaps offer to stay behind to keep Lady Sarah company?' Regan asked Gabriel as they made their way across the courtyard.

'Good grief, no. I believe she intends to spend the morning assisting her Grace in the preparations for the Christmas Eve party,' he replied. 'If I was in her shoes, frankly I would rather take my chances with drowning.'

Regan chuckled. 'I was just thinking, had we wished to skate earlier, you could have asked her Grace to freeze the pond with one of her glacial stares.' This made Gabriel laugh aloud, something that startled himself as well as the rest of the company, such a rare sound as it was.

The pond was actually more of a lake, an artificial dam created for Gabriel's grandfather by the renowned landscape gardener Capability Brown, which had the dual purpose of irrigating the lower eastern fields and draining the upper ones for grazing. A picturesque little temple built on the banks served as a storeroom for the ice skates and the little wooden punt from which Gabriel and Regan had swum in summers long past. The folly had a small terrace, upon which later would be served hot chocolate.

The ice skates themselves consisted of a pair of heavy metal blades with a wooden shoe-shaped platform, which were held in place with thick buckled leather straps that Gabriel insisted on checking—a procedure that had Lady

Lucinda blushing wildly and taking refuge in her vinaigrette at the prospect of having her delicate little foot examined by the Duke himself. Having arrived convinced that she would never fulfil her mama's dreams and become the Duchess of Blairmore by snaring the Duke, Lady Lucinda had in the last ten days been first in awe of her host, then smitten by his charm, and was now, in the face of some unexpected encouragement, quite terrified by the prospect of actually succeeding.

Gabriel was just about to escort her onto the ice when he caught Portia's disappointed expression. 'But perhaps it would be best if you skate with Lady Lucinda, Portia, for you are both much the same height and will be able to support each other better,' he said, earning himself a selection of approving looks, from Portia, Lady Lucinda and Regan.

Lady Olivia, a competent skater, was already in the middle of the pond, with Land skating somewhat falteringly beside her. Jack, wearing skates several sizes too large for him, hovered on the edge of the ice, torn between a natural desire to be as bold as his brother and an equally natural fear that he would make himself a laughing stock by falling over.

'Come, you must show Regan and me the way,' Gabriel said, smiling at him. 'See, you can skate between us and help keep us steady.' He was rewarded with a grin that nearly split Jack's face, not to mention a silently mouthed *thank you* from Regan. He wasn't sure that was responsible for the warm glow that suddenly bathed him, but it was a pleasant feeling regardless. Unfamiliar, but undoubtedly pleasant.

The three of them made uncertain progress, with Jack's skates barely touching the ice for the first lap of the pond, though Gabriel's firm grip kept him upright with his pride intact. By the second lap, he was skating with more confidence. 'I think I should go and skate with Land now,' he said at the end of the third lap, slipping his hands free. 'Only don't let Regan go, will you, Gabriel, because she's wobblier than a—a jelly.'

Laughing as she watched his erratic progress towards his brother, Regan turned to Gabriel. 'Perhaps you had best go and skate with Lady Olivia,' she said.

'I fear that Jack would take me to task if I did so,' Gabriel replied, taking her hand, 'I cannot leave you on your own to wobble like a jelly.'

'I will have you know—oh, dear!'

Lady Lucinda had taken a tumble. 'I am perfectly all right,' she said, when Regan and Portia finally managed to help her back to her feet—she was too embarrassed to allow Gabriel to assist.

'Your clothes are soaking. You must let me escort you back to the Hall,' Regan said.

Lady Lucinda shook her head. 'No, no, I will be perfectly all right on my own.'

'Are you injured?' Gabriel asked. 'Where does it hurt?'

'Nowhere!' Lady Lucinda said vehemently, unable, for the life of her, to think how to politely make reference to her bottom, which was throbbing painfully.

'Let me come with you, Lady Lucy,' Portia said. 'Then we can work on—on that thing,' she said with a conspiratorial look.

To this offer, Lady Lucinda smiled her grateful assent. Regan, telling herself she was being very silly, tried valiantly not to show the little spurt of jealousy caused by the worshipful gaze her sister cast her ladyship as the pair, with their heads together, walked slowly back up the path towards the Hall.

'The fickleness of youth,' Gabriel said. 'You must not blame the child.'

Regan smiled wanly. 'Oh, dear, was it that obvious? Of course I don't blame her, Lady Lucinda is so pretty and so gentle with her.'

'And you, of course, are neither of those things, are you?' Gabriel said mockingly, as he led her back out onto the ice. 'You know, if you would take my arm properly, we would make better progress.'

She knew as she allowed herself to be pulled closer that it was a mistake, but she could not resist. Gabriel's arm rested on her waist. His other hand held hers. In this fashion they made two circuits, their skates making a clacking sound on the ice. Land's laughter echoed over the lake. Lady Olivia and the two boys had retired to the pavilion and were drinking hot chocolate. Tiny flakes of snow began to fall, like a sparkling gauze curtain. Gabriel pulled her closer. She could feel his breath on her cheek. His hip pressing against hers. His thigh, too. Wherever they touched, she tingled. She had to work hard not to allow her head to drift onto his shoulder. In the hush caused by the falling snow, they felt quite alone, cocooned in their own silent, snowy world.

'It's like being in a fairy tale,' Regan whispered.

'I wish we were,' Gabriel said enigmatically. There was snow on Regan's lashes, for it was falling more heavily now. Her cheeks were flushed with the cold and the skating. They could hardly see the other side. At the farthest part of the lake from the pavilion he brought them both to a halt in the shelter of a cluster of trees. 'Look at it, Regan. The world looks magical, doesn't it, with everything blanketed in snow? A fairy tale, you say. Well, I wish someone could wave a magic wand and make some sort of happy ever after out of this situation, for I cannot.'

'Gabriel!'

'I cannot pretend that I do not find your company, and that of the children, captivating.' His mouth quirked into a little half smile that melted Regan's heart. 'In your case, much more than merely captivating. But I cannot change who I am, Regan. This thing, this attraction between us, it will pass. It will fade in time, become a memory, a very pleasant memory, but nothing more. It must. It has to, there is no other choice.'

'Gabriel, there is no need...'

'There is every need, dammit! I know what I must do and yet I find it almost impossible to act on it. Why cannot I take the first step and choose a wife? Regan, there are times—when I look at you—it's like a madness. I want you, I burn for you, I desire you passionately. I cannot stop thinking about you. It makes no sense.'

'Oh, Gabriel…'

'I know, I know I should not say such things. When I am not with you, I can persuade myself that I will follow the course I have set, but when we are alone together like this, that self-same course seems unutterably wrong. I am tormented. Why is that, Regan? What the devil is it that's happening between us? Do you feel it, too?'

Shock, not only at his words, but at the way he looked, the tortured tone of his voice, was making her icy cold. For a fraction of a second, the time it took for a snowflake to melt on his cheek, she allowed herself to hope. But she knew him too well to allow it to take root. 'Gabriel,' she said gently, taking his hand, 'it makes no difference how I feel. You've said it yourself, it changes nothing.'

'I know. And I know I have not the right to ask you, but it matters all the same.'

He clutched her hands in his. His look was so full of the yearning that she herself had been feeling, he was so bewildered, and so desperate, that Regan could not deny him this little comfort. 'Oh, God, Gabriel, of course I feel the same, but…'

'Do you? Do you dream? And want and need, as I do?'

'Yes.'

He kissed her cheeks. Her hair. He kissed her eyes. The tip of her nose. 'Do you burn from it? Is it like a fever in your blood?'

'Yes. No. Yes. Gabriel—'

But his kiss put a halt to her flow of words. A fevered

kiss, all cold skin and warm lips, gloved hands frustrated by layers of clothes. It was too much and not nearly enough.

A voice made them spring apart. Land's voice. The sound of his skates as he approached must have been muffled by the heavy snow. He was beside them before they were quite disentangled.

'Lady Olivia sent me to look for you,' he said, looking anxiously from one to the other. 'She was worried some mishap had befallen you.'

And she was right to be worried, Regan thought abjectly, *for a grievous mishap was indeed just about to befall us.* Racked with guilt, shaken by desire, utterly and completely confused beyond thinking, she took her brother's hand. 'My s-skate,' she stammered. 'It had become caught in my gown. Gabriel was helping me untangle it.'

'Come and have some hot chocolate,' Land said. 'It warms your tummy up and it's quite delicious.'

'Then we must go and have some directly.' Keeping up a stream of inane chatter, Regan skated back across the ice with Land, leaving Gabriel to find his own way, wondering morosely if he ever would, ever again.

Chapter Six

Alone, Gabriel skated in ever faster circles as the snow fell in a heavy cloak of thick white flakes. The blades of his skates sparked on the ice, his coat tails flew out behind him, but his brain grew ever more tangled as he sought to clear a path through the morass of feelings that were swamping him. Only two weeks ago, everything had seemed so clear. An estate finally free of debts. Time to secure his future. Stability. A wife. A child. A family.

He dug his blade into the ice, gouging out a deep rut, and came to an abrupt halt at the edge of the lake. He wanted a family, not just an heir, a family to drive out all the bitter memories of his own childhood and replace them with happy ones. He'd assumed that would be enough. He'd thought that it would make him happy. Until Regan came along and asked him if that really would be sufficient.

And what of your happiness? Dammit, her questions

had sown some very unwelcome seeds of doubt. *You will be a husband before you are a father*, she had pointed out. He could not imagine being a husband. Not to any of the Three Graces. He did not want to make love to any one of them. He wanted to make love to Regan. That would make him happy.

'Temporarily, perhaps,' he said to himself as he stripped off his skates, 'but it would inevitably pass. And there is the single salient fact that I cannot love her and she would settle for nothing less.'

Logic. It had always seemed so incontrovertible before. But as he made his way back to the Hall to assist with the preparations for Christmas, Gabriel could not stop a nagging voice in his head asking the same question over and over again: *What if you are wrong?*

The Yule log arrived that afternoon. The trunk of a huge oak tree was brought to the Hall along the now snow-covered drive on a specially made sled with metal runners. It was drawn by two cart horses and escorted by a small army of estate workers. Portia, Land and Jack danced excitedly behind the sled in the company of a swarm of other children, all waving branches of mistletoe. Watching from the shelter of the portcullis, a lump lodged in Regan's throat as she remembered herself and Gabriel doing the same thing, with Papa at the head of the team of horses.

As the log was lifted from the sled by a group of the burliest estate workers and carried carefully into the long gallery before being placed on the huge hearth, a silence descended and all eyes fell on Gabriel. Though he wore only a plain frockcoat and his customary buckskins with top boots, he had an air of authority about him that made him stand out from the crowd. He gave a brief, witty vote of thanks. Admiration and respect emanated from the throng, Regan noted with something akin to pride, as well as affection. Even the Duchess looked as if a smile might just crack her glacial demeanour, until Gabriel produced not one but three spills, and beckoned forwards Portia, Land and Jack, and the Duchess's face froze into an even deeper-than-usual expression of disapproval. Oblivious, thrilled to the point of stupefaction, the three children carefully lit their spills from the candle Gabriel proffered and, in turn, used the spills to light the kindling made from the remnants of last year's log.

As Portia threw her arms around Gabriel and unselfconsciously planted a kiss on his cheek, a cheer arose and Regan dabbed frantically at her eyes, noticing that Mrs McGlone, presiding over the long trestle table of plum cake and Derby cheese, also seemed to have something in her eye. Gabriel took position behind the huge bowl of wassail punch and Regan went to assist the housekeeper with serving the food.

'Lighting the Yule log,' Mrs McGlone said. 'It must have done your heart good to see the little ones given such an honour. His Grace has a way with them, doesn't he? Who'd have thought it, when you remember what he was like when you first arrived not two weeks past?'

Regan smiled wistfully, but the many mouths demanding cake and cheese prevented her from replying. She was surprised to see Lady Sarah making her way over, even more surprised by her offer to help, for her ladyship, while perfectly polite, had never made any effort to cultivate her company. Her motives, Regan realised quickly, were not to aid, but to impress.

'The Duchess has told me how important it is to understand every domestic detail when it comes to running an estate like Blairmore,' Lady Sarah informed her in her most condescending tone.

Regan grimaced. Gabriel might not yet have made up his mind, but it seemed the Duchess had a firm favourite. She could not like Lady Sarah. She did not like to think of Gabriel spending his life with such a cold fish. She stopped in the middle of cutting a slice of cheese. She did not want to think of Gabriel married to anyone. Realisation struck her with almost sickening clarity. She didn't want to think of Gabriel married to anyone else because…

'Oh, dear,' Mrs McGlone said. 'Best get that attended to, Miss Stuart.'

Regan looked down in surprise at the blood dripping down her finger, which she had managed to slice with the cheese wire.

'Go on, now,' Mrs McGlone said, giving her a little push.

In something close to a trance, Regan wrapped a kerchief round her finger before making her way through the gathering crowding the length of the long gallery, walking quickly along the dark, narrow corridor that led to the children's wing, her heart beating like a trapped bird. Once safely inside her own bedchamber, she leaned back against the heavy door and closed her eyes. There was simply no escaping it or denying it.

She dragged herself over to the window seat and stared out through the ancient flawed glass. The snow was a thick carpet of white now, the trees frosted. She was in love with Gabriel! How had that happened? How could she have been so incredibly foolish as to allow that to happen?

A tiny smile tugged at the corner of her mouth. It didn't matter. She loved him. He was her heart's desire. He always had been. She loved him. She loved him. She had always loved him. For a few precious moments, she hugged the knowledge close, letting it heat her. No wonder she craved his kisses. No wonder she yearned and longed and dreamed. No wonder she felt this urgent need to be with him, just to be with him, always. She loved him. Deeply. Completely. Passionately. With a desire which could too easily burn out of control.

She clutched her hands to her breast, feeling the erratic beat of her heart. She loved him so much. The tiny curl of a smile faded, and tears burned in her eyes as reality crept stealthily back, because no matter how much she loved him, it was pointless. He wanted her. He desired her, he had said so, but he did not love her. Would not love her. Could not love her. Duty, and a deep-rooted resistance to love, led him down a path he was set upon keeping to, regardless of his doubts. No matter what he felt for her, he would never marry her. A steward's daughter, with no dowry, no accomplishments and three very real encumbrances. Never.

A soft knock on the door interrupted these miserable thoughts. Regan hastily wiped her eyes.

It was Portia. 'Gabriel was worried,' she said, 'he asked me to come and check on you.'

Regan sniffed. 'I'm fine, darling, honestly.'

'You're crying. Are you sad like Gabriel?'

'Gabriel?'

'Land was just saying that he wished we didn't have to go home so soon after Christmas and Gabriel got a bit angry and said he didn't want to talk about that, which wasn't like him because even though we all thought he was scary when we first came here we like him now, lots, and anyway, then he sort of got sad and looked a bit like you do now and then Jack gave him a hug and asked him if he was better now and Gabriel said yes, thank you very much, and then he noticed you'd gone and that's when he asked me to come and find you.'

'I'm not sad, I promise,' Regan said, torn between laughter and tears. 'I just cut my finger, that's all.'

'Let me look.' Portia carefully unwrapped the sticky kerchief and tutted. Her little mouth was pursed, her eyes concerned as she examined the wound, which had already stopped bleeding. 'It should be cleaned,' she said firmly.

Watching her bustle over to the washstand, the concentration on her pretty features as she washed away the dried blood, Regan felt the tears rising in her eyes again. 'It's nothing, Portia dear,' she said with a watery smile. 'It doesn't hurt, it's just you look so serious and grown-up when you concentrate like that.'

'I am grown-up, nearly,' Portia said. 'Lady Lucy says I set the neatest stitch she's ever seen. There, that is nice and clean now. Shall I bandage it?'

'No, thank you, Portia.' Regan kissed her sister's cheek and pulled her down onto the window seat beside her. 'I thought Lady Lucinda was teaching you to paint. Have you been sewing samplers, too?'

'Sort of,' Portia said, tugging at the sash of her dress. 'I can't tell you. It's a secret. You'll find out on Christmas Eve.'

'I shall look forward to that. Mrs McGlone tells me she's boiling the king of puddings tomorrow for the Christmas Eve party.'

'Yes. We're to help stir in the token for the King of Fools. It's a gold sovereign. There should really be a Queen of Fools too, I suppose.'

Following her sister back to the long gallery, Regan thought, with a sad smile, that perhaps there already was.

Regan had claimed a headache in order to avoid dinner, afraid to face Gabriel while her love was so new and so raw, anxious to protect its fragile nature from harsh reality. The first part of the night she had spent foolishly dreaming herself a duchess, the second she spent chastising herself for being so foolish. Dark shadows, heavy eyes and a very real headache made her eschew the pudding-stirring ceremony next day, but she knew that hiding away would eventually elicit comment. She knew, too, that, painful as it was to see Gabriel, it would be infinitely more painful not to. Consequently, she donned a bright smile and joined the others for the traditional mistletoe hanging.

A huge pile of the vibrant green branches with their tiny white berries sat in the banqueting hall, delivered that morning. All week garlands made of holly, bay, laurel and rosemary had been hung over mantels, woven around staircases and even draped over the suits of armour and Roman busts that lined the long gallery. The mistletoe was already tied into bunches, ready to be hung in doorways and alcoves. Children and ladies together selected places for it to hang, estate carpenters trailing in their wake with hammers and ladders. The Hall rang with the clatter of nails and running feet and stifled giggles as footmen snatched kisses from unwary maids.

Disappointed to note that Gabriel was not present, Regan wandered off by herself to one of the turrets, which sat above the kitchens. It was used for storage, for the heat from the ovens, which were burning full blast in preparation for the Yule party, filtered up through the old boards and the open fireplaces. This was the room that she had described to Portia, but it seemed that, in all the excitement, they had both quite forgotten about its existence. Until now. Regan smiled. This had always been a magical place, a veritable paradise for a little girl who adored dressing up.

She closed the door behind her and lifted the dusty lid of a chest. Dresses, just exactly as she remembered them: rich brocades, heavy damask, the skirts full, stiff with whalebone, the bodices ornately embroidered, strewn with seed pearls and semi-precious stones. Dresses that were fifty, a hundred, years old. In another chest farthingales and hoops, panniers and corsets, which made her own stays look decidedly flimsy. In yet another, capes and gloves and tippets, ruffs and feathers.

Quickly unlacing her own robe, Regan slipped in and out of one beautiful gown after another, until she could resist no longer, and, with shaking fingers, opened the *special* chest. It was still there, still wrapped in silk, looking every bit as richly alluring as it had all those years ago, the red-velvet cloak with its fur trimming. Clad only in her chemise, Regan wrapped it around her, shivering with delight at the caress of the fur on her bare skin. The cloak, obviously made for some grand affair of state, no longer swamped her, but still trailed out behind her onto the floor as she stood on a small table the better to admire herself in the mottled mirror above the mantel. So engrossed was she in admiring its regal glory that when the door opened, she jumped.

'Gabriel!'

He paused on the threshold, taken by surprise at the vision of her, clad in velvet and fur. Clad in very little else. She had taken the pins out of her hair, for some reason. It tumbled over the cloak, its fiery lights putting the crimson velvet to shame. His mouth went dry. She looked delectable.

'I'm sorry, I was just—I didn't expect…' Gabriel closed the door. 'You've been avoiding me.'

She was still standing on the table, like some beautiful statue come to life. 'I thought it best, given the circumstances,' she said.

He put his arms around her waist and lifted her down. The cloak fell open. Regan tried to pull it back, horribly aware of her state of undress, but Gabriel caught her hands and pulled her to him. Her breasts brushed against his chest. She shivered.

'It's a coronation cloak, I think. The Blairmores like their pomp and ceremony. No doubt whichever Duchess it belonged to wore it over a gown of cloth of gold. I think I prefer your less formal style.'

'It suits my less formal status,' Regan said with a sad smile. 'The steward's daughter playing dress up.'

Gabriel flinched. 'Regan, you know—'

'Don't, Gabriel. I don't want pity, I'm just stating facts. Besides, we commoners have one big advantage over you aristocrats, you know. We can marry to suit ourselves.'

'For love.'

'Or not. Marry, I mean. I doubt I will. I know you must. There is no need for us to go over it all again, Gabriel, if that's what you came here for.'

'I came here because I can't seem to keep away,' Gabriel said. 'No matter how many times I resolve to do so. I came here because I thought…' His smile was twisted as he pulled the sprig of mistletoe out of his pocket. 'One last kiss, I thought. Tomorrow is Christmas Eve. It has long been my intention to announce my betrothal at the Yule party.' He dropped the mistletoe to the ground. 'One last kiss. A damned stupid notion. It would never be enough. I would rather starve than taste what I cannot have. I would rather cut my tongue out than make you promises I cannot keep.' He stroked the long silken fall of her hair. 'Please don't avoid me, Regan. You will be gone soon enough and then there will be a lifetime of forced avoidance to look forward to.'

He turned away and headed for the door. She stood, frozen to the spot, her heart pounding. 'Wait!'

He paused.

'Gabriel, I…' Regan swallowed. It could not be wrong, not when she loved him so. He did not love anyone else. He had not yet pledged himself to another. It was her last chance. Her only opportunity to snatch some happiness, however fleeting. She took a deep breath and picked up the sprig of mistletoe. 'Gabriel, I would rather not starve either.'

He turned. 'Regan, I could not ask such a thing of you.'

'I know.' She smiled, more confident now at the rightness of what she was about to do. 'I know very well you would not, Gabriel, but I can give to you what you cannot ask for. To you and only you.' Her hands shaking, she allowed the cloak to slip from her shoulders, spilling around her on the floor. She was flushed, she was acutely nervous, but she was absolutely certain. Tossing back her hair, she looked at him unwaveringly, and held out her hand towards him. 'It can be my gift, to both of us.'

Gabriel caught his breath, humbled by the generosity of such a gesture, stunned by the sensual beauty of her, the proud, clear gaze, the regal way she held herself, though he could see the effort she was making not to shake. He strode towards her, and gathered her in his arms. 'I could not. I would not, no matter how much I want to. I will not let you. It is too much.'

She wrapped her arms around his neck. 'I want to, Gabriel. I know what I'm doing. I want to.'

He caught her face between his hands. 'Are you truly certain?'

'You will be—careful?' she asked, blushing.

'I promise.'

'Then I am truly sure.'

Her smile twisted at his guts. She had no idea about that smile of hers, so innocently sensual. Gabriel pulled her roughly to him and kissed her.

Passion ripped through them as soon as their lips touched. They drank deep of each other, drawing flames, licking heat, a wild, roaring heat that threatened to engulf them. Breathing raggedly, Gabriel drew back. If this was to be their one time, he wanted to make it last as long as possible. Stroking her hair, her cheeks, he fluttered little kisses over her brow, her lids. Casting off his coat, he pulled her down onto the fur lining of the cloak. He kissed her throat, his mouth lingering at the pulse behind her ear, at the delicate hollow of her throat. Murmuring her name, he kissed his way down the creamy skin of her arm, the crease at her elbow, the pale blue veins at her wrist, finding every pulse, roused by the taste of her skin, the way each kiss made her pulse flutter more erratically. As he showered kisses over the swell of her breasts above her stays, he felt himself swelling, hardening. He tugged off his neckcloth and cast his waistcoat aside. He loosened the strings of her stays to free her breasts and feasted his eyes on her beauty, before his mouth captured one perfect pink nipple and he sucked greedily.

Regan moaned with pleasure. Liquid pleasure, trickling like warm honey, from her breasts, down to her belly, down. She felt as if she would melt, as if she was on fire, as if she was being coiled tight, all at once. She had not thought, not dreamed, never, ever, ever, that it would be like this. Her fingers trailed through the silk of his hair, under the open collar of his shirt to find skin. Warm, male skin. Such a breadth to his shoulders. The muscles rippled under her fingers. He licked his way round the soft underside of her breast and over to the other nipple. Her pleasure became a burning need. She wanted, desperately wanted, more.

Skin. His skin against hers. She plucked at his shirt. He pulled it over his head and it was her turn to gaze transfixed at the rise and fall of his chest, the soft smattering of hair that led her eyes down, to the dip in his stomach, down. Tentatively, she touched him. His breath became jagged. She touched him again, tracing the shape of him, memorising him as a blind person would.

Kissing again, their mouths clashing, lips hungry, hungrier. Her chemise gone. His mouth on her stomach. The pulse at her ankle, the back of her knee, the inside of her thighs. She was so hot. She was so very hot. Urgently hot. Inside her, a coiling tighter and tighter, shivering heat, and then his mouth fastened on the source of the heat and she gasped, arched up under him, felt herself thrown, spiralling, thrumming, pulsing into the air, into the heavens, into a sparkling diamond place where she flew and flew.

Just when she thought she would fall, he kissed her mouth again, whispering her name again, and she opened her eyes, and he was there, covering her body with his, asking her if she was sure.

She clutched at his shoulders. Pressed kisses to his throat, his chin, his mouth. Colour slashed Gabriel's cheeks. His eyes were dark. His skin seemed tight-drawn, stark. 'I could not be more sure,' Regan whispered, her heart so full of love that she was certain it must be etched upon her face. 'I want you, Gabriel,' she said, because she could not say 'I love you.'

He had never wanted anyone so much. He ached with wanting and ached with wanting to please. He did not want it to end, but he could no longer postpone its ending. Carefully, he eased himself into her, kissing her, stroking her, murmuring her name, slowly, pushing achingly slowly past the last barrier and into the glorious, delightful, delicious centre of her. It was almost too much. He paused, breathing heavily. Then carefully, his gaze fixed on hers, he began to move, waiting for her to find their rhythm, watching her eyes widen when she did, tightening unbearably as she began to move with him. So sweet, so perfect, so incredibly intense. At her urging he thrust harder, higher, deeper, thrust again as she moaned her pleasure, digging her nails into his back, his buttocks, bucking under him as his climax seized him and hers caught her up in a second wave, removing himself just in time, though he wanted, as he had never wanted, to spend himself inside her, because it felt right, as it had never felt right before.

Afterwards, Gabriel's kiss was softer, more tender, on her swollen lips. She kissed him back, pouring her love into him, holding him to her, knowing utterly, completely, that this was right, as utterly certain that when it was over, her heart would break. She wanted to close her eyes and to float for ever in this blissful cloud their lovemaking had created. But she could not. Regan opened her eyes. 'I need you to promise me you won't regret this,' she said softly.

Gabriel smoothed the heavy fall of Titian hair from her cheek. 'Never. Unless you do?'

'Never.' She kissed him, willing the tears not to fall. 'It's best if you go now.'

'Regan…'

'Hush, Gabriel. Don't spoil it. There is no more to be said.'

There was something he had not asked. Something he should know, but he could not think what. He wanted to stay locked in this turret, making love with her. But tomorrow was Christmas Eve. The self-imposed deadline he must meet. He dragged himself to his feet and quickly dressed. One last look at her, hair streaming out, body flushed with passion, eyes gazing up at him, then, quickly, before he could change his mind, he left.

'I love you, Gabriel,' Regan whispered to the closed door. She lay on the cloak, slowly reliving every second of their lovemaking, until she began to shiver with cold. Outside, dusk had fallen. Tomorrow was Christmas Eve. Tomorrow, Gabriel would promise himself to another. But for tonight, for this one night, he had been hers.

Chapter Seven

Regan greeted the dawn of Christmas Eve morning with mixed feelings. The rosy glow of what she had shared with Gabriel lingered still, but its residual heat was tempered by the knowledge that today would see the announcement of his betrothal. She was resigned to the fact that he was set on a marriage of convenience, but had no appetite for witnessing the deed first-hand. Her instinct was to flee, but how could she, since she would be depriving the children of the highlight of the festivities? She had no option but to keep her own counsel and suffer in silence.

Portia, Land and Jack were out gathering wood for the huge bonfire that would be lit at midnight. In the banqueting hall, the Duchess was supervising the setting up of the tables for the feast. Lady Sarah accompanied her, clutching the table layout showing who would be sitting where.

'You will be seated with the children at this table here,'

she said to Regan, pointing to a spot halfway down one of the long tables that ran at right angles to the top table.

'At the steward's table,' the Duchess said, smiling her usual frosty smile. 'I felt it the most appropriate location.'

Though her barbed remarks had in the past made Regan curl her nails into her palms, today she felt only pity for the woman, whose status was about to be usurped. The Duchess's reign at Blairmore Hall was soon to be over, and though she might delude herself into thinking that Lady Sarah would welcome her continued residence and Lady Lucinda could be browbeaten into agreeing the same, Lady Olivia would likely not tolerate her interference and, more importantly, nor would Gabriel. So Regan bobbed a curtsy. 'Thank you, your Grace, it will be an honour.'

'Our other guests will, of course, be seated at the high table,' the Duchess said.

'Most fitting,' Regan responded sweetly.

The Duchess's eyes narrowed. She resorted to her quizzing glass. 'There is something about you, Miss Stuart, that I cannot warm to. I tolerated your friendship with my son only because my husband placed such faith in your father, but even all those years ago there was about you something of the upstart. Do not think I am oblivious to the way you have been flaunting yourself at Gabriel these past weeks.' The Duchess let the quizzing glass fall. 'If I had my way, Miss Stuart, you and those noisy, ill-mannered brats would be on the stagecoach to Yorkshire as we speak. My son, unfortunately, does not share my view and his sense of loyalty towards you would be touching were it not misplaced.

But be assured—whatever hopes you are cherishing in that Jezebel bosom of yours are about to be dashed for ever.'

Regan paled. 'I cherish no hopes, your Grace, I assure you. I want—have only ever wanted—Gabriel to be happy. Which is more than you ever did,' she could not resist adding.

'Gabriel is the Duke of Blairmore,' the Duchess said haughtily, 'I fail to see how he can be anything but happy.'

'I know,' Regan replied with a withering smile, 'and that is exactly my point. Gabriel is your son. The fact that he is also the Duke of Blairmore should be entirely irrelevant.'

Her Grace's face seemed to sharpen. 'You are impertinent.'

'No, I am simply truthful. I'll tell you another truth, your Grace. If you treat Gabriel's children with the same indifference as you treated him, you will find yourself unwelcome at Blairmore. You made his childhood miserable. That is one tradition he intends to put a stop to.'

She did not wait on the Duchess's reply, but turned on her heel and left the room.

Gabriel was sitting in the estate office with his steward, being regaled with the seemingly endless list of preparations that were still to be completed before the night's festivities could begin. He was only listening with half an ear, however, his mind occupied by a maelstrom of conflicting emotions. Since he was usually the most attentive of employers, anxious to understand every last detail, his steward eventually asked him if his Grace was feeling quite well.

Assuring him that he was in perfect health, Gabriel abruptly pushed back his chair, muttered something about fresh air and strode off out into the gardens. The snow came up to the tops of his short boots in places. He had neither hat, gloves nor topcoat, but did not notice the cold. Brow furrowed, head down, he took the path that led to the graveyard. Leaning over the bridge, it came to him, the question that had been niggling since he left Regan in the turret room. Why?

Why had she made love to him? A gift, she'd called it. One she said she could only give to him, and him alone. Why? He scooped up a handful of snow and formed it into a ball, which he aimed at the overhanging branches of a tree by the river's edge. As the snowball burst against the bare branches and showered down on to the ground, Gabriel realised there was another question he should be asking himself. Why was it still so damned difficult to make up his mind? Three perfect candidates, yet he could prefer none. Three women who fitted every single one of his criteria—though perhaps Lady Sarah had not the maternal qualities he sought? As he pondered this question, Gabriel realised something else. For all his intention had been to observe how they behaved towards the children, when he tried to recall the many occasions when they had all been together, he could form no clear opinion, conjure no specific instances.

Regan. All he could recall was Regan. Which led him to pose another question. Why, when he knew and was utterly sure that the logic which had led him into this situation in the first place was inescapable, did his mind refuse to come to any logical conclusion? And another question. Why did he feel sick in his heart when he tried to force the issue? So many questions, so few answers.

Gabriel formed another snowball. The biggest question of all burst into his mind as the snowball splattered on the boulder at which he had aimed. Not why, but what. What was the name for this feeling, this passion, this need, urge, compulsion?

There was only one name. Only one answer. Love.

Regan would never have given herself to him unless she loved him. It was not simple carnal passion that motivated her, as he had claimed. It was love. She was in love with him. And heaven help him, but he was in love with her.

Gabriel braced his hands on the snow-covered parapet of the bridge, his head drooping. Illogical, irrational and completely impossible as it was, it was also irrefutable. He was in love with Regan. Wanting-to-be-with-her, unable-to-contemplate-life-without-her love, just as she had once described. The very notion he had once scorned. There was nothing ephemeral about it and nothing transient, either. He was in love. Would always be in love. How he knew it he knew not, but he knew it now for a certainty. Regan completed him. He loved her.

'Dear God, what on earth am I going to do?' Gazing out at the river, he threw back his head and laughed, a deep, wild, slightly crazy laugh, because the situation was beyond absurd. He, who didn't believe in love, was in love. He actually loved. He could actually love. Only love would make him happy. He could not be happy without love. He loved. He loved. He was in love. And was loved in return. Of that, he also had no doubt whatsoever.

His laughter faded as he contemplated the tangled web of the situation he found himself in. The Three Graces. The three children. His mother. The family name. Regan had no dowry, no connections—none who acknowledged her—she was hardly the biddable, tractable female he had sought. She was in every way the antithesis of the wife he should be taking. She had nothing that in the eyes of the world would make her eligible.

Except that he loved her. And she loved him. And the existence of their love changed everything. It would be a sin not to claim the happiness that they could share. As Regan said, it was a gift. The most precious of gifts. To be cherished.

Gabriel threw another snowball, and then another, arcing them up into the air without aiming at anything in particular. They flew, soared, as he felt his heart was soaring. A wonderful lightness of spirit imbued him, seemed to cast a glow around him. Despite all the difficulties, the single fact of Regan, his love for Regan, her love for him, made the world a very bright, wonderful place. To hell with the difficulties. He would overcome them. He had to see her. He had to be with her. Now and always.

Gabriel set off back across the bridge as if the devil were at his heels. He arrived back at the Hall breathless and agitated. His steward, his mother and his butler awaited him. Lady Olivia, Lady Sarah and Lady Lucinda awaited him.

Portia, Land and Jack called out their greetings. Everyone except the one person he sought was gathered. Various pairs of eyes looked at him expectantly. He bowed. 'Later,' he said, with an airy wave of his hand and promptly left the room.

He found Regan eventually, thanks to Mrs McGlone, in the stillroom. 'I've got something important to say to you,' he said, grabbing her hand.

'Your mother is looking for you, and your steward, and the children want to know—'

'Never mind that,' Gabriel said, dragging Regan out of the room and up the nearby backstairs, 'I am the Duke, after all, and one of the benefits is that they must all wait on me. Not a privilege I often exercise, mind you, but I am *in extremis* and needs must.'

He was walking so quickly she had to run to keep up. There was a gleam in his eye that made her heart bump. She couldn't help but smile when he looked at her like that. He looked different. Younger. Reckless. As he used to look when about to embark upon something outrageous. His mood was infectious. 'Gabriel, where on earth are we going?'

He pulled her to him roughly and planted a brief kiss on her mouth. 'You, too, must wait, but just for a moment. All will become clear directly.'

Along the long corridor that ran across both courtyards. Past the kitchens to the turret. Up the stairs. Through the connecting chambers to the one containing the clothes. He pulled her in, pushed shut the door and threw open several chests before he found what he wanted.

The red-velvet cloak was draped around her shoulders. 'Now you look the part,' he said.

'What part? Gabriel, what—?'

'Regan. Regan, Regan, Regan.' He took her hand and pressed a kiss to the palm. 'I've never done this before. I never want to do it again, so be sure of your line,' he whispered.

'My line?'

'I will ask you a question and you will answer, and the answer you must give is yes.'

'Gabriel?' Hope, wild, improbable, fantastical hope fluttered and soared like a flock of starlings in her stomach. She couldn't breathe She daren't think. He dropped to his knees before her. Blue-grey eyes looking up at her, suddenly very serious, glittering with intent. Her heart stopped. The air stilled.

'Regan, I love you. I've fallen head over heels in love with you. I'm in love, just as you said it would be. I want to be with you always. I need you to be with me always. I love you deeply, passionately and completely. I love you with all my heart and soul. Be my Duchess, Regan. Be there for me first thing in the morning and last thing at night and all the hours in between. Be my lover, Regan. Be my wife.'

'Oh, Gabriel.'

'That's not your line,' he said, trying to smile, though he was quite terrified for a horrible moment, wondering if he had misjudged the situation.

'Do you mean it?'

'Dear God. Truly. Utterly. Your line, Regan,' Gabriel said, a little desperately.

'Yes.' She dropped to her knees and threw her arms around him so violently that they toppled over. 'Yes. Oh, Gabriel, yes. But, Gabriel, you can't. What about—?'

He laughed and kissed her. 'I don't care about anything else. At least I do, but only if you'll be my wife. If you won't, nothing will have any meaning. If you will, anything is possible. Am I making any sense at all?'

'Perfect sense. I love you so much, Gabriel. I can't believe it.'

'Say it again.'

She was crying and laughing at the same time. 'I love you. I'll be your wife. I'll be your Duchess. I'll be your lover. I'll be anything you want me to be.'

'Just be Regan. My Regan,' he said, kissing her.

'My Gabriel,' she said, kissing him.

'My love, my very own love,' he said, pulling her hungrily into his arms.

It was over an hour before they could disentangle themselves. 'We must now go and face the music. Which is likely to be very loud and dissonant music, I'm afraid,' Gabriel said with a rueful smile as he watched his future Duchess struggle to pin her hair back up. 'But you know, I don't see why I should justify my actions to anyone. I love you. I will never love anyone else. I want to announce to the world that I love you, but I don't owe the world an explanation.'

'After all,' Regan said with a smile, 'you are the Duke.'

'Precisely,' Gabriel said. 'And you are going to be my Duchess, and no one will dare say a word against it, or they will answer to me.'

'Yes, but in all seriousness, Gabriel, I'm hardly the stuff that suitable matches are made of.'

'Listen to me, Regan,' he said sternly, 'that is the last time I will tolerate such comments, even from you. I know I've been the one pontificating about breeding and lineage and whatever else was on that damn-fool list of mine, but I was wrong, just as I was wrong to think that I could not love, that love did not exist. I was wrong about it all. What matters is that I love you and you love me, and that makes us a perfect match. Now that is an end of it, do you hear me?'

'Yes, your Grace.'

'We will be a family, Regan. You and me. And Portia and Land and Jack. A ready-made family. I need you to know—I want them to be my family because I have come to love them for themselves, not just because of you. But I also need you to know that it is you, and will always be you, who holds first place in my heart. Now what have I said to make you cry?'

'Nothing, everything. I'm not crying. I'm just so happy,' Regan said and promptly burst into tears.

Tears fell again when she retired to her bedchamber to dress for the Yule party. Laid out on the bed was the most beautiful evening gown she had ever seen. The cut was deceptively simple, a fitted bodice of claret velvet, puffed sleeves slashed with cream silk, a full cream-silk skirt and a deep ruffle of claret. A pretty paisley shawl embroidered in golds and reds lay beside it, along with a pair of long kid evening gloves. There was even a pair of claret-velvet slippers. Regan held the dress against her in the mirror.

'Do you like it?' She whirled round. Portia was grinning from ear to ear. 'We made it, Lady Lucy and I,' she said.

'But how? It's the most beautiful thing I've ever seen. How on earth…?'

'I said to Lady Lucy about how you were fed up wearing the same gown to dinner every night, and she said did you not have another and I said no, and I said how you felt like Cinderella. Which you did, Regan, you know you did.'

'Oh goodness, Portia, I know, but I did not expect you to repeat it.'

'But it was true, Regan, you *were* like Cinderella, and Lady Lucy said how sad it was and—you don't mind, do you? Only we meant it as a surprise, and—did I do wrong?'

Regan laid the dress down on the bed and enveloped her sister in a warm hug. 'It's beautiful. The most beautiful dress I've ever seen. And you are the most thoughtful sister I could ever have. And Lady Lucinda is most kind.'

'She had me measure your other gown and she sent express to London for the cloth and then we had to do some adjustments,' Portia said, 'to the sleeves here, and the neck—the deco—deco…'

'*Décolletage*. Dearest Portia, thank you. Will you help me dress once I have bathed?'

'Yes, but we have to hurry because Gabriel has arranged for me and the boys to be in the parade and I don't want them to set out without me.'

* * *

It was the tradition for everyone on the estate to join the parade, carrying flaming torches. Portia, Land and Jack set off in a horse-drawn sled driven by one of the grooms, to meet the main procession at the end of the carriageway.

Gabriel, resplendent in black evening clothes, stood at the steps, waiting to greet the crowds. Beside him the Duchess. To his right, the Three Graces and Regan. His Regan. Time after time he found his eyes straying towards her. A tiny knowing smile passing between them. It was an agony, this waiting. The pulse at her ear beat wildly. If only the procession would hurry up.

Finally, the flicker of the flambeaux grew. Singing, laughing, the procession made its way over the hump-backed bridge, along the final stretch of carriageway and through the portcullis. The sledge containing the children—with several new friends in tow, Gabriel noticed—pulled up at the rear. His mother bid everyone welcome. He bid everyone welcome. His butler threw open the doors to the banqueting hall and a small army of his footmen made sure that everyone took their places according to the Duchess's careful seating plan.

With four exceptions. Portia, Land and Jack were placed at the far end of the high table. Regan was placed at his right, ousting Lady Sarah. Only when she saw what had happened did the Duchess begin to have an inkling of the rather more earth-shattering news that was about to be announced.

'There is no place at high table for a governess,' she hissed.

'You are quite right, your Grace,' Gabriel said blandly. 'It is as well she is about to discard that role.'

'What the devil…?'

'Your Grace! Such language, and at high table, too.'

Turning to help Regan into her seat, he pressed a quick kiss to her neck. An action noted with utter astonishment by Lady Olivia, who until this moment had been quite certain that tonight would be the night she would be declared the future Duchess. Lady Lucinda, who also noticed the kiss, was immensely relieved. Not even the handsome Duke could compensate for the vast responsibility that being his Duchess would entail, nor the terror that being the Duchess's daughter-in-law would bring. Lady Sarah, whom the Duchess had quite persuaded would be Gabriel's choice, did not see the kiss, and consequently was the person most shocked by Gabriel's announcement, for Mrs McGlone had long hoped, and the Duke's staff had long guessed, which way blew the wind.

Upon the nod from his butler that all glasses were filled, Gabriel got to his feet. His speech started conventionally, with thanks for the hard work of the year past and best wishes for the year to come. 'But before you raise your glasses, I have a special announcement,' he said. 'For five years now, Blairmore Hall has been without a mistress. These five years have been hard for all of us, and a lonely burden for me. I know many of you, my mother included,' he said with one of his most charming smiles, 'have been wondering whether the Hall will ever ring with the patter of little feet. Well, it is my most pleasant—'

Gabriel broke off. 'You know,' he said, abandoning his formal tone, 'it's much more than pleasant. It's my absolute pleasure to introduce you to my future Duchess.' Casting a quick glance along the high table, he saw with relief that both Lady Olivia and Lady Lucinda were looking at Regan. He had been careful never to give either lady reason to start buying their trousseau, but they could have been under no illusions about the reasons for their presence here. Lady Sarah, however, was looking at his mother. Who was looking like thunder.

Gabriel returned to his audience. 'My Duchess,' he said with a grin, 'is a woman whom many of you will have known as a girl. Whose father knew and loved this estate as much as I do. Ladies and gentlemen, I give you Miss Regan Stuart.'

As he helped Regan to her feet, proudly noticing that the clenched grip of her hand was the only thing to betray her nerves, the banqueting hall filled with the sound of applause. Chairs were scraped back. Halloos were bellowed. Portia, Land and Jack, their faces shining with astonishment, came running to join them. To his mother's chagrin, Gabriel lifted each onto the table. 'The patter of not-so-tiny feet,' he said, causing much hilarity. 'My new family.'

Lady Olivia then, making an admirable attempt to smile, offered her polite felicitations. Lady Lucinda hugged Regan, tears sparkling on her lashes. 'I'm so happy for you. You look so lovely.'

'Thanks to you and Portia. I hope you are not disappointed?'

Lady Lucinda giggled. 'Oh, goodness, no. That woman terrifies me.'

That woman was at that moment being reluctantly forced to her feet by her son. 'Unless you wish to be banished, you will now and for ever accept my choice of wife and treat her with the respect she deserves,' he said firmly.

The Duchess did not smile, but she nodded regally. Later, Lady Sarah, loyal to the end, would pass the Duchess her vinaigrette and offer to burn feathers. The Duchess was apparently heard to mutter that she would prefer to have a certain person burned at the stake, but most likely that was just a malicious rumour.

Toasts and more toasts followed. Goose, roast pig, a whole roast ox, and then puddings were consumed. A whoop from Jack heralded the finding of the golden sovereign. To his delight, he was decked in a laurel crown, crowned King of Fools, and passed from shoulder to shoulder along the room to cries of 'All hail his Majesty'.

'He'll be insufferable after this,' Land muttered.

'You don't mind, dearest, coming to live at the Hall?' Regan whispered to Land later, as they gathered round the fire in the long gallery to listen to the estate children singing.

'Mind? It's the most fantastical, wonderful thing. Does that mean I am to be a lord?'

Regan laughed. 'No, but you shall live like one.'

'Will you still want us when you have your own family, though?' Portia asked.

'You *are* our family,' Gabriel said.

Regan cast him a glowing look. 'Thank you.'

He put his arm around her. 'You don't have to thank me. You just have to love me. Always.'

For the third time that day, tears of happiness filled her eyes. 'Darling Gabriel, that is the easiest thing in the world. I love you. Always.'

As he pulled her into his arms and kissed her soundly, a cheer went up.

A similar cheer went up two months later, when he kissed her again, outside the church on the estate on the occasion of their marriage. And another, even louder cheer at the Yule party exactly a year later, when he held up the tiny bundle who was his first born, the Lady Cordelia Portia Lucinda Olivia Sarah Beatrice Toward, named in memory of her maternal grandmother, for each of her four godmothers, and—finally—for her paternal grandmama who doted on the child in a manner both heart-warming and bewildering to all who knew her.

'I'm afraid we've failed to produce your son and heir,' the Duchess of Blairmore said, taking the lustily squalling babe from the Duke. 'We'll just have to try harder.'

'I'm looking forward to it already,' her besotted husband replied with a loving smile.

* * * * *

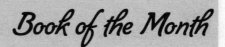
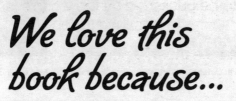

Come home to the magic of Nora Roberts

Identical twin boys Zeke and Zach wished for
only one gift from Santa this year: a new mum!
But convincing their love-wary dad that their
music teacher, Miss Davis, is his destiny and
part of Santa's plan isn't as easy as
they'd hoped…

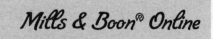